Sandra New.... .... but has
lived in Germany, Russia, Malaysia and England.
Her professions have ranged from academic
to professional gambler. She studied Creative
Writing at UEA, and her first novel, *The Only
Good Thing Anyone Has Ever Done*, was short-
listed for the *Guardian* First Book Award.
She currently lives in New York.

SANDRA NEWMAN

Cake

VINTAGE BOOKS
London

Published by Vintage 2008

2 4 6 8 10 9 7 5 3 1

First published in Great Britain by Chatto and Windus in 2007

Vintage
Random House, 20 Vauxhall Bridge Road,
London SW1V 2SA

www.vintage-books.co.uk

Addresses for companies within The Random House Group Limited
can be found at: www.randomhouse.co.uk/offices.htm

The Random House Group Limited Reg. No. 954009

A CIP catalogue record for this book
is available from the British Library

ISBN 9780099428824

The Random House Group Limited makes every effort to ensure that
the papers used in its books are made from trees that have been
legally sourced from well-managed and credibly certified forests.
Our paper procurement policy can be found at:
www.rbooks.co.uk/environment

© Mixed Sources
Product group from well-managed
forests and other controlled sources
www.fsc.org Cert no. TT-COC-2139
© 1996 Forest Stewardship Council
FSC

Printed in the UK by CPI Bookmarque, Croydon, CR0 4TD

For Robin and Jennifer

One

We met her when she crashed our party.

I had just bought a house and Todd decided that before we cleaned it up, we ought to have a party for our rougher, druggy friends, the Hackney crew. All the junkies, squatters, failing students, all the people who might hit an artery or run amok or die at someone's party. So you couldn't ask anyone *except* the kind of rabble you don't even want in your house, OK.

Except, I did tell this one CFO from work, Mark Keynes – who I'd run into at a Plan 9 gig once and we had kind of bonded. Like, got throwing-up drunk but didn't fuck then. So, he's alpha at my work, he does karate, he's attractive – I would blurt shit at him just to say something. I blurted, *oh, this party cause I bought a house cause I'm so fucking brilliant* in so many words. But I added that he shouldn't come, I didn't want him there. He laughed and said that he was 'uninsultable'.

Then, catastrophically, he came, but.

The house was a Victorian terrace; three floors and a concrete garden with a dead potted palm. Cheap cause, falling apart. The dust so thick it was dirt; a broken windowpane was fixed with duct tape; mushrooms on the ground floor. Entering, you had to step over a ceiling rose.

It had three bedrooms. One for me, one for Todd (Todd is my friend from home, an overgrown skateboard kid who came to me when his parents threw him out for having no career plans, and being thirty. Cause we have this history, and

Todd said he'd work on the house, he was into that, too stoked – in lieu of paying rent. So, this thing, where I knew he was a lazy stoner but, if I didn't give him somewhere to live, he wouldn't have a place to live. He was a charity case.

I

I was just housing him and when I grocery-shopped I bought for two. That's how it has to be) and one room for a lodger. Rent £100 a week – to cover Todd's keep, a built-in inequality that meant we couldn't like the lodger, at all. It wasn't going to work, right.

Anyhow, it was in Islington, the house. I had a lot of money suddenly which is a long story. We had this party and invited all the people from the dispatch company where Todd worked and his scratchy 'artist' mates with no art-school degree and my ex-fucks.

Eleanor crashed this party with her temporary boyfriend Mark – the CFO from the Plan 9 gig. Then she moved in with us and that was my life gone. It has kind of its own logic. Right,

this party was only at eleven o'clock, the doorbell rang and I ran down the broken stairs and got the door and it was Mark Keynes and Eleanor. As I opened up, she'd lost her balance and he had her by the shoulders; they were lurching in tandem like a maladroit pantomime horse, drunk. She was hiccoughing. He was unfocused, shy, ill at ease and

because she was so pretty, and Mark Keynes a CFO, or because she was wearing some black slip dress, green eye shadow, diamonds I thought were rhinestones,

I took her for a tart and didn't want her in my house. She was too pretty and too young, like shiny, and long blonde hair. (I want to fuck Mark Keynes, OK, although I'm not allowed to fuck him. Anyone. Fuck anyone, I can't. He is attractive, he is alpha, blah blah, and I had problems with just fucking people randomly. I had to quit it.)

'Tanya, hi,' said Mark Keynes. 'So it was the right house. Ha.'

'It was.' I smiled. But then I got hung up, just watching

the trees buffeted by the rainy wind, their leaves lighting up and going out again with wet. I was a little stoned. I thought my problem might go away. It didn't. Then

across the street I noticed, like a pink kite straining in the air, a second-storey window; seeming doubly pink cause you could see men in pink-spattered work clothes painting hot pink in there: one man on a ladder, and the other standing with a beer. They were talking, I assumed they were a gay couple and imagined they would be my new friends. I felt happier and thought how most of life was taken up with stupid fantasies like that — if you had good ones, you had a happy life out of the starting gate.

Then I was like, 'Hey, guys, come in,' but in that time the scene had changed cause she was crying.

She put both hands on her face and sobbed in jolts. The windy backdrop was *Wuthering Heights*-ish, trippy. You noticed that the stars weren't moving in the wind. And that fact seemed very sad and profound.

She wept, Mark Keynes had stiffened, mortified. I almost not quite reached out and touched her. Now I took her for a tart who was much deeper and more real than anyone I knew. I thought, That's how I would cry, if I were whoring, far from home. Stand weeping in the street. Fuck the world!

I loved her suddenly. Like I could have held her in my arms. I felt just so unbalanced and I wanted to slam the door or have us all sit down on the floor, like when children camp out underneath the dining table.

He patted her arm unwillingly and said, 'Come on, come on,' I stepped aside, they tumbled in and I had shut the door behind them.

Two

We breathed, close in the dark, dust-smelling stairwell; El and Mark sat on a step. I put my foot on the busted ceiling rose and leaned against the wall.

Then I lit a cigarette. I turned away from them to smoke. Then I was smoking so that standing in the dark hall was its own activity. Above, in the party, *OK Computer* played – like the soundtrack of forlornly hiding in a closet.

Then Mark started saying he and El had been seeing each other quite a bit 'since Jan moved out', and he thought I wouldn't mind. That I would like El, anyhow, that we would get along. 'Met at karaoke, hilarious, really.' I was looking at El, who'd introspected and leaned over dabbing her tears with the hem of her dress.

Then she spoke, clutching her skirt and speaking haltingly, 'I had . . . pretty desperate news on the telephone. It's actually nothing.' Her voice was high-pitched and faint, girl-child *à la* Marilyn; the accent mid-Atlantic. Pensive, she licked her mascara-grey tears.

And by the time she got her hiccoughs stopped, and we climbed the stairs into the noise that shuddered faintly as it settled over us like a ponderous cloak

I felt as if I'd come with them, and we were going up to face a room of strangers.

Three

I moved to London in the fall of '96. I was twenty-three, just out of college, and I got a job in London cause I'd done an internship that wanted me back. It was a guarantee of work, and I needed money then because my father lost his job. Or, was thrown off the Ayer, Massachusetts Police Force for taking one too many bribes, and being hated. So I had to send him money so he wouldn't lose the house.

But he spent my salary on restaurants and going to the dog track: lost the house.

Then I was paying his rent. I paid the landlord direct although I had to wire it and it cost a fee, I couldn't trust Dad. My brother Vinnie told me that the family discussed it and decided this 'castrated Dad so totally he'd never get a job, the way he felt'. Then Vinnie asked to borrow a grand. It was like comedy without the humour.

So, then they both died, my brother Vinnie and my father, dying slowly with no medical insurance just to fuck me. So they cost me every penny that I earned and still I have a lot of debts from when my dad was dying and he'd call me on the phone to spew vitriol because I wouldn't come home and nurse him in my spare time from earning for him. Till the brain tumour robbed him of speech. So when they totally were dead I was elated and said to Todd, 'I'm going to buy a factory with all that money that I'll save. I'm going to buy a Greek island.' Todd got all excited like I meant that literally. He said, 'Do the Greek island.'

And if you want to know how Vinnie died, it was drugs. So his rehab bills forever plus emergency care. He was always overdosing and being revived at great expense until the time he didn't come back to life.

It was a hill of money for my family to slowly die. I

used to cry until I threw up a lot. That couple of years I took sleeping pills every night, and some weekend mornings.

My brother Dana and my sister Dawn are still alive. We used to call them Dungeons and Dragons. They were evil twins. I've fallen out of touch since they both moved to Miami.

Four

And El and Mark and I came upstairs into the part of the house where the electrics worked and there was Todd standing in the hallway, kind of standing there, holding a shoebox of animal bones. His friend Annette boiled these bones and sold them off to other artists at parties. Todd was looking for me to give Annette ten pounds.

'Hey, Tan. Tanya. Look.'

I said, 'It's chickens.'

'No, it's a whole rabbit. Except its ears.'

'This is Mark and Eleanor.'

'Do you like my bones?' said Todd. 'I mean, the ones in the box. Not my main bones, my body bones. What would you call them, Tan?'

'Your . . . I don't know.'

Eleanor started to cry again. Todd looked stricken.

I stood there gulping. I was feeling nauseous cause I have these stomach problems tied to state of mind. I said to Eleanor, 'Why don't you . . .' I said to Mark, 'You could take her to my bedroom. It's not furnished or anything but . . .'

'There's a bed,' said Todd. 'I'll take you there. I guess I'll put my bones down here. I'll put them here on the old magazines, the old tenants left these motorbike magazines. I wouldn't buy motorbike magazines unless I really had a bike.'

I said, 'I'll get you drinks, I'll get you wine. Do you want wine?'

'Please,' said Mark Keynes. He put his palm between her shoulder blades and I turned and walked away from them. Once you got into the sitting room it was hot and noisy. People sweating. I thought about melting into the crowd, forgetting them because, fuck them.

The wine was in the kitchen, in the new refrigerator.

7

Someone had written WASH ME in dirt on the refrigerator cause it was the only clean thing in the house. There was a couple of artists with a cake-mix box on the kitchen floor, bitching cause there wasn't any oven. They had cake-mix powder on them. They were pouring it into their mouths. One was saying to the other, 'Nah, she's binned him now cause she's got confidence because she's shagged.'

I didn't talk to them, I got a bottle and went back and got to the bedroom hurried. And I put the bottle down and said, 'Shit, I didn't get . . . you need a corkscrew.'

'Glasses,' Mark said.

'I could do that,' said Todd, 'I'll get it.' He walked out with me and said quietly, 'She's gorgeous.'

I said, 'Oh, fucking hell.'

I went back to the kitchen. The cake-mix people had gone. I was alone and put both hands over my eyes and slowed my breathing. It made me feel nervous like I wanted to bite. I don't like cake-mix cakes so I decided on the spur of the moment to make a real cake. I dropped my arms and looked around kind of violently angry.

I'm a good cook because I cooked for my family. I can make a cake without a recipe. A yellow cake or coconut but I had no desiccated coconut so it was yellow. I had butter, sugar and eggs.

In the sitting room, framed in the kitchen door, people were dancing stuffed together in too little room to dance, one lane was cleared where an OD girl was being walked by men who chanted, 'She's cool, she's all right,' dreamily, a guy with no hair or eyebrows danced with a plastic lei around his neck along their lane, doing laps behind them, I was digging in the cupboards where I'd put my groceries yesterday. Lennie Lee came in the kitchen

in a shirt with silver lightning bolts on red satin,

8

threadbare; he steals all his clothes from the pavement in front of the Oxfam shop on principle, although he owns his own house, he went to Oxford. He has wild black hair like a joke wig, but we go way back anyway, he's like a friend.

'I thought you'd left,' said Lennie.

'It's my house.'

He was drinking sambuca from a mug. I could smell it. The mug said 'Stoke Newington Festival' on it which made me feel depressed. Like if you ever tried to go to those festivals, the fucking Scottish people on stilts, it makes you desperate. I found a wooden spoon that had the cardboard still on it from Sainsbury's. Lennie said, 'So, how are you doing?'

'It's been good, ever since I closed on the house and my family is dead, it's been a chance to regroup. I really feel OK.' I took the mug from his hand and drank a little. Then I drank it all. I said, 'I fixed my credit rating. That was like a Finnish saga, cause I co-signed on my brother's car in 1996 and he was living with me in Rhode Island when he went to prison? You don't care.' I gave the mug back empty.

Lennie held the mug against his lip, making eye contact. He said, 'Some people would be irritated by you just drinking their drink. But I like it. I love it when you're really selfish. Kiss me.'

'No. You're going to have to leave the kitchen if . . . I'm in a serious mood. I'm trying to have a real life, I can't put it into words.' I looked down at the flour bag, it was King Arthur brand with a cartoon of a knight.

Lennie sighed. 'I'm so depressed. I'm more depressed than you. It's agony. Do you have any sambuca left?'

'Check under the, the thing there, it's an EasyCrate,' I said. 'I'm making a cake.'

'Fantastic,' Lennie said on hands and knees. 'I'll throw it on the floor.'

'I don't care. I'm not *eating* the cake.'

'Fantastic. I love you. There's two bottles of sambuca here.'

'I'm rich now. I'm not joking. Drink it all.'

'I love you. Give me thousands of pounds.'

We made eye contact again, high to low.

'Give some money to me,' he said. 'Or sleep with me.'

'No.'

Lennie handed me a bottle up and I drank more sambuca. It was making me drunk. Kind of frightening. I said, 'I feel much better since my father died,' and sighed loud. My hand was shaking and I had to put the bottle down. 'However that sounds.'

Lennie stood. 'I think you're perfect. Perfectly evil. I mean that as a compliment. Kiss me.'

'Oh, Lennie, fuck.' I stooped down and got a bowl.

I felt him watching my skirt ride up. I wear skimpy clothes, my face is ugly, so I compensate. It's not a come-on, it's cause my eyes are too close together. I'm a dog. I mean, I don't *wear* make-up, what does that tell you. But I feel uncomfortable if anybody looks, so it's neurotic. It's a give-away. I said,

'I'm trying to get over that, anyway. Fucking everybody constantly.'

'Make an exception.'

'I'm serious. If I slept with you, I'd sleep with some sales rep tomorrow night, I can't face it.' I chopped butter off a block and started pouring sugar onto it. I did it by feel because, no measuring cups. It wouldn't probably work. I didn't want a fucking cake though. I crushed the sugar into the butter.

I said, 'I could really just lie on the floor and scream.'

'I'll join you.'

Annette walked in, saying, 'Lennie, if you had to have sex with an animal –'

10

'Deer,' Lennie said. 'I already spoke to Dominic.'

'Tanya, if you had to have sex with an animal, what animal would it be? It's for an installation.'

'I don't know. Toad. Salamander, given my luck.'

'No, you get to choose, it's what you'd prefer.'

'It is not!' I said. 'No, you don't get to choose! The salamander fucks you and you don't get to choose!'

I broke an egg, I was weirdly excited. But we all laughed cause what I'd said was pretty funny. Lennie said, 'I'd *love* to fuck a deer,' and I scattered flour on the butter sugar egg mix. He said, 'It would be lovely to fuck a deer.' Annette said, 'It would shit in your bed.'

I picked the mixing bowl up and realised I didn't have an oven. I was saying, 'This is just the kind of conversation,' laughing, and I took the bowl into the sitting room. Everyone was dancing in there. It must have been one o'clock. Our friend Nick had brought a kind of strobe light that sat on the floor so it was strobing in there against the dirty-white skirting boards, feet feet feet. It smelled like people and I had this bowl. I pushed through, let the bowl shoulder through the dancing people.

I paused in the midst of it and had a spoon of batter. It was good batter, I don't know. I thought it ought to have drugs mixed in, but otherwise it was a cooler thing to offer at a party than a cake. I walked on through, feeling as I left the crowd and, in the cool hallway it was like I had been made suddenly visible. I stood there feeling my naked legs and bare feet. The salamander fucks you. Haw haw.

I went on and opened up the bedroom door with my hip.

Her bare breast shone like a lamp. One leg was hooked over his shirted back, a slender, poised limb like a listening doe. It was Eleanor being fucked by Mark. I stepped back. The door closed by itself.

It would shit in your bed. I ate a spoonful of batter. Todd came walking towards me with a framed photograph of the Dalai Lama hugging Todd. I said, 'No,' in a strangled tone.

He said, 'I was going to show her this, cause we . . . we had this conversation and I thought she might be interested.'

I said, 'You should leave them alone.'

He read my face and we stood facing each other with our objects. I'd made them a cake and they rejected it. It was as if.

I said, 'My God, you think all these people are ever going to leave?'

'We should go back and try to . . . I saw you talking to Lennie, did he decide about my show?'

'He'll let you have a show, don't worry. We should move away from this door.' I put the bowl down on the hallway floor and stepped away from it. Todd leaned his Dalai Lama photograph against the wall beside the batter bowl.

He said, looking at it, 'That was retarded good that day.'

I said, 'I was at work, I couldn't come because I had that meeting.'

'No, I swore that you were there.'

'I was at work. I might go over to the all-night gym now.'

'Tannie. Like, no.'

'I don't feel good.'

'What am I going to do?' said Todd. We parted ways and I couldn't get my gym clothes because they were in that bedroom and

the rest of the night I danced some and took an E off Jeremy that gave me a short mild panic attack and got in one of those political scraps with Em, who assumes I'm a Tory cause of my job and she was something on the *Rainbow*

Warrior before she had her kid as if that made the Earth a paradise, is all. I'm not a fucking Tory. Just

I get these negative feelings. When I went back to the bedroom, they were gone. The others all were leaving, they were going to a club.

I lay on the bedroom floor and pulled the duvet down to me. I watched our friends pass going out. I watched them sideways from the floor. Some people waved. Then Todd came in and said,

'Do you think we did OK?'

I rolled my eyes. '*I* had a good time.'

He sighed, appreciative and sheepish at my pointing out his blunder, his neediness. He said, 'Yeah ... I had a good time, too, kind of.'

And he went across the hall to his room, to his inflatable mattress I had bought him; I could hear him plug it in, and the moaning engine that inflated it. At last I sat up on my haunches and felt across the mussed sheet. There was no wet spot. I got in. The mattress engine stopped and I heard our friends quietly, obliquely, from the bus stop outside, saying, 'Get a kebab? Three, I reckon. Place on Kingsland Road is open.' Then the roar of the bus and it swept all the noise away with it.

Five

Next week, I'm at work and my cell rings with the caller ID saying HILTON and I think it's a client who's in town from Liverpool, because we have this contract pending for some fertiliser people which would open doors for us if it happened but it's Todd.

It was six, that's a lull for me before the building empties. I was sitting on Nick's desk, eating shrink-wrapped sushi from the vending machine. We had our paperwork under the sushi and, complaining. We weren't getting anything done.

Nick's an accountant from the downstairs company, Sofanet: we got to be improbable friends because we both work later than the rest of the building. Nick has a bad home situation, and I work constantly because. And cause I own my own company, me and a partner. So that's my excuse, like this is fate and unavoidable, although I really work constantly because I do.

When I started as an employee, our business was providing mailing lists. If you retailed diet dog food, we'd find a list of fat dog owners you could mail your catalogue. But we got some craze for diversifying cause we never had the scale of business that could keep my whole family in meds.

So first I offered Sofanet an all-in catalogue package at some cost that wouldn't earn out in the fucking Sudan, but it 'opened doors for us' – then we'd do a whole catalogue, or send someone to second-guess your catalogue staff; we created a marketing IT 'arm' cause you can always sell new computer packages to business since existing packages are full of bugs because computers don't really work.

But I'll do anything, I even do some fucking day-trading in the evening after people have gone home. That's a hobby, really, with the company's money, but. I mean, I'm not expected to, but. It's unexpected on the whole. But that's what owning your own business means.

It means you don't have a real job. OK.

Cause we don't have the personality to be employed by anyone. Like Alan who is kleptomaniacal and violent, who's the founder. And he's always in a taxicab drinking from a bottle saying *fuck fuck fuck* in an accent like Prince Charles, or like a basset hound. One year he even sniffed glue. I mean, at forty. It was how he cheered up after his testicular cancer.

That's all I really could say, and then the cellphone rings, OK.

It's Todd. He's at the fucking Hilton Intercontinental, he says,

'Hey, Tan. I'm with that girl.'

(I turned my back to munching Nick and sighed. I was looking at, on Nick's wall, he'd taped a poster, 'Sporting Fish of the Americas', with all the fish like marlin or bonefish sportsmen catch, drawn commercial-art style in rows, all facing in the same direction, mouths agape. Beside it, smaller and framed, was a photo of his older sister, facing in the same direction, mouth agape, dressed to play the part of Desdemona in a tragedy nightgown.) I said,

'Todd, don't fucking call me at work. Unless there's something.'

'But she's going to take that room,' said Todd. 'I totally am not bugging you, I promise.'

'Did you get the plumber?' (This was from an earlier fight where he didn't get the plumber.) He said,

'Yeah, I'm getting the plumber tomorrow. So it's two good things. That's cool you reminded me, the plumber was good, too.'

'What girl?' Then I said, 'Thanks with the plumber. Thanks.'

'The crying Eleanor girl from the party. Who was with your Mark.'

'Shit,' I said. Todd said, 'Yeah. She needs somewhere to live.'

'She doesn't like the Hilton?'

'Yeah, this is the Hilton. It's kind of awesome,' Todd said. 'It's pretty crazy luxurious, though, like not my thing. But you should come and talk to her. You should come over now. I mean, it's eight.'

'I'd have to come and go back.'

'It's eight, you shouldn't ought to work beyond a certain hour. I cut you out that article. It wrecks all your Arcadian rhythms.'

'I'll come. But not . . . OK, I'll come now. I'll get a taxi, OK.'

'Well, yeah. Come over. We've got sausage pizza from the In-room Dining. But they call it Pizza Saucisson. Get it?'

'No.'

'I mean, they don't call it sausage. It's called Saucisson cause they're pretentious.'

'Oh, shit. Goodbye,' I said hanging up.

I asked Nick why I had to be burdened down with retards. He laughed equably and started cleaning up the sushi mess. I cleaned, too, and Nick had his own problems, he was sort of a tame bloke, very chubby, pink, unattractively blond. He told me once his sister 'got all the money', admiringly, the way a modest person might say, 'She got the brains, she got the looks.' She got the money when their father died; he was living in her basement, and she acted in the RSC and called Nick 'Nigger'. But she always had since they were small. That made it all right.

I'd got a scrap of ginger onto Nick's copy of the autumn

catalogue, it clung there. It was like a tiny handkerchief. Or like a snot, it was thematically confined in what it looked like. I threw the last garbage away, I felt a little crazy, what's new, and

Alan came storming in, barking, 'Fuck! What are you doing down here, you lazy cow?'

'Nick's 'puter wouldn't let him in the nineties.'

'Fix your fucking machine, Nick,' Alan said.

I said, 'But now I have to get a cab.'

'Thrilled to hear it. I can get a ride with you and you can pay. I'm just assuming that's all right. Night, Nick! I'll ring for it, are you off back to Islington?'

'No,' I said, 'And anyway, I'll actually walk.'

'Fuck off!' said Alan, outraged, so I told him to fuck himself, and this was the basic conversation that we dusted off each time we saw each other. It was heart-warming if it wasn't dispiriting. He left the room without another word.

I left the office soon after. With a fiver only so I'd have to go back. That was how – I had a house, now, to pay for. No peace for the wicked and etc.

And I walked through the streets. The rain stopped as I walked and I recalled

When I was eighteen I went to Prague for a month. I went to Prague because it was the cool place and this was when I didn't have expenses. So I spent my money and I went to Prague.

It was a great place, totally batty and gentle and permissive, but

the point is that I went to this bar, called Asylum, that was run by expatriate American kids, they had bad bands there and showed bad art.

I was there this night to see a girl from Michigan, Melyssa, who I met at a concert in Petřín Park, I had been kissing a stranger in the bushes and I walked down the hill disoriented, tousled, with leaves in my hair, and Melyssa was there. She told me that my shirt was buttoned wrong, in English. The stranger came staggering after and she said to him, 'Pyotr, are you coming to my opening tonight?'

He said 'No,' in Czech, Melyssa said to me, 'He's so mean. You come,' then the Kraków Orchestra began to play Martinů downhill.

So I went to Asylum where I met

Melyssa with a Czech girl, Sharka, who was beautiful, a leggy white-blonde with that unearthly beauty of intelligent beauties, she was really really beautiful; wearing jeans and a man's shirt.

Melyssa said as I joined their table, 'I'm sick, I swear I've got a fever. Feel my forehead.'

Sharka said flatly, 'You should be in bed.'

Melyssa said, feeling her own forehead since we didn't, 'I don't want to go home. I'm just feverish.'

'You should go home,' said Sharka with the cold tone of someone declining to play games.

'I just said I don't want to go home. God.'

'If you are sick, you should be at home.'

And Sharka went up to the bar and did not come back.

Melyssa said to me, 'God! Do you believe her? We *just made up*? Cause only yesterday when we were walking home, I slipped and fell on the ice, OK? And then, my hip was really hurt. And this was in the middle of the road? So I said to her to help me cause I couldn't get up. And she just says in this voice, "*Get up*." And I said, but I can't get up, I'm really hurt. And by that time there was a car coming, headlights coming towards me, and I said, could you help me, and Sharka only said, "*Get up*." And I was, look, there's a car coming, I'm really crippled, could you give me a hand, cause this is shit, and she just goes "*Get up*."

'So, I got up. And then, we were walking to my house and she stops and turns to me and says, "I am finished now with you and your friends. You are *evil*. You are *like Satan*."

'But I saw her here tonight and I thought she was over it,' Melyssa wrapped up with pained eyes, with her head cocked. I looked across the room at Sharka.

Sharka was looking at me. She smiled knowingly. I realised abruptly they were lesbians. And that month Melyssa was found in a Hilton room, dead. It wasn't murder, probably, but it was an OD which didn't seem like her. And I remember I thought about Satan, and hell. I saw Sharka after at Bunkr, Radost, rave clubs, but she wasn't beautiful. The beautiful was something that had happened to me.

Seven

I had come to Park Lane, I was tired. There the Hilton was, with its plaza of lit cabs, like a lap full of cabs. The stock glass/plush hotel, deluxe luxury for pigs. It was good to walk up to it on foot, it made you feel like an interloper.

I kept thinking they would stop me in the lobby, but they didn't. It was room 312, DO NOT DISTURB in English, Japanese and Arabic.

Todd opened, high to see me. It was, 'Tannie! Isn't this cool? It's too cool,' El was sitting up in bed in a Hilton bathrobe saying, 'Oh, no!' and laughing and

the room trashed. Stockings, dresses on the floor where someone'd sat there playing chess on top and left the board out. Cigarette ends planted in a dried chunk of lasagne. There were so many orange–flavour Tic Tac boxes that they brightened the room. A brunette had gotten a haircut in the bathroom while eating McDonald's. There were Polaroids of mutts shagging stuck to the mirror with (El did this later at our house) the nicotine gum she chewed wherever you can't smoke. On the floor lay three rose bouquets, still in their cones of paper, in three different stages of dead.

I said, 'You want to move in with me and make a mess like this?'

Todd laughed, lovingly like he knew I meant no harm. He said, 'Duh!'

I sat on the bed and Todd was pouring me a Glenmorangie. 'Not for me,' I said, but he just put it in my hand. He said, 'It's so great, try it.'

'I've had Glenmorangie,' I said. 'OK, it's great. I have to work after this.'

They said, 'No!'

I hate when people try to stop me. Like, when people try to fucking stop you, I was tired suddenly. I said, 'So, to the point, you want the room?' I turned to Eleanor, I hadn't met her eye till then. (Her hair spread all over, one tress of it ran all the way across the neighbouring pillow, one ran into bed beside her body. Blonde. She had absolutely brown freckles on her white skin, her nose was pink as if she'd been crying, intense. And she was that intensely pretty that, you could not see behind it to her face, to who she was. I didn't know what was in front of me.)

She said, 'I'm skint, is the terrible thing. Todd said it might still be OK?'

'Skint?' I said, 'But, where are you living now? Here?'

'Probably.' She reached under the covers and pulled out a sudden stuffed animal, a maned lion.

'You don't know?' There was a pause, I said, 'Are you still seeing Mark?'

'Mark Keynes, no.' She furrowed her brow. 'I think he had some problems cause he left his wife. He's down, in fact. You'd have to ask him.'

'Who are the flowers from, then?' There was a pause, I said 'Is it a boyfriend? Are you dating?' El coughed, there was a pause. I said, 'I want to know because,'

'I don't see anyone,' she said. El turned her stuffed lion so it looked her in the face. I said, 'Who's paying for the room? Cause,'

Todd said, 'This is so not right.'

'I'm only asking.'

'Like a *hundred questions*.'

I said, 'I have a right to know —' he said, 'You weren't going to rent it till the painting was done, and then she'd have it by then,' I said, 'Just don't, because I wasn't going to rent it so I'd get some quiet —' he said, 'You lie so much!

You're such a liar! That was like the opposite of what you said!' I said, 'It wasn't! What do *you* think I said? Fuck this!'

Then we clammed up. Hot. El was blinking hard. She fooled with the bathrobe – she was wearing something under it, fucking white negligee thing. Lace daisies. And she had on a scarf, white wrinkled crêpe wrapped five times around her neck and clumsily knotted.

I said, 'Not that any of that is so vital.'

'You got to change your mind,' Todd muttered, sullen, and lay back.

There was a moment where I peacefully *saw* playing chess on the floor – I'd be lying on my side on a heap of clothes and laughing at something, smoking. Her lacy gear and schoolgirl affectations; she would hide her face in her hands when I got checkmate. And I sipped my Glenmorangie – I had finished it –

I said, 'Well, come and live with us. What the fuck.'

Todd sat up saying '*Cool*,' El blurted,

'Only, I won't ever have the money, that's the truth. I'd like to say I will but that's bullshit. I never have the rent, so if you need it, you should say no.'

Something in her then was so Vinnie. I got hung up by it cause, I couldn't tell, was it her smirk (my brother Vinnie used to smirk every time he said anything that passed muster, making it immediately stop passing muster; the accepting faces at the restaurant table cooled, expressing distaste, and Vinnie *noticed*. Vinnie started shaking, stammering, he was so hurt, he would

go to the men's room and I think shoot up.

I'd say, 'Damn, you got to cut Vinnie slack, he only just got clean,' and people'd go, 'We didn't do anything, we didn't say anything,' they'd act insulted. People have no fucking charity) and I looked at her, imagining a world that had charity, and failed to understand that what reminded me of Vinnie – she was lying.

And Eleanor said

Eight

'I once earned pots of money. I used to dole money out to others, I had people who depended on me. No one believes that now.

'I was an artist,' she said. Then she put the lion down, carefully as if it might tip over. There was a silence while we tried to picture Eleanor being an artist, or an artist having money. She said,

'It was from being beaten, that I stopped. A drug dealer who was in love with me. He had been a drug dealer, but he got Aids. Then people didn't want to buy from him, it's funny. And he was ill, he had neuropathy, you know, from the treatment.

'Anyhow, I gave him diamond necklaces. I used to have diamonds and rubies, I still have, mostly, from having all that money. We'd pretend he was borrowing them to cheer up. Then he never gave them back, he was pawning them. He needed lots of money for his habit, cause you can't judge people for taking painkillers with neuropathy. I didn't mind giving him my diamonds at all.

'I wouldn't sleep with him, though. He said that didn't matter. I actually believe what people tell me, it's daft.

'So this night we were talking about dreams, we used to sit in front of the gas fire talking. And I said he didn't seem like a person who would dream about flying. That was truly all it was.

'But he went mad. He beat me, he was thrashing me with a chair. Of course, you didn't know he could, he had seemed so weak. And we were mates, we used to make a fort from blankets, it was actually a magical time. His name was Brendan. But he broke my ribs, I had concussion. It was serious.

'I had to stay in hospital, and then I couldn't earn. Someone helped me out and got me this.'

She looked around at the Hilton room, its mess and its respectable appointments, its TV. She hugged herself and said, 'It's paid for three weeks, and it's got to be two and a half weeks now. Then he found me here, anyway, the drug dealer. The flowers are from him ... God, I wish that somebody would hold me.'

Todd cleared his throat. We heard the room's hush against the traffic below, a cop siren drawing its wavy line. Todd cleared his throat and said, 'I would if you were serious.'

She said, 'I don't even mean I'd never have the rent. When I get upset, I say things out of fear. I'm in the Hilton, after all. I do all right.' She crept out of bed, not looking at us. Got the Glenmorangie from the floor, not looking at it, and she drank from the bottle. Clumsy with it, like a child helping an adult. She put the bottle down and said,

'God, I need your help. I don't want to tell you how much, because I'd frighten you off. I need a safe place. Last year, I was doing so well. I need to do well again, I'm thirty.'

'You're thirty?' I said, and Todd laughed at the tone of my voice. Then he said, 'Wow, sorry. I don't know why I laughed.'

El said, 'You'd genuinely let me stay with you? You won't just say it to my face and phone me later on to say you changed your mind?'

'No,' I said. 'Ask Todd, I say what I mean.'

'Tanya totally will hurt your feelings,' Todd said. 'It doesn't bother her.'

'Thanks,' said El. 'I feel like I can relax now.'

Then we shut up, it was like rushing energetically to open a door, and it's locked. Todd and I sat back. I was checking out a mash of scars on El's neck, partly hidden where she wore the crêpe scarf as if to hide those scars. It looked like someone tried to cut off her head. It was Frankenstein bad. El stirred and brightened and said,

'I want to draw you a lion. Can I? I draw very well, you'd be amazed.' She got up and fished a pencil from a bowl of pistachio shells. 'I only draw for certain people. If I like people, I want to draw for them. Oh, I don't have paper, shit. Oh −' She got a passport from an open drawer, an American passport. She sat on the edge of the bed and opened it, drew dashingly swift with an air of magic trick, like plucking coins from the air. I leaned close and

'Whose passport is that?' I said.

'Don't worry, I'm not wrecking someone's passport. It's mine.'

'Where are you from? You're American?'

'I don't know.'

'Somebody said you were Dutch,' Todd said.

'Oh yeah, I'm Dutch,' she agreed. (She was American.) And she was drawing a lion on the Comments page. I said, 'You know you're not supposed to do that,' she said, 'No, it's OK,' and

had drawn this fucking outstanding lion. It fit within the design of the page so it looked like a unified masterwork. It had the bulk of its weight on its back paws. It squinted, drowsy and cross. Todd was staring cause he tries to draw. He's an artist, if you get to decide if you're an artist. And his mates whose 'sculptures' look like a Mexican yard sale, who can't draw. She was done so fast it was like signing her name.

El said, 'Keep this,' and said, 'Then I'll believe that I'll see you again. It's my only passport.'

I said, 'OK,' because I didn't know what to say. Her lip was trembling. I took the passport from her hand. It felt solid and fine, like an antique. El was crying.

And she said, 'You know I was never an artist.'

I said, 'No, I believe what people tell me. You were saying you believed what people said.'

'But this is obvious. It's not a lie, it's so obvious. I'm a whore.' She sobbed hard. Todd got up and rushed to the bathroom. Then he was back with a bunch of napkins stamped with the Hilton H. He thrust them into Eleanor's face. She pushed his hand and said, 'I don't want any tissues, fuck. I want to have not just said that.'

'It's all right,' I said, with the passport trembling. 'I mean, it's all right.'

'Yeah,' Todd said.

'No, it's not all right. It's like being raped every day for money.'

'We didn't mean —'

'That's why I need a place. I need to get out of this. I need to *be safe.*'

'It's all right,' I said, and I was bending the passport, clutching it.

She said, 'I'm only crying cause I'm so glad you're here. It makes me vulnerable. I don't know what I'm saying.'

And she said, 'God, you'll never even like me now. I fuck everything up. I shouldn't say that either,' and she said, 'I want to set myself on fire! I want to fucking die!'

Nine

And I stroked El's back and held her hand and changed the subject; I would help her, I would give her a break. She would be safe. The blond light in the room was cloying. Todd breathed deep. I wanted to crawl in bed beside her and forget. I wanted like I seldom let myself, to have a good excuse

to have her in my house.

She dried her eyes. I started chattering, telling stories meant to be funny, though

I felt sick. It was nine suddenly and I got up. They were protesting (laughing) and the room seemed to be full of twinkling glass, it was like Christmas advertising, lavish. (Passing the ajar closet door, I spotted, on the inside doorknob was a bracelet, bling, that could be diamonds or fake. Prostitutes don't wear diamonds, it's a young girl's fantasy of being a courtesan. She could be a rich kid or that bracelet was 2.99 from Boots. And I asked El again who had paid for the hotel room, she turned bright red and covered her mouth. She said, *I can't tell, because I actually promised.*)

But the story I had told while we all were still sitting there, it was how I met Todd. We were fourteen then. About us being in love. It has an unhappy ending I didn't tell. Todd kept interrupting me excitedly to say what I was saying was true. Then he left with me.

We took the lift down in silence. It was like we were being one person, digesting an experience alone. We faced the doors. Then Todd took a deep breath and wistfully sighed.

I said, 'We shouldn't have done that, fuck.' He said, 'Oh, *Tannie.*'

And when we got to the street, and the lights and noise and rain were overhead like a storm, Todd hugged me suddenly hard. He said, as he sometimes does, for reasons more of his own, cause what it means to me doesn't come up, and I don't know what it means to me,

'Love.'

Ten

When we were fourteen, Todd and I were tennis friends. We used to play tennis, and I had a crush on him cause his parents had a tennis court. We were both gifted, serious players. People find this humorous now.

Really it was my first crush on money. Cause Todd's house had a tennis court, he had a tennis coach, these were essentials if you wanted to be pro. Because I didn't have them – had to use the public courts, which were a drive and no one wanted to drive me – I was finished. Achievement was a luxury denied my class.

Todd's parents had a heated swimming pool and a gym. The tennis coach and personal trainer came to them. They had a time share in a Lear jet: Todd slept full length on his way to junior tournaments. One of those ironies: Todd had a sponsor, and some of his fabulous gear came free.

In the Lear jet, Todd went to Tanzania with his mother. She took him there to celebrate his straight As. They sampled grubs and shared a grass hut; and their jeep was charged by an actual rhino.

Being charged by a rhino was a luxury denied my class. And beyond the exclusive rhinoceros, the cheated hope, raisin in the sun, whatever – the worst sting was my personal conviction that a family who loved me was a luxury denied my class.

One day my father went berserk. He pissed on my bed. Called me bastard for the thousandth time. Told me if he fed me, it was like a birdfeeder, like throwing crumbs to pigeons. He said, now on, he was putting rat poison in my food, to prove if I was part rat.

I never had a meek nature: I am for me. And nothing cows me, I walloped that prick, I'd never learned how to fight and thought somehow, this time, if I hit him with both joined fists that would work better. He caught my arms and threw me to the floor, head first. That opened my old scab on my brow and I saw blood.

Then we just whaled on each other.

I fought him, shouting, scratching, and feet, till I rang numb with blows and he stopped to vomit.

There was a pause while I sat on the hall floor. Dad was going to the kitchen for a beer. I sobbed but no tears came. Dad was opening and closing drawers and swearing in the kitchen. I had noticed a stray dull blue glass marble, poised in a crack in the floorboards, that I could maybe convert into a weapon

when my brothers came home. I said to them, 'I'm fighting Dad.'

They jeered, 'You and Dad, that's so perverted. That's demented. Why you wanna,'

Dad came back with his gun. I shrieked at my brothers till I couldn't breathe,

'You Benedict Arnolds, fuckin traitors, you can live with him, you live with him, you're like his dead abortions, you're shits he took.'

Dad was saying, 'You rat, fuckin bastard rat, I ought to killed your slut mother but I'll get you.'

I screamed, 'Do it!'

He shot the ceiling so my brothers yelled 'WHOA!' They dove behind the couch, the table. They were laughing high-pitched, thrilled; plaster fell and rose again as smoke. For a minute it was just my dad and me, facing off like two adults.

(And I saw how I could leave. I had the one idea I ever had that mattered, that sufficed, to change my life. I knew, as if somebody handed me a key – in Todd's world, fathers *can't fire guns* at kids.)

'I'm out of this dump. Fuck you,' I said, all quiet because I was free.

'Where you going, rat, to yaw fuckin rat hole?' Dad shouted, his voice afraid, 'Don't you leave *this house.*'

I ran to my room I shared with Dawn and shoved the TV set she got for her birthday to the floor so it smashed. I decided not even to pack. And I stood over my soiled bed, where my father's piss was surprisingly odourless;

ran away from home.

I walked the three hours to Todd's house, a three-storey Colonial on ten wooded acres. To his tennis court and weights room, the image in my mind of their quarter horse, Maiden Voyage, put down for her equine arthritis, and Todd's mom cradled Maiden's head in her lap as she died. The vet gave the shot and the mare had buckled and gone down on her knees, not understanding. Then the whole family and the girl groom stroked Maiden's flanks and cried. Everybody understood Todd wouldn't go to school the day after the horse died.

Walking in the brisk night felt so beautiful. I cried a lot, I was still in love with my brothers for that one night. The trees were black to high overhead. I made it from street light to street light. When you were under the light, your eyes would stiffen, and heading back into the dark was like going downhill. When I saw Todd's house, the tiredness hit me in one go, my knees were jittering. Then I started running, and crying, it was just like I'd thought.

Eleven

'We're not sending you back,' Todd's father Craig swore at last, jaw set, thumbs hooked through his bathrobe belt-hooks. 'You don't have to be afraid any more.' (And Todd's father Craig was a professor of French and semiotics, with a beard, at Tufts. He made a joke of calling things he found comical – rider-mower, Hoppity Hop, nose ring – by their French names.)

'I still say we should call the police,' said Todd's mother Janet and she shook her head. 'I'm taking you to buy clothes *tomorrow*, don't worry, you don't have to face that man again until you're good and ready.' (And Todd's mother Janet was a tiny brunette who stood up like a toy soldier, who was an early adopter of Pilates. She once came home in tears from town cause a drunk had called her 'white bitch'. It was her money, old wealth.)

Craig said, 'Then we're agreed.' He looked up sentimental at his wife. Her face waned and doted. It was still tan from Africa, from *Tanzania*, that pun niggled at me like pinching clothes. Todd's bare arm appeared in my peripheral vision; it had been there all the time and only *seemed* to appear when I thought 'tan'.

He had tennis muscles. He had green eyes and a well-appointed gym. He had blond Greek-god hair, and a potent air of being well fed. It was like his country was at peace and mine was at war.

After Craig and Janet went to bed, Todd was getting fresh sheets for me, his undershirt riding up to show brown, and he turned to me, sheets heaped in his arms, and said, 'Except, it might be weird for me, you being here, because. I mean, I really like you, Tanya? Like, I *like you*.'

'Like?'

'I don't know. As a girlfriend?' He shrugged. He studied me unhappily and shrugged and said, 'That's cool. If you . . .'

'No. I mean. I like you, too. As – a boyfriend.'

It went from my soles of my feet to my scalp. I looked at him as if he were a wonderful restaurant, and somebody told me *order anything, it's on me.*

Todd dumped the sheets on the deep pile carpet. We made out, with the frank agility of tennis players. I was thinking as I shut my eyes how I would rather Sauconies than Nikes this year, because the Nikes didn't brace the instep for my shape of foot, if I'd get Janet to the mall they had them at the Foot Locker that would speed up my game great

(The sheets were Todd's old childhood sheets; they had a print of astronauts on a blue ground. Each astronaut was braced with his snowman arms in a falling posture, and the line that should have led back to a spacecraft was chopped off, clear for the next astronaut. If you stared at them while trying to sleep, you realised they were cut off from their crafts, eternally falling, a crowd of astronauts just far enough apart they could not help each other; in neat ranks, they were lost in space.)

as my body lit in Todd's arms and I was *flying.*

Twelve

And I walked away from Todd as we both walked away from the Hilton. The rain was raw like I could actually feel the rain. 'Love,' Todd had said, ringing false because it went without saying. I couldn't remember being someone who didn't love Todd. I walked past Green Park, vacant and grey in there as if the trees had been switched off for the night. The sky had worn through to blue at the top; bats flickered and swung. I got the Tube and

on the train read Eleanor's passport. There were no stamps, just the lion and her photo, there was nothing to read. But in the photo she was nude to the waist. I got out by my office, Old Street,

but went to Hutchinson's.

Jamie Hutchinson was an ex-banker: fifty, supersmart, gaunt, money to burn. We first screwed when he was still at Goldman Sachs and I was twenty. Then we fucked a lot, he was the only person I could show up on his doorstep and he'd be home. His place was walking distance from my work. So, he got to be like a friend.

I slept there plenty even now. I never screwed him any more, but we watched videos and shared a bed to satisfy some urge to share a bed. We held hands. We said, 'I love you,' meaning anything we wanted at the time and used each other, OK.

But I've never been good at going home. I just don't like it, going home is not my kind of thing, I'm like the wrong type and so this night I went to Hutchinson's to talk. To watch some movie I would never watch ('Iranian cinema') and drink great port. Sometimes he plays piano; he's some pianist manqué, and this is what I loved when that was all my luxury I had. I'd go there from some filth and having worked a hundred hours on the trot. I'd go to use his nice shower. He'd phone up for Indian. We had this thing that only we liked vindaloo, so that was what we had, we got both prawn and chicken. Opening a bottle. God, I used to just relax.

'There was a point to this. Oh yes, I found this bit in Heidegger –'

He always had women drifting in and out. Women liked Hutch, it was a problem how they wanted him to marry them etc. And he was romantic, yearned outspokenly to fall in love. He always thought he was. So he'd tell me he had fallen in love, and then he'd never mention that Annabel, Jo, Beth, again.

So I'm sitting in an armchair in his bathrobe I wear at his house and he's standing (cause he stands to talk to you, it takes some getting used to, but he can't sit for long because he broke his hip badly as a boy), I'm saying,

'There's this sexual envy, cause you have to understand men fall in love with her beauty. And I've had men fall in love with me, but not for my beauty, cause, well. OK. And then I feel like, if it's not for your beauty, that doesn't count. I want to be the fucking *princess*, but now I want the princess too, for myself. I kind of want to fuck the princess. No, it may not be that,' I said, with a sense what I was saying was bullshit. I couldn't understand what I meant. The words were bugging me, I tried standing up.

'No,' I said, and sat down again. 'Shit. She gave me her passport, you know? But it's counterfeit. She's naked in the photograph. It looks legit, but.'

Her name there was Beautiful Boots. It was like a passport from the country where porn films happen, which implied some shit too warped to get into tonight. I stood and wandered over where Hutch was pouring port. I put my hand on his elbow, sighed and leaned my head against his shoulder. I saw him smile in the reflection in the shiny fridge. We were happy like that, it kind of broke my heart. How great these people are, who aren't a 'real relationship'.

He said, 'I had a fairly rocky week, too. Re: Fran.'

I started smiling in the fridge. I said, 'Is it over now?'

'I don't know,' he said thoughtfully. 'I might never see her again, of course.'

'Did she sleep with you, at least?'

'I'm not ready . . . did. But she hated me, after. It was rather disconcerting. Tell me something. You never . . .'

There was a pause while he thought about what he was saying and handed me wine. I drank, and he said, 'I never liked to mention this, but I thought it strange I never saw you naked.'

I laughed so abruptly I got wine in my nose. I imagined like, if I had a tail or I could have gills, secretly. (It made me scared as shit to talk about. I never talk about this stuff.) I said, 'Yeah, so what? So if you saw the real me, you'd be revolted, right? Whatever.'

He said, 'Truthfully. It bothered me. It made me concerned about you.'

I caught my breath and poured more wine for myself. My stomach hurt and maybe I should stop drinking wine. My stomach hurt and I was staring at the nice designer frames on his kitchen wall. There was one picture of me.

I was sitting with Hutch's late cat, Sabrina, on my lap. I had a big milk moustache and she was licking it. I looked really actually nice.

Hutch said, 'Because I do encounter this, that women have difficulty with sex. Men, too, I know, although I never

37

had . . . I never saw the difficulty. That's the one thing that never was difficult for me.'

I said, hoarse, 'But you know why I wouldn't be naked.'

'No, I don't.'

'No, you have to,' I insisted. I wanted to pull the bathrobe tighter and tie the belt into a knot. I kept imagining doing this. That would be such a giveaway. I said,

'Look, you *know*, when I was in LA, when I was living with Vinnie in that building. It was a really pretty fucked–up time cause Vinnie had his thrombosis and his other leg was broken so he got to be wheelchair–bound? I mean, I had all this shit going on. I ended up scoring drugs for him once and then I changed my mind and flushed them down the toilet and you know.'

Hutch was looking at me mournfully, vigilantly. He had his glass of wine up stiffly like a torch to see me by.

I spat out, 'That's when I got my plastic surgery. You *must know*. I mean, you can't *not notice*. You *must know*.'

'I know. But I didn't . . . never realised that was a problem.' His eyes darted up and down me. I shuddered, feeling slimy and lost. I said, 'Jamie, look. It's not that that's the problem, cause . . . I mean, it's gross, yeah. My brother egged me on to it, OK. I don't know *why*. But I thought it would make me feel all right, I couldn't stand even being in a bathing suit, and this was California?'

I got breast implants and lipo on my thighs. I economised and got a job that makes me look like a plastic blow–up doll. I guess it's not really as disgusting as I think. I have to get the breasts replaced this year but I keep putting it off. What the fuck, I look hot in clothes.

I haven't had sex with the lights on, ever. Never put on that bathing suit.

Hutchinson put his hand out to my forehead and pressed

down there. Sometimes men do this, they press your head down, I never could decide what it meant. He said, 'I could tell about your breasts, but I thought the aim was, to look good.'

'You mean because they feel like styrofoam.'

There was a pause. Then he said, 'I never knew what styrofoam was. It's an American word.'

'They don't feel like fucking breasts!' I was having trouble breathing again. I said, 'It doesn't matter, really. I don't know. But you're not the only one, no one ever gets to see me naked, I look like some fucked Barbie.'

'Can't you get it undone?'

'No! Some of it I could, but then you're not the same . . . you can imagine, I don't have to say all this, God.'

'Don't be angry at me. I don't care if you want to have sex hanging upside down or in a . . . tent. I'm at your service, as you know.' Hutch smiled at me. When I caught my breath, I could see he wasn't upset. It seemed incredible because I had just hated him so much I was weak with sweat, fuck.

I pulled the bathrobe tight and tugged the belt close, tying it into a knot. 'Well, whatever,' I said. 'I forget, what does this have to do with your girlfriend?'

'Fran's not my girlfriend,' he said. 'No fear of that! I think she's only nineteen.'

I laughed. 'Nineteen. That's a little extreme.'

'She's a very old nineteen.'

'Yeah! Do tell! Where have I heard that before?'

We were both laughing hard again, in our own shared safe world again. I went off to the bathroom and when I came back he'd started the DVD of people having similar crises to our dumb crises, only in Tehran and that was weirdly consoling.

We lay on the settee in each other's arms. It was a movie

so slow you couldn't tell when the set was on Pause, and we had seen it before. Some scenes, the characters walked down empty streets, not talking, and the only action was when breeze ruffled their hair. Once he got up to get a bottle. The movie ended and I lay with my head on his chest just thinking and looking at the spines of his books. He said, 'It's odd to have arrived at this age. I guess it will be odder yet to be *dying*.' I said, 'Well, it was *fucking odd* being nineteen.'

Then I felt mortally tired and stumbled off like mortally wounded to drop off in his bed in some circling feeling of loss, *I'm dying now, I'm disappearing now.*

Thirteen

Eleanor moved into my house. My life was never the same. I don't know why, but.

The day she moved in, a whole truck turned up. I wasn't there but Todd was home with flu, watching all of *I, Claudius* on video, and said the movers kept on going from Augustus right through Caligula, it totally ruined *I, Claudius*. They brought

a king-size bed with pink everything, a canopy, and tassels. Antique teak mahogany drawery things that locked with keys. Her armchair was gold velvet, and there were candelabras and Japanese fans. There were framed butterflies that had travelled, whose frames looked chewed, that sat on their pins askew. Two sets of matching luggage had clothes, gowns, princess-wear. But she had no books at all and no stereo.

She had no real-life clothes. No jeans or T-shirts, only party frocks and lingerie. No socks. She had a fleet of scarves, all kinds, all lengths, and she was never seen without a scarf. She dressed to the nines and had the nine kinds of perfume, jewels, diamond earrings underfoot in nests of underwear — her room.

There were five oil paintings of herself, in allegorical style, as Faith, as Salome, Pandora, they were opulent; gold tones seeping through reds and browns. They were unframed. She leaned them up against the wall. But they were perfect like they could have been forgeries.

When I asked if she had painted them, she said, 'Don't be daft.' Who had painted them was something she had promised not to say. Signed RH which I would go through and couldn't think of any artists starting RH, although I wanted it to be a clue. Todd said it was Damien Hirst with a weird D, trying to be funny.

And she could not do things. She couldn't do anything and couldn't learn how. Boil eggs. Hammer in a nail. Drive. She didn't know her times tables. Eleanor wasn't illiterate but was dyslexic and could barely, haltingly, read.

Asked to fetch something, Eleanor came back an hour later in a change of clothes, *sans* the thing. She watched with a rabbit-in-the-headlights face when I showed her how to use the washing machine; tried to smile, but wrung her hands and kept looking at the floor, distressed. Finally, she asked if I minded cause she wouldn't if I minded if she went and took a bath now? I said, 'Please.'

And she drank like a Russian wedding. Smoked till the house stank out to the street. Weed too. Pill-popped till her whole head sweated. She beat a path from the bed to the toilet; El's nose ran and her pupils were a disconcerting size. Some days El slept clean through and on through the night.

She brought us whisky and chocolates, Es, CDs, but couldn't pay rent. 'I'd *love* to pay rent. I would have more self-respect, I think. But actually, when I have money, I spend it on drugs. I'm a terrible addict,' she said, looking down at her breasts, a mannerism El had when she felt sheepish, 'But I'm trying to stop, enough.'

When I asked her what drugs, she said 'I'm not using heroin now,' and giggled.

But she changed the flavour of my life, to good. To strange, to sweet like aniseed. Once

Fourteen

El went to Café Flo with me after work. I used to go for the steak frites. It was in our first week.

It was hard just getting her down to the corner, this was Eleanor's barefoot phase. She had thrown all her shoes away without explanation. So she brought bathroom slippers, that were all she wore, that were no good to walk. Walking barefoot on pebbles, broken glass, whatever, didn't bother her. In the restaurant, you realised what she looked like, wearing some prom dress, wet from the rain, and dirty soles showing, where the slippers hung, half-on.

She was euphoric, crushy with me, when I talked she looked at my arms and hands. And she said she was glad Todd hadn't come. She liked Todd, yeah, but some people were people you talked to privately. You knew that you wouldn't be judged.

I said, 'I always get the steak frites.'

She said, 'I must remember to tell you –'

I said, 'I do judge, though, I'm really judgmental,' and 'Good,' said El, and laughed, and said,

it was something she'd remembered in bed the night before. She was so grateful to be in my house, there was a sound the radiator made that felt very safe, and she'd remembered her best friend Rosie.

Rosie had carried her through the streets once, when she was too afraid to walk. When El killed her parakeet, he was the only one who didn't think she was sick, who never lost faith in her. Rosie would fight in a war or burn down houses and cities for her. If he'd discarded her, ever, it was El's fault. She had to remember that now. And she said

you could only *love* two people – with her intense brown eyes that made brown look like an unusual colour, like purple eyes that saw through Islington and le franchise chic of Café Flo to Rosie, who was a person she *loved*. You thought you loved all kinds of people, Eleanor said, but that was shit. In your life, you could love two total. That meant you would give your life for someone. That was the definition.

I said, 'I would give my life for seventeen people, and counting. I got a fucking list, no shit.'

She laughed, it was one of the ways she was quick-witted, taking a point. She said, 'I didn't say that I loved you *yet*.' And she covered her face with the menu, pressing it to her nose, and said, 'I didn't say that.' I said

when the waiter had come and taken our order and gone, and we were more calm, watching cars strip through the wet in the night outside, 'You're kind of a kid. That's cool. I can deal with people who never grew up.' And we were silent a lot of that dinner, and it was cool. I asked her, did she see Rosie now, and she said, 'I don't know.' She said from nowhere she'd never bring punters to my house. Then I talked about my 'sex addiction', though I didn't call it addiction. She looked me deep in the face and drank my words.

And she had that childish magic, candour, where it was human to be too scared to wear shoes. To walk home barefoot, jumping in puddles with both feet, and it was irrational how it was sweet. That was the week

I near as dammit called Peter. I had had the conversation in my head. Peter Rabbit, I had got as far as looking for his number.

Fifteen

Peter Rabbit was the new successful artist people hated. Nominated for the Turner Prize, Saatchi bought him – plus the Tate commission for the Turbine Hall. From Pittsburgh originally, wasn't even British. His perfect American teeth got mentioned, proved to many his work was shallow.

Thirty-nothing, he photographed great. *Time Out* ran a feature where he rated gyms. Radio 4 always got his take on art, the US, and Beatrix Potter.

He was *our* celebrity. Thea shagged him at St Martin's. Back when he was still a carpenter, he botched You's doors. Nick still had Peter Rabbit's umbrella. When they worked together at the Dog and Trumpet, Layla told him, 'They'll never let you make it here in London as a Yank.'

He wasn't that successful. Radio is not television. Ten years into his career, he was a New Face. He wasn't any Lucian Freud, be real. He still used public transport.

His work was portraits of beautiful girls nude – pasted with crosses, silk flowers and coins, stuck on/in the paint – it was the way it was done, and the materials. He had a subtle taste that was real. He could work the Pre-Raphaelite thing or an aesthetic like the cover of a book about elves.

Sometimes he painted the pictures, sometimes he hired commercial artists. It was 'decentring the artist as genius', but the ones he painted were better, were genius ironically. Sold for twice the money. Possibly by still another, wonderful, commercial artist, who was paid a premium to keep shtum. Critics who didn't like Peter said that, that 'one suspects the other postmodern shoe is set to drop'.

He was famous for girls, meaning 'beautiful girlfriends', and also fucking in a closet at parties. 'Girlfriend' with Peter didn't mean the same girlfriend twice. It was all that gossipy, exploits–of, shit, the best was about the slave girl. Exquisite but never spoke, that chick was jumpy, *you just felt wrong about it* – held to be a sex-trafficked Pole, but by my time, she had vanished, and people stopped telling that story, in gradual stages.

Lennie and he were on inviting terms. He put in appearances at Lennie's private views. A medium-sized man with Nordic features, he had flaky skin, dandruff, everything that never showed in newspaper spreads. None of his clothes were in one piece, they all had sentimental value; he had things from being sixteen he wore, he wore some old ex-girlfriends' T-shirts too. He was good-looking if I didn't mention that. He looked good in real life and photographs. He looked good like steak tastes.

I never tried to fuck him cause he had his pick. I didn't want to be the one who got no for an answer, this is all my shitty vanity. God knows I wanted him. Like kind of a crush. I'd met him at Lennie's and we started to talk once. He'd run away from home like me.

Then we started to, I don't know, date. At least I thought they were dates. I never dated, so. We used to go to movies together.

And what Peter was like, he just apologised for everything, for walking funny when he didn't even. 'You're looking at my teeth? Ugly, right?' If you mentioned his fame, he looked astonished, lost, misunderstood. He checked your face to see if you were making fun of him. All the time he had big arms, he was being good-looking, I mean.

I never got to know him much. We went to these films. We'd go when fight movies were playing at the Prince Charles, we saw *The Seven Samurai*, *Natural Born Killers*, and we'd come out excited even if the movie was naff. We had our popcorn and we'd share a cab because his studio was near my work. My office came first so

I never saw his studio. I wanted him to want to paint me. That would mean

and Peter never fucking asked. And time passed.

I think I got — no, because we didn't fuck, I didn't have my real defences up. I got in weirdly deep. How it ended,

this night we went to Lennie's fancy dress party. Not together. We'd been to see a matinee and mentioned meeting there. Because I knew I'd see him, I didn't wear fancy dress.

He wasn't there. I started drinking and I kept on drinking. Once I was talking to this guy for twenty minutes, he was in a pirate costume and I didn't notice till I got up he had thalidomide arms. I almost shook his hand, and then he didn't have one. That drunk.

I kissed a couple men. You just realise you're lying on the floor beside your can of beer, kissing. Stopping kissing, you're surprised who it is. I always leave with dust in my hair. I find phone numbers stuck all in my underwear.

And I was on my way out. I couldn't walk so good, a dude was helping me, the stars were overhead. I guess I had my head tipped back so everything was overhead. The way that drunkenness can be like hanging upside down.

The skinny bloke helping me was saying about sharing a cab, that we were in the same direction; when I saw Peter. He was with a blonde. She had some crocheted halter top. They were sitting on the garden wall, drinking Campari from those fucking individual bottles.

And he said, 'Tanya.'

I freed myself somehow and went to him. I feel as if I had a dog expression on my face, naive dog, and I said, 'Peter, Jesus Christ. You left me here.' I gestured at the party, but he didn't hear. He gestured at the blonde and said,

'Diddy here's making a documentary on the female orgasm.'

The blonde looked at me, bland with power. I said, 'Bully for Diddy,' and looked back at my man.

I took that taxi with and went.

I spent the night. We had this sex that was like working at a Burger King. I worked at Burger King for one week once, and sucking that guy's dick, fucking him, was like that job. I had to fight to keep from staring at the clock. I still remember what his clock looked like, and what the Burger King clock looked like.

I stopped fucking people. That was six months ago.

Peter never called again. I couldn't call him. Todd said that was shit, I could, but Hutch agreed with me and Hutch is my authority. You can't

Sixteen

except I thought of calling Peter, now I felt more mature, or whatever I felt. Then I didn't have his number. I turned out not to. Eleanor had nicked my address book, my little black book that was actually little and black as a joke.

Before she stole the book, she used to read it sitting on my bed. I'd have to explain who people were, some dudes I had no memory. There was a Larry who escaped me, and others. Then the book disappeared. Since I was trying not to fuck those dudes, it was part good.

Only then this lawyer, Patrick, who I used to shag when I used to travel to Leeds, emailed that he never knew I had a sister. That she didn't look like me, and he was sorry but he hadn't lent her money, in case. Days later, uptight Giles Hughes mentioned El by name. She'd come to his office in a see-through shirt, barefoot. He was pissy about it, read the incident as some get-back from me. I said, 'Mad person, OK?'

And wrote a long note to El (who had vanished for a couple days, because she used to vanish) saying, *fucking don't do that*, ten ways. The dodgy communications from my ex-fucks stopped. But the black book never reappeared. (El stole. I started hiding things because they walked. Not even valuables; I'd find my tweezers, dictionary, junk mail in her room. She'd be wearing my bra. If I left my handbag out, El cleaned out the small change. Not to spend, she was keeping it in Sainsbury's bags, it was sentimental value gone mad.

'*Should* you need anything back, you must tell me,' El said when I complained. I said, 'Give me everything back now.' El laughed like that was humour, cause I couldn't really want my possessions back, right.

'God, the way you just say that,' Eleanor said. 'You're brilliant.') And she wouldn't admit she had the little black book. I told her about me and Peter Rabbit while her face got blanker. Finally I said, 'Leave it somewhere without telling me.' She'd do that kind of thing. That time she didn't. It was just as well I couldn't call Peter Rabbit, though. He didn't want me, my eyes are too close together, and I have a beaky nose. I look as if my name is Alice. I can't stand the way I look. And I don't want a relationship. Like actually, relief

Seventeen

and with just El, work, the house which I was going to fix up soon,

the world was real to me again. Rain looked like my first rain. As if the sky was falling in its sleep, I don't know what. At home, my broken stairs were chestnut by the naked bulb, euphoria. You came in from the wet, and there were voices in the kitchen. Somebody already had the gas fire on.

I started making chocolate pudding from scratch. I would do it some mornings before work. Todd and El were sleeping and the quiet made the house seem unusually full of air, like on a spring day. I listened to Dylan albums that I hadn't played since Hollywood, and stood stirring chocolate in a double boiler, thinking of the old days and making faces. Each minute I hadn't left yet became precious, laden with wonderful juice, so safe. Then I sat, deciding to be late, and had a cigarette, the happiest moments in my life so far.

The month El came to live with us, I played tennis for the first time in years. It was Sue from work, it was a two-hour lunch. Above, the sky was white like it was listening to us. I don't know why people don't mention white skies more, when it's warm out; my favourite sky. Reaching at an instant of poison-green ball in sharp focus on two blurred hours of sky. My arms felt strong like my arms again. It started raining and we played a long time in the rain – till when you hit the ball, it sprayed you. Then, when I went back to work, too wet to be in any office building, smelling like wet clothes

Mark Keynes was in the foyer. When he saw me, he

lit up like he'd been hunting for me everywhere. He said just, 'Tanya, good to see you. Haven't seen you since your thing.'

I said, taken off guard, 'Hell, I asked you not to come!'

He bust out laughing and looked gratified. I back-pedalled, 'But I don't mean, you know, because I did. I did, you do remember that, although it wasn't,' and he muttered, 'Really, I'm a thorough masochist, do your worst,' beaming. Then I got into the lift and he was staring at me so hard –

he did karate, alpha at my work, he was attractive and I wasn't going to fuck him. I could just let it go. I had a lot of work then and I was high. Was not the same, like,

The people in the building, I'd avoided them for years because they knew about my fucking everyone – now I talked to them, normal. Secretaries stopped at my desk when they had boxes of candy. The mail guy told me all about his surgery. Suddenly I was included in leaving drinks, asked to sign Get Well cards, called 'Tazza'.

To cap it all, one night Nick and I had dinner at a Cuban restaurant, instead of eating vending-machine food. Waitresses flirted with him, there was Cuban music playing and et cetera. Somebody came in with a parrot: life! Nick dropped into conversation that he'd started to go to Al-Anon, 'Because I don't know if I ever mentioned that my sister has a problem. And I've realised it impacts on me. That is, the relatives . . .' I told him stories then about Vinnie. We got bashful and frowned at the dessert menu like we really might get dessert. And

Nick cleared his throat noisily and said he'd had a pony as a boy that reminded him of me. 'She trod on my feet, to show affection.'

I said, 'Am I really like that?' crestfallen, pleased; he

amended it to say I'd been much calmer since the Islington house, and that.

I said he didn't have to say that, and 'technically Hackney', and told him I'd played tennis that week with Sue Blue, the work experience, who'd been pro as a teen, as if he'd know what I meant. He watched me telling this and drank his Cuba Libre happily. I must have spent a half an hour telling him. He said at last,

'We'd better get back, but this is better than the vending cack, if you had time another time,' screwing up his napkin.

'I do, I would, yeah,' I said, and felt bizarre. He'd drunk too much, he said shyly I was 'silly as arseholes', and we giggled a lot in the street,

walking back.

And El talked to me. I came home, she'd be at the top of the stairs, shy, joyous, overcome. Cocking her head, in a crumpled dress, she'd often dragged her blanket with her. 'Oh! That's so glorious you're here. Are you coming up?' I don't know what I wanted, but I'd go. I put in long nights on El's bed, her talking while I often shut my eyes. I'd got her a boom box, and she let me play my compilation tape Vinnie made for my thirteenth birthday, labelled 'Blue's' though it was teen idol pop. She used 15-watt bulbs with pink lampshades, it was love-scene light. Rum and cola was our drink. I'd put my bare toes up on her drawings, testing whether the pencil had dug in, not even that stressed if she had wrecked my wall. (Eleanor started drawing on the walls a few days after she moved in. It was one mass, spreading from the head of her bed like ivy. It was pencil with pink highlighter and blue ballpoint. It was perfect.

The pictures together made a maze with elaborate tiny mazes in it. There were animals, children with no arms, 747s and bananas. There were scenes from the kitchen with me and Todd; there was Eleanor in an empty city. There was even a section where she'd drawn her old stuffed lion countless times in snaking columns, and the draughtsmanship was perfect. It gave you a funny-bone feeling, like love, like art does times that you actually look.

When I mentioned it, she said she would paint over it, she had the paint. She'd talked to someone who had paint, she meant. (And tears were welling up, right.) My stuff was precious to her. 'I make such ugly things. I'm ugly inside. I know, you don't have to patronise me,'

until I had to say, 'I love it.') Really pencil doesn't dig into plaster. So I was tracing while she talked and talked. I'd tell her stories too but I had done very little, fucked guys and earned, it wasn't much life. I'd go through my memory and it was like an empty drawer with a couple paper clips and a dusty sock. El had had this life.

Eighteen

It started with, being a homeless kid. The home she had left was never in it, whatever early traumas sent her out in the street. The story began with El fourteen and sleeping in car back seats at night. Some people left their cars unlocked deliberately for her. There was a time she ate from the garbage, you'd get whole loaves of bread with one mouldy corner. She had a blanket she'd named 'Lizabetha', and loved; it had saved her life.

The winter she had no coat in Vermont, shacked up with Schizo Mal in the woods for warmth. He called her Uriel. The snow was thin on the hill nearby, and once she walked SOS into it, imagining a plane would save them. Once he brought a pizza back and they were so happy till they fought. At last he chased her away from his lean-to with a piece of firewood.

Her boyfriends at fifteen were the small-time drug dealers/addicts, one pimp who never put her out cause she was that age and small. 'Don't want no problems,' he would say, but she fooled herself he loved her. 'What a prat,' she said of herself and laughed. The city was easier, though she guessed what she had done there to live had turned her into a freak.

She hitch-hiked and crawled in suburban windows, looking for food. Used to go from church to church and the people were lovely, they would feed her at their own table. Elderly Christians put her up. 'But they never stuck me long, well, no one can. One couple bought me a bike before I was suddenly out. I'm always out.'

And she told London tales of being a rich man's trophy, dancing off Es in Tokyo Joe, waking up in a limo alone and trying to find her clothes. Waking up in hospital. Waking up in a hotel room and going out and it was in the middle of

Scotland. Businessmen from twelve-odd nations kept her, in hotels or flats. She liked hotels because you could order flowers on the phone.

She'd met Mick Jagger once but they had to tell her it was him. Mick and she were the same *exact* height but he was not impressed. 'I borrowed matches from him and he asked for them back in this voice.' She had also met Princess Margaret.

She told me anecdotes about car crashes, being stabbed, gangrene. An overdose in a pool. Being raped by high-school-age kids four hours straight. A lot of her stories featured being left for dead.

Men had whipped her with hangers and she had been left for dead in a dumpster concussed and torn 'down there' — she pronounced with raised eyebrows, like saucy humour. She would laugh about being beat, she had no rancour. 'Oh God, Micky! He would always get in trouble with that temper of his, you know? I reckon he'll be dead by now, it's a shame.' She would still shag anyone for a bed, that was actually her level.

I swore she'd never be out with me, just lying, I don't know how you make these promises

when you're sprawled in someone's bed, blissed out on perfumed linen, her bare foot resting on your stomach and a current of her runs into your gut, your central vein. You feel her life; what it was like to get that bike. You write a happy ending.

I told Eleanor she could start again. Get on her feet, now she was with me and Todd, who totally loved her. I could get her work, a couple hours at first. Or she could just stay anyway, forever, fuck it. But if she did work, she would feel loads better, that was all.

She'd fix her eyes on me and need to hear. She'd rest

her head on my stomach, scared, and mutter, 'Go on, I'm listening.' I'd make promises till they were pretty true, they sounded true to me. She'd interrupt:

'God. How I love you.'

And was that confidingly loving, like a pet. You could not see the wrong. You couldn't mind she had no character. Was trouble.

Once Todd and I sat on either side of Eleanor, braiding her long hair into two long long plaits. She cast back her head – her eyes shone hard, impetuous, as she held still for us.

Nineteen

This day had started with a rotten taste, one of those days when you lose your keys and miss your stop. You get the paper and it has all bad news: lime Jell-O gives you colon cancer; a kindergartener was found in five bin liners on your street; the 'voice of Goofy' died today and even that seems like a doleful sign of the times. And I had paperwork all day, when

Mark Keynes says 'Knock knock' in my doorway.

I looked up wanting to say 'Who's there?' but knew it wasn't funny. So I just looked at him thinking this. Feeling kind of, also, do not even talk to me because I *will* fuck you, only I'm not allowed. He said,

'I wanted to get you something as an apology, but I was luckily spared.'

'Oh?' I said not understanding a word. 'Yeah, that's OK.'

'I mean, that is, Nick mentioned that you'd lost your PalmPilot, and it so happens I've had two for the last year, so I erased my info off of this . . .' He started blinking, he was smiling and blinking. I realised he was holding up this PalmPilot and I was supposed to —

I said, 'Oh, that's really . . . that's so thoughtful of you, great.'

He stepped forward as if stepping out onto a stage and placed the PalmPilot gingerly on my desk. I put my hand on it.

He said, 'I wasn't sure if you'd have got one, or if . . . Nick thought you might want to buy your own, he said, he actually said you didn't like most people.' Mark made a face at himself for having said this.

I said rather flatly, 'No, I like you all right, don't worry.'

We laughed but I was feeling cornered cause this shit

dynamic remained which I could only describe as him knowing I had fucked everybody in the building without showing any sign of the beginnings of a finer feeling such as ever thinking of those people again, and yet he wanted me to be his girlfriend. It was obvious. The guy had some diluted version of the 'slave' fantasy that drives the older version of him to a dominatrix. It was sad, especially because he did karate, etc etc, you wanted him to have

I wanted to fuck him. Just infuriating, totally. He wanted me, was waiting for me to make a step towards *dinner or a drink sometime*, I sighed heavily and picked the PalmPilot up. It had the email and, you know, features. Nice. CFO gear.

'Yeah, that's genuinely helpful,' I said, 'Thanks,' and waited. I was waiting him out.

Mark waited out competitively. Haunting the doorway, telegraphing readiness to go for an Indian or a quick drink, when it occurred to him —

'Oh, Tanya, did you ever know Curt Short? The timber supplier?'

'Sure, Curt Short.'

'He's been murdered.'

Twenty

Curt Short, so it's not like Curt was a friend. He used to drink with Forter and us in Star and Garter days. A Chicago Republican business type, he had the whopping gut, the rah-rah voice, the hot-pink skin. He couldn't say business was good without crediting God; he called his Bentley the Shortmobile. In our drinking crew, he played the babe in the woods; the game was, make Curt blush. His catchphrase: 'Boy, if I thought you were serious!' A 'self-made man', meaning, nobody was meant to know the money was his wife's. She was from Surrey, bleach and tanning-booth coloured, with a face that would stop a clock. Felicity. We used to say, 'Felicity Short, vita longa.'

And every year, as a fellow Yank, I was invited to his Fourth of July 'bash'.

He had catered pig roast under a marquee and professional fireworks. Other Yanks would toast the 'freest country in the world'. People told inspirational tales about their gardeners and childminders, refugees from Castro. At last, everyone sang 'God Bless America', reading from stapled photocopies passed out by an intern. The party favours (coy keepsakes like 'willy warmers') bore the logo 'SHORT LUMBER' in red, white and blue.

At every bash, Curt would greet me, ask with a pout to be reminded ('Darned Alzheimer's!') of my name; I would remind him, he would be delighted, shout that I was getting younger. He'd sling an arm around my waist and name me 'Independence Buddy'. Finally I'd slip him, saying that I had to 'use the little girl's room'. I never minded Curt, though. I have no reason, there are assholes I fucking mind, I mortally mind. But him not.

He had three very British kids who treated him as an

eyesore. He'd built a trophy case for their sporting medals, and every guest had to have the cups explained. He actually preened himself because he gave his old truck to the RSPCA, it made your heart bleed, he was a fool. Once I met a bitter Short cousin at the bash, who said Curt could only stay married twenty years because 'the man lacks all imagination'. It made me sad that it was so true, poor fucking Curt.

Now he'd died with no imagination, ever. Some people aren't heavyweight enough to die; their dying strains any faith you had in an afterlife. Curt fit right in on Earth.

He was bloodily killed, the murder weapon a Stanley knife. His throat was cut five times, high and low. Then his head was beaten in, his face was beaten off, the killer smashed a table on him and tracked blood around the house to find a baseball bat and beat him more. Several bones were broken after Curt was good and dead.

Only then the house was robbed. There were red hand-prints inside the shattered trophy case, the robber dumb enough to think the cups were real gold.

I almost cried when Mark told me, I mean I kept swallowing. He looked at me admiringly although I guess I didn't feel that bad. I mean, when he left, I just went back to work. I'd got stuck with photo returns because Sue was off.

Then Alan came in yellow with shock.

'Curt Short, did you hear? It makes you want to . . .' He shook his head.

Then I was outraged. Cause Alan was more traumatised than me, it wasn't fair. *His* humanity, *his* big heart, it doesn't bother me usually.

'Yeah, you hardly knew him,' I snapped. 'Curt.'

Alan grimaced. 'That was a description. What you just

said, curt. You don't need to be fucking curt with me, it's not like you were his . . . No, you never fucked *Curt*?'

'No!'

'Good, the last thing I want to know! Christ. But come and have a drink with me, I can't work today.'

'No way.'

'Fuck off, you're meant to enable me.' He wagged his finger. And he said, 'Cut Short. Cut Short, I just thought of that: macabre.' And stormed out, hunched, blamingly. I got up like a shot and like I never ever,

went home at five.

The house was silent when I got home. Because no one was there, I noticed all the dirt, the ashtray spilled on the floor, places grease had dripped down the kitchen wall. I had wanted sausages as comfort food but now I couldn't. Sausages had to be eaten in conditions of pristine cleanliness.

I went to bed and slept in my clothes. I mean, I always do. That time I felt it, though, 'I'm sleeping in my clothes.' And I felt like a neglected building, derelict and cold.

Twenty-One

I started sleeping in my clothes when I was nine, when my mother left. I slept in Dad's bed with him, in my clothes. I was the favourite then, before I was the scapegoat.

My mother left to live with a man named Bert Best, an unemployed realtor from Houston, Texas. I was old enough to know that Texans didn't all live on ranches and they weren't cowboys. Still I was excited for Bert to be my stepdad, hoping I would get spurred boots.

I never saw my mom again.

Dad started taking me out driving nights. He'd take me out till 1 a.m. and I'd get Dunkin Donuts or a cone. Once I got two cones the same night.

Out driving nights, we used to go to Lowell, to the parking lot of Bert's condominium. We didn't take the black and white, we took Mom's Pinto, but my father strapped his holster on over his street clothes. He took his gun and nightstick.

I ate doughnuts. Dad let me play my favourite *Saturday Night Live* cassette my friend made. She'd tape-recorded it, this was before we all had videos. It included a nonsense song about fish heads. In the song, the fish heads were *never ever seen drinking cappuccino in Italian restaurants with Oriental women.* To me, that line was about adultery. If you mention fish heads to this day, I think adultery – from a child's point of view, as something mysterious, fatal and macabre.

I only went to school if I wanted. Most days, Dad and I watched TV. I remember game shows and *Rocky and Bullwinkle*. Dad didn't care what we watched. He drank. He took painkillers too and a kind of speed pill.

I told my friends my mother was in Texas. I said she had a snow-white stallion named Alabaster. By the end it was three horses, and an oval pool. Then my friend Maura saw my mother at the Purity Supreme and said she'd never ever trust me again. I lost those friends and had to be the solitary kid at recess, pretending to play.

I hardly went to school. I didn't go to school at all. I ate what I wanted. I read Dad's porn. I used his wallet as my own and smoked his Winstons. Maura didn't know what she was missing. They would all be my friends now, except I wouldn't ask them. I never forgave, like Dad didn't ever. When I grew up, I'd be a cop.

I found Dad naked on the hallway floor. Because he was naked, I thought he was dead. I had a flood of energy, I ran downstairs and drank a whole Coke before I checked his pulse. Then I was smart enough to call 911.

I spent the night in the Emergency waiting room. Gathered around me was an African-American family, the Waters, who were waiting for a grandfather who had had a stroke. Matter-of-factly they expected him to die. Through the night more and more Waters came, some from as far as New York City.

They made me 'coffee' which was like a drop of coffee in a cup of cream and sugar. One of them had brought cheesecake from a bakery whose logo showed a chef on a bicycle because they delivered. The good-looking brother told me I was real brave.

They were my first black people: that made me feel grown up. They hadn't seen each other in a while, and they had a blast, cracking jokes about past funerals. 'Don't mind us, we just tired and a lot of sadness,' said the mother, naughtily grinning.

There were mustard-coloured plastic chairs in the waiting room, fixed to a fat metal beam, that you could crawl under; still it wasn't dark. There was nowhere you could go that was dark. In the background, you always heard voices, and the rubber-soled footsteps of nursing staff, the clinking of equipment that was meant to save lives. I think that night is why I still like fluorescent lights.

At last a candy striper took me in charge. Because she, too, was black, I thought of her as one of the Waters and tagged along happily. I told her my mother was in Texas, and she coaxed me to admit I had an uncle who could come and get me. 'Do you have an Uncle John? Do you have an Uncle Ron? Do you have an Uncle Ned? An Uncle Ted?' My parents were both only children, but I liked the game so much, for a long time I faked that I had something to hide.

I called home and got Dana. He'd just come home from football practice. When I told him, he said, 'Great job taking care of Dad, Tampon.'

Dawn in the background said, 'What the fuck? What's going on?' and when Dana told her, she said, 'Oh my God my fucking God my God,' and Dana shouted, 'Watch my frigging guitar! I'll give you something to cry about, idiot!'

The phone went dead. I told the candy striper they were on their way. I slept on the floor and in the morning Grandpa made the drive from Maine.

Grandpa took me out to Chinese alone at the place with the Siamese fighting fish. I said that we could eat their heads and giggled cause he didn't know the joke. Because we never ate shrimp at home and I thought it was classy, I ordered everything with shrimp. We didn't mention Dad but I asked him if he thought there would be a nuclear war; that was related. He said my generation sure got dealt a hand of cards.

Dad was in the hospital a month. He'd taken an overdose and couldn't stop crying. Dawn and Dana went to visit him, they drove his cop car that whole month without a licence, but they wouldn't take me. He didn't want to see me, they claimed. I called them liars, and we fought about it so hard, I tried to brain Dana with a metal footstool.

The first week, my cousin Polly came to take us to their place in Natick. Only Vinnie went. Dana and Dawn were fifteen, and I already was just me, like a wild animal. Polly said, 'Like mother, like daughter,' sighing under the tree where I was waiting her out.

That month, Dawn and Dana had friends round day and night, smoking dope and drinking peach brandy. They cranked Guns N' Roses. They played Truth or Dare. I was still sleeping in my father's bed till Dana burst in one night a black freak ablaze and flailing in the doorway's painful light and pulled me out by my feet. My ass elbows head hit the floor. He was screaming 'What'd you do to Dad! What'd you say to Dad!' and kicking me. Dawn came to the door with her friend Kate. They both had Dad's police shirts on over tight jeans. Dawn was sweating so hard she looked as if she'd come out of the shower. As Dana dropped me, she shrieked, 'We all know what you did, Tanya! You can't hide!'

It turned out Dad had said it wasn't suicide, that I let Mom in, and she injected him in his sleep. Dana and Dawn went on believing this for years, perversely, as if they were really that stupid.

I mailed Vinnie my only copy of my *Saturday Night Live* tape and he never even called to say he'd got it. When he came home, he said it melted in the sun. I started crying and ran up to my bed. He called after me, 'Shithead! You couldn't hear that fucking tape anyway!' I cried until it felt like pneumonia, like I'd turned inside out, I was clammy my whole flesh through.

Vinnie knocked on the door that night and gave me my first joint as a peace offering. We sat on a smiley-face hook rug Mom made from a kit, on the floor of the girls' bedroom only Dawn had slept in before, and got wasted. 'I guess Dungeons and Dragons were giving you a hard time,' Vinnie said. 'But assholes always suffer worst in the end.'

After that we hung out together. We had the same friends that were really Vinnie's, that were all a year older. We went through a demon-worship phase where we were trying to conjure Beelzebub, using a ritual we found in a library book, but nothing happened. We slept side by side in sleeping bags in the basement. Vinnie used to put on Alice Cooper make-up sometimes to sleep.

He told me our cousin Polly had molested him; 'You want to see how?' I said, 'You perv. Not,' and couldn't stop laughing. But we did that anyway, that was a thing we did. I'd lie there looking at the ceiling tiles that were like all other ceiling tiles as if there only ever was one ceiling-tile factory that made just one line of tiles. I don't remember what I thought. (Years later Vinnie asked if I remembered it, and when I said yes, he looked stricken and tired. He said, 'Shit, I swore that you were going to say no.'

He asked if I forgave him and I said, no biggie. He asked if I thought it caused my problems that I had with sex. I said, 'What problems?' Then we looked sad and couldn't help it and he shook his head and swore to God he'd never done that, if he'd known.

But kids don't know any better.)

Dad came home. He started AA, he was back at work. As if by prearrangement, he and I didn't speak. I used to go straight to the basement when I came home. After a while, we didn't flinch when we saw each other, we could walk right past.

Once Dad took me out to dinner with his new girlfriend, Shannon, who did bail bonds. Shannon asked me questions about school in a loud voice, as if children were deaf, the way some people speak up to cripples. After dinner, she had a beer so Dad had a beer. They had another. Shannon said to me, 'You're a smartie, I can tell. You're like my sister. She got the brains, I got the boobs.'

I went to the ladies' room four times – really smoking joints in the parking lot. When I went to the ladies' room for real, I found blood on my panties – my first period. I wound toilet paper around the crotch and thought that I was resourceful, I wasn't a whiner. I was the kind of person who would survive if there was ever a nuclear war.

I went to the parking lot again and saw the waiters smoking on the side by the staff entrance. They were Puerto Rican and Dana's age; they looked at me furtively, one at a time. I could smell their cigarettes that far away and it was magical like it only is when you're that young. I didn't know that they were ordinary people. And I dreamed that they would kidnap me. I mouthed my only Spanish, *Buenos días*, and dreamed.

Sometimes after that, I raided Dad's stash of painkillers. But I never got really into them like Vinnie, who had his first withdrawals at thirteen.

When Dad started hitting me, it was just me. He left the others be. I didn't mind. I'd had enough by then, I loved to hit him back. Hitting back was like the ice cream you got when Mom had left, when Dad was in the hospital; the pleasure of your brother's hand in you, when your body was seized and strange with fear. It took the top off your head like coming.

I'd say to Dad, 'Kill me.' Then I'd take a deep breath and go

I ran away from home. That drew a solid line between me and my family. From a safe distance, I watched their sick boat sink. When I grew up, I paid and paid money like I owed my life to them. I cried about them, wasted tears.

But now I will not mourn them when they're dead. That much I earned the right, I hate them now they're dead.

Twenty-Two

It's the dark of 3 a.m. I wake alone, the bed cold, the covers balled in my arms. Outside there are voices like your parents fighting. A woman screams *please, don't*, and there's the pretty sound of shattering glass.

It's El's room. That's her headlong crying. You only hear the high notes, so at first it sounds like hysterical laughter. A man yells, fearfully, *don't, make, me*, and something booms like kicked metal. El swears.

I'm on my feet. I'm going to bust in and save her. In my head I'm just about to. Then I hear him running down the stairs. Our front door slams.

I hit the window just in time to see him run out, so fast and far below he appears to drain from the house. He runs across the street and stops. He wheels. I had been thinking, *That's the drug dealer. That's the dude who broke her ribs.*

It's a man in a black leather jacket like everyone. He looks up from the street, it's pissing down, a brute downpour that rains so hard he gets smaller in it. And stands for it. He stands still, bright with tenacity. He watches Eleanor's window.

He seems familiar though I can't make out his face. I'm thinking of Brendans I might know, I might have fucked, drug dealers. A black Irish guy once from the Star and Garter. He said he was the only black kid in his town but no one gave him any bother. Maybe that was Brendan's whole rage, he had bother. That dude isn't black. He looks too buff to be sick from any Aids medication.

I'd swear he's crying though, how could you tell, just stand there weeping in the street

fuck the world. Like she had done. I could have held her in my arms, the same street and rain. And I could fit the stalker guy with me inside that hiding feeling of that night. He could beat her with a chair, and it be love. There were places it was love, where I had come from, too.

I said, 'That isn't Brendan,' aloud. My voice was petulant, and I stepped back, the scent of rain in my, everything, goosebumps having that steely taste. I had to see El.

In the hall I still heard rain. I heard it rushing down on him. Her door was open a scratch, that parting on light. I went in like she was going to want to talk about the guy, I had these expectations.

Eleanor was crouching on the floor in her underwear. Her eyes were fierce and insane and red.

First, the broken glass fucked me up: a flash of Curt Short's trophy case. It was her big mirror, flat on its face and bashed. A painting had been kicked in so the frame buckled. Psychedelic dust surrounded it, and Salome was blurred, scuffed through to the yellow underpainting, though John the Baptist's head was fine.

Her room was its posh mess. Your eye went straight to the knickers and bottles. The duvet was twisted where they probably were fucking. On the floor, there was something, it was clothing but tangled in a

spotted with blood. It was a dress but it was patched in blood and she

on top of it a knife from our kitchen, from her hypersharp knives she brought when she moved in. And once I saw that, I saw that El was cut on her face and her neck. Her fucking *neck*. That took me long enough to notice, then I noticed she was covered in scars.

It fucked with me because I somehow knew but not specifically that she would be covered in scars. There were round buttons down her thighs so like cigarette burns that's what they were. The cut-throat lines on her neck I saw bared for the first time. Hacked-up arms like an old school desk; a big gouge over her bra, her heart.

I sat on the bed, where they had definitely fucked, saying, 'Jesus Christ, are you all right? Should I call –' as she rubbed her eyes and reached for that knife. Then she left it and stood, fast. Like a flame standing up from a sudden match. She said,

'I want you to leave,' as if she needed me to stay, her voice weak.

'Are you all right? I mean, you got –'

'I'm perfect.'

'Who's the guy?'

'I don't know. Why should you think there was a guy?'

'I saw him run out of the house. Come on.'

She went and plucked a robe from the floor, it was a black silk robe with gold dragons. In it she was different, almost sane. She faced me and got out a cigarette, she had Camels in the robe pocket. Then she was smoking and the cut on her neck moved over the muscle with her inhale. It wasn't that deep. And there was one on her cheek, not that deep. They'd stopped even bleeding.

I said, 'Are you still a prostitute? Was that a punter?'

'I was never a prostitute,' she said with distaste. 'God. You don't understand me at all.'

'You told us you were. I'm not inventing it. That's what you said.'

'I don't remember why I said that. I must have lied.'

'Look, that's totally insane.'

'I can't control what you think of me,' she said, and looked at the cigarette, wrinkling her nose. Her face had lost all trace of its sweetness. She was the street kid who'd done things to live that turned her into a freak. The one who slept in cars and got left for dead.

'So,' I said, making my voice as even as it would go, 'where do you get your money then? Come on, sit down.'

'I'm an artist.' She glanced at the drawings on her wall.

I looked at them, too, superstitiously, freaked. Now they looked like too many scars to be OK, they meant perverse acts behind closed doors. I cleared my throat. 'You mean, you sell your art? You said, once.'

'No, I don't get my money from there. I don't know.'

'Where do you get your money?'

Her shoulders changed. She said, 'I'm not up for a session now, thanks.'

'I didn't need a *session*,' I said. 'I'm just trying to calm —'

'What do you *need*? What do you *need* from me now?'

'What's wrong with you? I'm only talking.'

'I can't service your needs.'

And then I needed, I did need. It's cool to need. You need people to

She said, 'You fuck yourself with your needs. I fucking hate you.'

I felt cold and white. I got up, I was shaking all over. I said, 'Just, do you want a doctor?'

'No! I don't want a doctor! What is that, code for cops? You go and call whoever *you need* to call.'

I was heading for the door while she said,

'I know you, I know people like you —'

I slammed the door behind.

I went downstairs and she would have to leave, I couldn't go on with this. You couldn't, and work, and have a life. I'd never had a life. I'd bought this house and now. I'd made her promises, her life was just as valuable as mine but. I swore to God I had to fuck someone except I couldn't, just to hold someone in bed, I *needed*.

My head was going going, my toes twitched like a dreaming animal's.

At last there was only the homely scent of my own four walls, my stinky house. And the rain had stopped. I saw the bright outlines of drops resting on my windows.

So I stand in the dark and breathe fully so my chest grows. I let all the bad scene out.

The television's left on in the sitting room. By its dodging light I put my leather jacket on, I get my sneakers. Creep downstairs where my bike is, one shoe on each hand and my bare feet experience the cold grit on the linoleum as unmediated reality. I tie my sneakers on bare feet, leave

and there is no man standing on the puddled sidewalk, only a scattering of wrappers where he (maybe someone else) was eating Starburst fruit chews. I raise my gangly bike to my shoulder and go down my steps:

Twenty-Three

there's Lennie walking up the street. He lives two streets down, he has to pass my house on his way from the bus stop, a thing I'll have to get used to now I'm in the neighbourhood. We're looking at each other as he comes. It takes a long time, we smile on and off. At last he stops in front of me and says,

'Sweetheart darling. I've just been at a party for a dreadful poet's birthday with some robots from the ICA. I'm horribly depressed. Tell me you don't hate me.'

'Lennie, not now, I got a lot on my mind.'

We both look up at my house that looks especially like someone else's house in this morning dark. It's just some house. I don't particularly like it. Lennie says,

'I was looking for you, actually. I have a message.'

'I have a cellphone. No one can look for me who's not retarded.' I reach into a neighbour's hedge and get a crumpled Planters Peanuts bag. It has some barbecue crisps in it, but I don't wonder how they got there at that time. They're dry despite the rain, and their smell is incongruous; like something imported from exotic lands, I insert the bag back in the hedge, just as it was, as if to cover my tracks. Lennie says,

'It's Peter Rabbit. He wants to paint you. I ran into him down the road.'

Twenty-Four

Peter Rabbit had slashed El's face. He had run amok, smashing her room. Cut her throat, in a half-assed way, fuck knows. It was Peter Rabbit I recognised when I got woken by shattering glass, Peter Rabbit in the bucketing rain, I immediately realised.

He was sleeping with El. She'd had my little black book, and me going on like a prat, about Peter and me. She had sat there knowing. Maybe she had got him from the book.

For a moment it was just in my head, I was tripping from no sleep. Then it was real. I felt too slicingly real; a slight wind blew and stopped. I had chill where I had sweated on the nape of my neck. I had chill in the palms of my hands.

Lennie fished inside his jacket and held up a yellow business card. 'He wanted you to come to his studio. He must want to fuck you, or is that my filthy mind?'

I put my hand out and took it back. I didn't want the card. 'Except, does that make sense? I'm no Alissa.'

'Perhaps Peter wants a change of pace.'

'Dude craves variety.'

'You *are* ugly, aren't you? Conventionally. *I* don't find you ugly, but I'm strange.'

'Oh, I'm like a carved pumpkin, fuck it.'

I laughed hoarsely, picturing Alissa, who had actually jumped out of a cake for money once. Exquisite, blonde and fond of public nudity, et cetera, painted twice by Peter Rabbit in the character of Holy Mary. Those were her real breasts. She was the twin of El.

I was holding the card to my surprise. It read:

peter rabbit 200 old street

76

and that's all. I gave the card back but I remembered it. I said, 'I'm not fucking any fucking Peter Rabbit.'

'He likes *you*. It's a shame you don't like *him*.'

I looked at Lennie. His face was pursed, intense, maudlin.

He said, 'I love you, Tanya,' and it went down my spine like a slipping ice cube. I said,

'This was supposed to be an OK morning,'

and rode to work. I stopped on the way to have a cappuccino standing up, near Smithfield's in a swanky cobbled micro-street. It kind of rained, making craters in the cappuccino foam. You felt tough standing there, like the lone cowboy that couldn't be hanged with a cappuccino; partly because my life was chaos, right.

Bankers walked past, looking hangdog, poetically lost in their suits. My head felt bright from cycling. And Peter was fucking El, he was in love with her. I could shut my eyes and see his glazed veined cock slipping out of her and in, I didn't have to shut my eyes. He was probably paying her way. I could go to his studio for her back rent, meaning I'd fuck him. That wouldn't be the end of the world. He was on my way to work, I could fuck him and still get in by eight. If he fucked me, though, it was only to get to her. He had slashed El's face.

I could do what I liked, you didn't have to make good decisions. You could make bad decisions, as long as you earned your own living. No one could tell you shit. This kind of thinking had got me into this mess, my life, although my life looked pretty good now, to me. I could go home later and braid El's hair.

That day we braided her hair, she was telling us, like she liked to say, that she was evil. Killing the parakeet featured. She'd killed this parakeet with one hand; El held the hand up, making the fingers cramped like they felt the blot. That was why she felt so vile with leather, because she'd killed. It was what psychopaths did, she said, with an air of facing facts. They tortured animals when they were kids, though she hadn't tortured the parakeet, just squeezed it too hard, in a crazy moment. Then the tears and the whole nine yards,

Todd roped into hugging her. Eleanor peeped up over his bicep, cute.

I had to live in reality finally. Except I didn't know what to do in reality. I got back on my bike and rode, and worked late, is all I ever learned how to do and

that night was Curt Short's wake bash
which Alan had to go to, so I went.

Twenty-Six

Curt Short's memorial do was a catered function in a hotel ballroom. There was live harp music from a lady in a gown. There were waiters bearing wine which they identified by year, grape, vineyard as they dipped the tray; and there were waiters bearing canapés. A cake to make children dream, boat size. The grieving widow in Chanel. The Short kids were chubby, affable, nice, but like nobody had told them what the party was for. I kept wondering what my dad's funeral was like.

Of course Curt Short wasn't there, this was the public reception, not the funeral. The funeral party had *come from* the funeral. I talk as if I knew this when I went, but I was disappointed not to see a coffin, not to see Curt Short, in any guise.

I wandered here and there, plucking 1982 Biggadongdong Shiraz from trays and so on, drinking too much. Eating pear balsamic sushi rolls, talking to people that I hadn't seen in. And saying things I hadn't said in. There was even Alex Forter from our old drinking crew, who is meat without a soul, and like a carved pumpkin. Just in a different way from me.

He said to me, 'You'd heard Mohammed Ziah was killed, too? Also in his home?'

Mohammed Ziah, my assassinated friend, was a tycoon dude I knew from Star and Garter days, the Soho offices. I fucked Mohammed Ziah. In his home. I said,

'OK. That was political, though.'

'Oh, that's all right, then!' Alex said, and brayed laughing.

I said, 'He had some finger in some pie with dissidents in Egypt.'

'In Iran,' Alex said, and sighed and spotted someone else and took his leave.

And Ziah was uncannily like Alex, now I came to think. Therefore also like a carved pumpkin. We had that in common, all three. Only they weren't ugly like a carved pumpkin, but

> scary, hollow, like a face on something other than a human
> like a carved pumpkin.

And my assassinated friend Ziah, who was my one man I slept with who might have been involved with al-Qaeda, had a private zoo. So when we fucked

Ziah had invited me to see his giraffe. It had been purchased at a Welsh safari park as a foal, but had to grow before it could be shipped. He'd owned it for a year, but it was living with him only two weeks, on his compound in Surrey, once the home of the Olympic stables.

Ziah put the moves on me in the monkey house. There was a couch there you could watch the monkeys, you know, jerk off and fight. Someone had spilled disinfectant on it so it made your eyes water.

While we fucked, the monkeys screeched and hurled filth at the cage wall. It made that jounce of hit chicken wire. Ziah said to himself: 'Fuck it good, fuck her. That's good.'

And walking back through the zoo we saw the famed giraffe. Like all hoofed animals, anticlimactic, it looked faded, unintelligent. It lacked drama. Needed steam-cleaning.

I said, 'Is there a rhinoceros?'

Ziah said, 'No,' disdainfully, like rhinos were sophomoric. Then he handed me a handkerchief and looked away, grimacing. I didn't know what I was meant to wipe. I tried wiping four or five things.

Now he was dead as a rock. As Curt Short and Dad. It struck me funny I would be the same kind of dead some day.

Unless there's hell.

★

So after seeing Forter there was Curt Short's wake cake. Cause, when I walked into the ballroom I had registered the table with a big rectangle and I thought it was the coffin. From a distance. When I got close, I did a double take. It was the right size, right, and it was chocolate so it could have been wood. It was brown and from a distance, in a moment of distraction.

Then I thought, my God, we got a cake instead of Curt! I decided I would have a slab of cake like a paving stone, just to show the widow, who I blamed for the frivolity of the event, that kind of plastic bitch. Then I was going to boycott the cake. But I was starving.

So I had a slice and it was so delicious that I had another slice

and a Short relative was talking to me while I pigged this cake, about the murder. He was saying people who opposed the death penalty were just, ignorant. I said I opposed it

and took a fat mouthful of cake. It was fantastic.

He said, 'Yes, but if it was *your* loved one,' dismissively, guffawing, 'I wonder what you'd say then.' (He was from some nothing fly-over state like Texas. He was like a Humpty-Dumpty with a mean streak. *Fuck* Texas.)

I said, 'Honey, my *mom* was murdered by her boyfriend, Bert. And if you want to know, it didn't make me want to murder Bert. I'm not *like* Bert. You want to be like Bert, don't pick and choose, just kill at random. Kill me,'

I said and got a chill remembering how I would say that to my dad. I had a mouthful of cake and wanted wine. The cake was wonderful.

I said, 'I mean, for real.'

He backed up, wanting middle ground, and said, 'I'm sorry to hear that. I guess that must be awful hard to get over, the death of a parent. In those kind of circumstances.'

I looked at him, I don't know why I get so angry. I said, 'Yeah, it's not as hard as peeling a hot hard–boiled egg. But it's hard.'

And I said, 'Fuck the death penalty. Fuck death,' and put the crumby plate down and walked away.

Then I felt this sick mixed feeling of pleasure from the cake and from the petty vengeance I had taken on the poor guy for holding a belief at variance with mine

(I wanted Vinnie back alive. I wanted Curt Short back alive even. Even Ziah. My poor deranged poor dad.

And I could puke this cake forever, puke my whole body out);

I took another pear balsamic sushi roll off a platter and my hand crashed into Mark Keynes's.

I looked up drunk. He was blinking, startled, flushed with excitement. He said, 'Hi. Hello.'

I said, 'You want to get out of here?'

Twenty-Seven

So, when I had my problems with sex, they were a problem cause

I couldn't stop fucking but

I stopped enjoying fucking and

I fucked every man I met, you'd be amazed the high percentage.

Then I hated them.

Some like Hutch I didn't hate and I'd have sex with if there weren't new prospects. I fucked Alan lots of times instead of lunch. There was a kid in dispatch.

I thought everyone was doing this. It was a generation thing, with women my age. I even used to speculate aloud about the causes of this social phenomenon. When people mentioned thoughtlessly that Aids had ended casual sex, I would become strident. 'That's a lot of bullshit from the media. That's such crap.'

My drinks were on the house. I went to concerts, the theatre, clubs. I never had money, so I'd think this was pragmatic.

'Fucking's good for your abs.'

'I've got to know all kinds of people.'

'It's a form of meditation.'

I stopped enjoying it. I kept lubricant in my bag. I had to leave right after, I would call a cab sometimes *before* we started fucking, so the cab would be there. Then I'd offer the cabby a blow job if I really felt

it. Whatever it is. That ruled me, what demon

makes you follow someone into the men's room and kneel. Whatever makes you think that's liberty, you are a renegade, that people envy you. That song is about you. You outsmarted them all.

★

And Mark said to me, as we came from the lobby to the cab rank,

'You know when I first noticed you?'

I said, 'When we met?' edgy, too harsh.

He laughed, beaming. Mark thought I was charming, it was fucked. And he said, 'Where did you want to go? Have you eaten?'

I considered eating. We could go and eat. We'd hit a Thai restaurant and have drinks, converse about Labour's fiscal policy or Plan 9. What do people say on dates?

What do you think about death? Does death frighten you?

I said, 'Why don't we just go to yours?'

He said, 'All right,' in an altered voice, and I looked back up the hotel's lit windows and asked if Mark had been the one who paid El's tab at the Hilton.

He said, 'No, that was Peter Rabbit, the artist.'

For a moment I had swallowed my heart, but it was stuck. I said, 'Yeah?' and swallowed it all the way down.

Mark said, with distaste, 'They have one of those relationships,'

and a cab swept into the bay where the doorman bent as if to catch it in his arms. He opened its door like a gracious crow's wing. We ducked in out of the lights.

Twenty-Eight

But there are moments in sex that are like the make-believe worlds you had as a child, a magic fort made of cushions. Because you believe, you can fly. When I was seven I dreamed every night about a castle. It was me standing in the tower, all alone, looking at this fairy-green landscape that faded in different gardens to the sea. There was a mystery about it, what the castle was and why I was there. When sex works, you're in the castle and you don't understand, but it means more than all of life you understand, except it doesn't work for me, for years, so why am I saying this.

Sometimes you just do shit that's wrong. Everyone should lighten up about it. Mark was not complaining, Mark was an adult, I never lied to Mark. I'm not responsible for other people's feelings. They should tell me if they're feeling something bad, I'm not a mind-reader.

'It means something different to your partner,' said a haggard wiser older woman, at my one and only Sex Addicts Anonymous meeting, at the coffee urn. I thought, 'Yeah, it means nothing.' But I knew that I was wrong.

I know I'm wrong. I lay there fucking Mark and knowing I was wrong. It was like chocolate cake over everybody's dead body. It was freedom

for a long minute.

What it feels like is someone digging in my crotch. Digging in me with an implement. My mind is ranting on about how great it is, my body goes through the motions like a *seasoned tennis player*. Usually I come, but, like a muscle spasm, something going on in your organs. It's unpleasant. On the borderline of itchy.

It's not my fuck as soon as it's done: I feel as if the sheets *got wet* and it's disgusting. I regret the energy I could have used for work, at the gym, constructively. I've got nothing to say and I am never sleepy.

They talk.

They tell you what attracted them about you when you first met. They talk about being lonely, watching telly night after night. They talk about whatever drove them to this, they say things you don't say aloud. Then they turn off the light, and ask if that's all right. Mark

talked about his wife.

I watched the shiny grain on his cheek, the black pores people get on their nose, petty signs of age. He had wild eyebrow hairs that sprang at angles to his face. Where he was leaning on his palm, the skin crinkled. They were details that made the body medical, you started to think about tissues and guts. I imagined his wife lying tired on a pillow and watching Mark with love, when he was younger.

She'd left him cause he couldn't give her children. His sperm were meagre, malformed, then the IVF failed. 'Jan never wanted anything but to be a mum. Her mum was just a mum, I knew that when I married her,' Mark said, stiff with hurt; 'I welcomed it.' He'd also had a minor affair, but that was not the reason, that was just a symptom, Jan's family might think what they liked.

He said he had a friend who, when his marriage broke up, he'd left his job and travelled round the world playing saxophone. He'd always played the saxophone, he played in a band – just a weekend band, this was in Bristol. Mark got a letter from him from Cuba, he was sitting in with Cuban bands and on his way to Zanzibar to some jazz festival. Mark didn't play any instruments.

He talked about sitting watching telly alone night after

night. And I was looking at the room, tense, in this despondency. The furniture was all from the Sofanet catalogue. The flat was on the twelfth floor and silent, weirdly monotone in temperature from double glazing. There were three framed film posters on the wall. *Manhattan. Pulp Fiction. Silence of the Lambs.*

I didn't like to look at those posters, they just got to me. Keynes never loved those movies, never saw those movies, maybe. He just needed something on the wall to stop it being white. A discount 'personal touch' replacing art the way our sex replaced his ten-year marriage for love. You could replace the partner of your life, your heart's daily bread,

with cake. That's why they have stores. That's why
I made him fuck me over again;
I don't know why I watched over him while he slept. I was intent, thinking nothing. Sipping rum in a measured way. And woke him after two hours and made him again.

Then he said, 'Where are you going?'
That's the story of my life. I got a black cab

Twenty-Nine

to 200 Old Street. In the cab I felt elated, I was high. I was going to phone Todd and tell him. He would laugh. He never gave me any shit.

The city circled me and I went through it like a pinball. I sailed through it unscathed, high. It means something different to your partner, and fuck them. Fuck you, Texas. Die in memory of Vinnie.

And the cab pulled up, I was buzzing, crazy. I jumped out and had to pay the guy, I was impatient as I handled the fiddly money, stupid paper. Then I turned away and looked up and

saw the lights on in the dirty windows, realising it was 1 a.m. But I proceeded.

(I had quizzed Mark about Peter Rabbit. And he said, 'Jan bought something off him. I suppose we used to see him for a while. Jan loved him,' he added on a flat note, and produced a smile like a crack in a plate, desolate and bitter. He had met El *through* Peter Rabbit, El and Peter showed up at this karaoke bar at someone's leaving do. Mark got pissed as a fart and sang 'Wild Horses' to her, it was *the week* Jan left. And Mark said,

'The grapevine has it, she's living with you?'

'Temporarily,' I said, and

I said, 'I suppose then Peter is the womaniser we all . . . ?')

I walked up the steps. I heard music from above, so faint I couldn't tell if it was classical. I thought that it was classical but couldn't tell. I rang the bell.

It was 1 a.m. There was no sound from inside but that music. I rang the bell and listened.

The door flashed open on a swell of country music.

Tall Peter Rabbit stood there, frozen.

He said, 'Oh, shit – *you came*.'

Thirty

Peter Rabbit's studio was one half of a former factory floor. Long and narrow as an alley or a bowling alley, it had no windows till the whole back wall Peter Rabbit had replaced with glass. When the sun went down, that mirrored the room, tilted up like a dream walkway up the night to the lit and golden windows opposite. By that glass wall were dozens of rugs, in sloppy layers, like a puppy litter of rugs asleep, where his easels were. His palettes were, his pickle jars with brushes knee-deep in turps were.

Hung ceiling to floor, on both long walls, were Peter Rabbit's paintings. Otherwise the room was bare. There was a balding, velvet, seventies-brown settee made up as a bed, no other furniture. The dishes were stacked on an army blanket on the floor. Ponytail holders bundled the forks, spoons, knives. The khaki refrigerator had a rabbit painted on it in white glue, and wasn't plugged in.

You could see where Peter sat, because he smoked. There were ashtrays and parts of newspapers on the floor where Peter liked to sit. I had the same sheet-metal valentine ashtrays cause Layla made a hundred when she went through her break-up. Peter read the *Guardian* and the *Star*, like Todd; Todd hides the *Star* though.

And heaped in one of those heart ashtrays were Starburst wrappers. And I looked for and found, on the floor in a corner, that black leather jacket like everyone wears, still overly black with wet. And, among the paintings was Eleanor as Pandora, gold and red, and signed PR in the same hand as her one was signed RH.

He was walking around turning all the lights on, apologising. I was just there, like a stick stuck into the ground, like when you know you ought to leave. I could feel my sloppy cunt from sex. All I'd eaten was cake and rum, I had that chilled small feeling when you need to be alone. Peter Rabbit was going

he was *so sorry* he came after me, with his lame message. Anyone would just pick up a phone, not him. I didn't think that he was psycho, just because he acted psycho? 'Probably you don't even *like* Lennie, right? I am *so sorry*. All I needed is photographs, I didn't expect you to sit there while I paint you for thousands of hours, were you worried I did? We can do it right now, no *problem*, only my friend Con Carne might bust in. He's here from LA, it's a pain in the *ass*. Sin gets here tonight, his wife, it depends what time her flight gets in, he went to the airport, right? If you're cool to do it now, though, they'll be cool, they don't have to sleep *that second* they come in. They never sleep so much, because they're usually tweaking, is the truth.'

I said, 'What's going on with you and Eleanor?'

Peter stopped dead. He was standing by a lamp he'd just switched on, his shocked face bright in the new light. He said, 'The cute blonde chick who lives with you? That chick?'

'I know that you know her, OK.'

'I know her,' he cautiously said. I said wearily cause people just make me tired, 'Have you known each other long?'

He smiled, coy, looking down at his toes so I noticed he was wearing huaraches. 'You could say that,' he said. 'I've known Elly since we were pups. In foster care in Pennsylvania, right?'

'So you're not –'

'Am I fucking her? No! I haven't fucked Elly since we were twelve! Thirteen! Since we were thirteen. Is that what she says?'

'No! Somebody said you put her up in the Hilton, is all. Mark Keynes did.'

'Oh, that dude. So, sure, I put her up in the Hilton. Yeah, I did that for her. I don't know what that dude cares what I do for Elly.'

He turned and walked off onto his rugs, like he was headed to meet his reflection that stalked down the glass wall, shaking its head. His reflection came to meet him from the night roofs opposite like a disconsolate tightrope walker. Peter stopped at an easel, and said,

'Yeah, I blew a lot of money buying Elly jewels, too. Is that what you wanted to hear? Cause she can't hold onto money, no way, I thought she better have something. Diamonds. Whatever, that's what she digs. She doesn't have to *put out* to get that stuff from me, she's the champ.'

'Anyway, OK, you're close?'

'What did I just say? What do *you* think?'

We faced off like duellers at twenty paces. Peter was wearing a T-shirt I remembered, Playboy with the bunny head. Someone had written 'Flopsy' underneath in Magic Marker; it was an inside joke that he'd explained, but I couldn't remember now.

I said, 'You never – we fell out of touch.'

He said, 'I know. I'm *so* sorry.'

'I didn't call.' I shrugged.

'There's actually a reason, but I can't tell you, is that cool? I shouldn't have told you *that*.' He'd turned to me, his face unsettled, coy. He said, 'I wasn't boning that girl.'

'Diddy?' I said, and to pretend this was the reason I remembered, 'That's a cracked name.'

'She was a *pest*. She was sweating me. I don't know what's going on with girls.'

'Sweating you to fuck her?'

'No. Maybe. But Elly isn't like that. Don't even trip on Elly and me.'

He started to tell me, then, about El and him growing up, about the foster-parents who were God-fearing folk. Who he hated, you could tell. He didn't say much, what you could say at twenty paces while standing, dying of whatever you were trying not to feel. Later, he would tell me details and the personalities. Now he wrapped up, 'Elly was always the coolest,' and crossed his arms tight, sad.

I walked to him. The rugs were piled so thick it made precarious footing, like walking on someone's back. My reflection moved towards me self-consciously, stiff in my peripheral vision. As I got to Peter, I lost my balance, and he steadied me with a hand. He caught my arm.

And Peter had dark hair so thick you thought about it as thick. His arms were big all the way to the hands; he had the exact right looks. But his eyes were bluish white. It freaked me out his pale blue eyes were a shade of white, for a particular reason. I turned to the easel, sharp.

The painting clamped into that easel, still wet, smelling good with turps, was of a plump white girl with hair so blonde and short it looked like baby hair, in a lumberjack shirt she'd opened to the waist; her tits were soft, unfocused, but the plaid exact. She'd dipped one hand into her cunt. She had her period and the blonde cunt hair was bloodied, her hand was bloodied and the palm held up. You could see the fingerprints marked out in red. The draughtsmanship so good, it was in poor taste, then Peter would add those big silk flowers like off a tourist's Hawaiian lei. And the girl was Amber Short, Curt's youngest daughter, which, a good thing Curt was dead, he was pretty Baptist. I said, in a hoarse, defensive voice,

'Hey. Did you slash Eleanor's face? Not slash, but, cut her?'

Peter's eyes went wide. '*No way.* She *told you that?*'

'I *saw her.* Look, it was at my house. I heard –'

'I was trying to *stop her.* She cuts herself, for *Christ's sake.* Did you ever see her *arms?* I wouldn't tell you that, but if she's going to pin it on me, fuck that.'

We held on a minute. My body believed him first; relaxed so I felt drunk again. It was so obviously true it seemed to solve my problems. Peter said, cheered up, 'Elly's a horrible liar. Damn!'

'Well, cool. Do you need, I guess I thought, you wanted me to pose for you naked?'

'Wow.' He ducked his head. 'That's what I do, anyway. Is that cool?'

We both inhaled and held it. We looked at Amber Short. He was barely meeting my eye, ashamed, his head was angled away. I said,

'No. Sorry, I so can't do nude photos. I never even take off my clothes in front of people, or not with the lights on, it's totally neurotic, I know,' I said. 'But, do you want to have sex?'

Thirty-One

El's real name was Rachelle Freespirit Lynch. Born in Philadelphia to teenaged parents, Eleanor was orphaned at one. Her father had left his child and child-wife to be an artist in New York where he became a drug addict and died. The mother died a suicide, Peter knew, but didn't know why there weren't grandparents stepping in. He knew Elly was in state care before she could walk.

Her first and last foster-parents were the Hortons. They were Christians. They were what you call 'important' Christians because they were outspoken and rich. Pa Horton had a chain of Christian-themed shops, and he ran a Christian interest catalogue. He had started with 'Books from the Heart', and the gift store franchise was called 'Art from the Heart'. On the facade of each store was hand-painted the old chestnut from 1 Corinthians: *Though I speak with the tongues of men and angels, and have not love, I am become as sounding brass* — and along the highway, billboards with this message were signed 'A reminder from the Heart of Pennsylvania — From the Heart stores'.

The high school had a Ruth and Douglas Horton Stadium. The hockey team thanked them before each game. The Coalition for American Pride was seeded with his money, as was an evangelical talk show. He toured to speak for abstinence and donated time to the Prayer in the Prisons movement. He was nothing but good works.

He was a model father. Both his blood son, Isaiah, and Rachelle got the best of the best things. His wife, Ruth, was a great mom and cook, and they had an Irish setter who could sit up and beg. Pa Horton wrote the *From the Heart: For Fathers* book for Baptist Values Press. Ma Horton was his 'co-pilot' on the title page of *From the Heart: For Wives*.

Isaiah, the son, was fifteen and big-tits obese. Pa Horton would say he'd have all the friends that you could ask if he would show them that prize-winning smile. Isaiah wore a ski hat year round, pulled down entirely to engulf his hair. He bred and sold parakeets, was all he had. The birds had names like Torquemada, Azrael and Sauron, but Isaiah was a well-behaved child otherwise, where no-behaviour is accounted good. He went straight to his room and shut his door and kept his mouth shut.

Elly fought. She'd breathe her whole self full to scream names. Her plate of food went on the floor. Her bites drew blood. She was the first girl ever sent home from her Sunday school for fighting: the Brownies threw her out for foul language.

Stick and carrot alike left Eleanor cold. She'd been through Ritalin, manners camp, and a Christian child psychiatrist. Under duress, Isaiah gave her a parakeet she unhesitatingly freed. She burned with hate like a cross in a midnight lawn, and burned and burned on.

When Peter came, it was a last bid to settle her. A cousin from a lesser, Alabama, Horton strain, Peter lost both parents in a freak accident. He was small, a kid who loved his chemistry set. Already he could draw and drew requests at family parties. A Charleston aunt, Althea, wanted him, but Pa pleaded specially — for El's sake.

'I was so bummed. Cause I wanted to go with Althea, that's my fun black relatives, all the Jespie side of our family's black. And they were so cool, all my cousins could hunt with guns, my cousin Elaine got a pickup when she was fourteen. They had a fireworks stand. I'd never met Ma and Pa, they were in Pennsylvania, it was like the dark side of the moon.'

97

Thirty-Two

It was Peter's first plane journey. The man sitting next to him explained how the engines worked, the landing gear. He pointed out what Peter ever after remembered as 'turbulence clouds', because the plane began to jig. Planes 'never, ever' crashed, the man said: he was a former pilot. Flew he paled to think how many missions in Korea.

Peter said, far as he knew, the worst could always happen. *Impossible* things had really happened to people.

'Twelve is way too young to be a nihilist.' The man's blue eyes dulled then, he stopped liking Peter. He was a real pilot who you don't contradict, and he flattened out his newspaper anew.

Peter hunched towards the rosy, bunched and glistening clouds that looked like real heaven where his parents were, in heaven. He'd land and his parents would be there, he wouldn't think about it. Planes were cool. He'd ask to go home on a plane for his thirteenth birthday.

A red-clad stewardess led him to his new parents. Pa and Ma Horton were fat. They had thin hair, they were wearing matching blue tracksuits. It was like clown parents. It was like parents painted on hard-boiled eggs.

'How was the trip, son?' Pa said, twinkling. Peter started saying, but they turned to go. They let him carry his own bags all the way to the car. Put him in the back of the Lincoln and said nothing on the drive. Ten minutes in, Ma put on her Barbra Streisand.

Peter sat on the edge of the car seat. He watched reflected lights flee backwards in the window. Since his parents died, sometimes his teeth chattered even when he wasn't cold. His teeth were chattering and he was jumpy, thinking the car would crash.

Peter Rabbit had seen his parents die. The family were going to a company picnic when the car broke down in a country lane. The parents left the twelve-year-old Peter sleeping in the back and headed down the road, presumably to find a phone. Fifty yards away, both were struck by a truck that kept on going. The parents lay flat in the road, turning red where they had worn light clothes. Flies circled as if concerned.

The noise woke Peter.

Missing his parents, he got out of the car disoriented, calling out. As he walked up the road, he was hearing the last sharp cries. But he didn't even know it was people till he got close.

'It was rough for a little dude. For months I didn't believe they were dead, even though I saw them all beat up. I thought they had gone into hiding or some little dude idea. Cause we used to sleep all in one room, we were tight, I never thought of them going away.'

Thirty-Three

The Lincoln pulled into a garage. An automatic light went on, displaying racks of skis, tools, fishing poles fixed to the wall — abundant like a store. Their shadows moved like cats as the garage door came down. 'Home again, home again,' Pa Horton sang. He opened his door and the car filled with no-nonsense cold air, sharper than the Alabama night at any season.

They would have gone up with Peter but they didn't like the stairs one bit. Once a day was plenty for those stairs: joints! Saying 'Elly's so excited to meet you,' Ma settled in her rocker-recliner and turned up her show. Pa headed out to the patio with his cigar, the setter frisking ahead.

Peter mounted the stairs. His palm trailed up the panelling, Peter was counting the grooves. The dark was warmer at the top of the stairs.

Under her door, a line of light was so concentrated it looked sweet; like light prostrate at her feet. It was an orange light because the carpet was. Peter already knew she would be pretty. He had seen her picture.

She was a 'hoyden', all the folks said at home. He had an idea that meant she took her clothes off for boys.

He knocked to the time of his knocking heart and she was at the door already listening. Elly opened standing on tiptoe. She touched down; her pink mouth set. Then she stalked back through the room, territorial, queenly. He trailed her as if entranced. They fetched up by her bed, where she pulled the sheet up with one twitch, erasing tangled underwear in the bed that left an after-image in him, left Peter weird inside and restless. She crossed her arms and stated,

'I don't want you here, even. *I don't.*'

'Who wants to *be* here? I wouldn't stay if you . . . wanted so bad.'

'But you have to stay,' she said. 'Or you're planning to sleep in the *garbage*?'

'You just *said*. You stupid *girl*. I ought to —'

There was a poster of a lion cub tacked to the panelling. He reached up as if to tear it down and she shrieked, 'You ever dare and I'll —'

'What?'

Then she berated him. Her voice was a Penn drone, flat-footed to his Southern ear, a language played on the nose. He crouched on the bed and hugged his chest, unstrung. There wasn't even any TV up here, it was a gyp. He wasn't going to cry. If he cried it was because he was tired, but she would never believe that. She'd think he was a fairy.

He started chanting, 'You suck, you suck, you suck.'

At last he had to stop. It was like he couldn't almost breathe. His teeth chattered. God had freaking stuff to answer for, he wasn't going to church any more if someone made him at gunpoint. They could shoot him, that would make God proud, Peter guessed.

And she had shut up. There was the deep bounce of El sitting down on the bed. When she did that, he felt hot everywhere.

And she said, 'Only, if you're not a spy, we could . . .'

Then it was a miracle, because she was crying. And he was sitting on the bed, and crying. There was the noise of Ma's TV downstairs, the cackling studio audience. There was the static of crickets. They held each other and cried, it was magic, it was something that he couldn't have done.

'Yeah, I was crazy for Elly from the word go. You know what Elly's like now. I followed her around like a dog. If she went to the bathroom, I'd just sit and wait. I didn't know how to be without her there, I was like she took out my batteries.'

And soon, like two months later maybe
    for the first time in the history of naked
    they made love: tin-eared, kid love that was real. In their bodies like brand new clothes, Peter loved and
    Peter said to her, 'I would take a bullet for you, Elly. I would fight lions,' in the dark. He swore he would walk through fire. He knew it; her hand grew damp in his. He told her he would give his life.

Thirty-Four

There were Passion puppet shows and Junior Joy choir. There were raffle tickets for the Mission Booster. Summer was potlucks after bake sales. Casseroles began with a can of cream of chicken soup.

Children did duty at functions in their fancy clothes, hand-finished by a Puerto Rican seamstress. What Peter remembers is having his picture taken. *Say cheese! Say Jesus! Turn that frown upside down!*

Ma kissed Peter for the eyes of other ladies. Since she never did at home, it was unpleasantly sensual; he used to blush and be the butt of jokes. 'The girls'll have their work cut out with *you*.' 'It's the quiet ones!'

Pa would rehearse the tale of Peter's parents' death. The night before the accident, Pa had a dream in which a present was put under his tree. A big and handsome present, with a mighty bow, the very best gift of all, called 'son'. He ruffled Peter's hair and said, 'The Lord giveth and the Lord taketh away.'

El watched from an armchair her pose made into a throne. She watched Peter like a searchlight and willed him to bite the hand that fed him. He was paralysed, needing her to look away cause

El stole. By night, El crept downstairs and stole
one item each of the family silver
anything left in the pockets of coats
cigarettes and booze
an enamelled box she decided was antique
records she didn't like, even.

El broke all the glass from a window, pane by pane, with a spoon handle. On the garage door, El wrote FAT PIGS in Ma's lipstick. She sat with Pa's review copy of *From the Heart: For Teachers*, drawing cocks and tits and cunts over the print.

With the cash from Pa's wallet, they took a train to New York City, where they wandered the streets, pretending that they weren't going back. They panhandled, getting not much, and spent it on McDonald's coffee. Whenever they saw a cop, they ran, imagining their pictures had gone out and

in the sun-laden street which smelled of bread there
as if sun smelled like baking bread,

he said to her, 'I would fight lions for you, Elly. I would fight dragons,' in the brown shadow of her neck. He said that he would give his life. Her breathing shortened as she knew that it was true. He had already given up what Peter had to lose, and on the train ride home they were headed to Peter's punishment.

Thirty-Five

Peter took her beatings for her. Pa Horton never liked to whip a girl. So it was Peter now, when the money vanished from the wallet, when the reading glasses turned up broke. The filthy graffiti that gave Peter bad dreams, he got beat for. They were mere belt-whuppings Peter got through no sweat because it was for her.

And he fairly earned them. Peter thought it was square. He might have never broken, stolen, done stuff, but he had known it. And he'd do it, if ever she asked. And El could hate the Hortons, he was right there with her, there was nowhere else that Peter could be. He didn't. Didn't want to rob Pa, didn't mind their homework and their dumb, make-the-bed rules. He would have been the very best gift of all, best he could and

was ashamed of yearning for it. Ashamed of admiring Pa's well-stocked garage. Ashamed of wishing El would lighten up and eat her pizza, shamed of doing all her dirty work, ashamed of her and them till

being beat was like a breath of fresh mountain air.

Once, Peter made friends with a girl in Bible study, Doretta, and he stayed late one day when Elly wanted to go. Doretta had a Shar Pei. If he played with her she'd let him come and see the dog, she wanted him to play four square.

That night El set his room on fire. The fire ran up the curtains like a squirrel, brisk. Peter woke to the pungent smoke that already made his skull ache. He ran out in torrential rain.

El was standing in the backyard, starred with water. She pointed at his window where the fire was gone. Pa moved there, dark.

'I hate you now forever,' El said, 'I sentence you to hell.'

Pa Horton came out with burnt cloth bundled in his hand. Isaiah was behind him, looking two feet taller than before. Isaiah hated Peter in those days.

Pa Horton said Peter's then name.

Peter said, 'It was an accident, cripes' sake, Pa.'

El shrieked, '*I did it*, you let him be, *stupid.*'

Pa Horton muttered, ' . . . for they know not what they do,' unbuckling his belt.

Elly stood trembling and mouthing words. The rain fell like clothes going on, it fit them. It was a warm night for Pennsylvania, it was May and when the rain paused, fireflies fringed the scene with their stumbling lights.

Thirty-Six

The night is a tale about fear. It is the black pit that opens
for children who misbehave. The night is ghosts and graves,
the night is murderers. Its cold hand fingers you as you pass
the door.

That's where you're going, to the night.

They pack her Simba the White Lion bag with clothes.
They pack his rucksack. Gathering food in the kitchen, they
are breathless. They must not wake Isaiah, whatever. Ma and
Pa would only shout down the wearying stairs, but Isaiah
would come, for sure, and see everything and know.

The cat follows them, down the stairs, from room to
room, purring, tilting his snout. The cat's name is Doubting
Thomas, because he's a tomcat and for his sceptical face, and
Peter used to nurse the fat orange cat to his chest. 'I heart
Thomas,' he would say to please El. (You shouldn't say you
hearted things in jest at the Hortons', Pa was sensitive.)

They bring Cap'n Crunch, muffling its rattle in a sweater.
Carnation Instant Breakfast they will eat with spoons, because,
the vitamins. Bologna and a lone potato that will later strike
them funny. A raw potato! Elly rifles the silverware drawer
and takes five silver knives that turn out later to be only
plated, and she has already taken Pa's wristwatch, to sell.

And suddenly there's nothing more. They don't look at
each other – as if looking must make noise, their feelings
roar. Their faces are bright and then Peter begins to go, as if
stepping onto a high wire;

(Pa was sensitive: those I HEART folks in New York
plain hounded him, when he was starting out. Got their
teeth in him for his using a valentine rebus in his signage.
Lost in court, so they published their article about him,
wanting to smear his name. He would never say he did not

have vulnerabilities. First and foremost, he started that Christian business when he had turned his back on God. He was a prodigal son, those were the long dark watches of Pa's soul. Years he lived as a hypocrite, selling his Christian wares with Pharaoh's mind. But when he gave to the world *From the Heart*, he opened one big door to grace. And he was proud as a mother he gave folks *From the Heart*, that meant the world to him, his gleaming legacy. Say what you liked, simple truths were best. El'd say,

'Easy money from the heart,' to him in unlovely Penn hatred, wreaking havoc, 'I heart the new Lincoln.' Peter never.)

Peter took the cold doorknob in one failing hand.

And for a moment she obstructed him; pressing her body against his, her lips to his cheek, she said in an artificial tone, as if she never meant it in the first place,

'I love you. I'm so glad we're doing this. I love you.'

Thirty-Seven

Peter Rabbit told me he and El had run away at fourteen. They stayed away, they blew the East Coast for good. He earned their keep by working gas-pump jobs on fake ID, he was super-responsible at that age. Only, they fought pretty quick though. Elly had a thing about sex, she'd sleep with anyone. He'd come home, she'd be with some fifty-year-old street bum, it couldn't last. 'Once, I came back, there were nine dudes. *Nine.* I freaked,' said Peter. 'I said, get these pricks to buy you your chow, get lost.'

And he said, 'I feel responsible, what happened to her, though,' and he shook his head and sucked on his new joint sadly.

We were on those rugs, we had just got done having sex. I was feeling my breasts, which, usually I won't touch, it makes me sick, or inconsolable more. I was feeling them through my T-shirt cause I'd never undressed. We'd fucked in the not-quite-dark, with shoes on, twice, then Peter started to talk.

'This is five years after, Elly turns up at my old place in Santa Monica. She was living in a damn hatchback with two white rap kids, like fifteen-year-old kids. They didn't have a *driver's licence.* Animal Boner and Human T-shirt. Those were their names. They were team-tagging her in this car, they'd park outside of my house. Cause it was Elly, I let them use my shower, you know. It was fucked. At last I told her, move into the house, this is fucked.' He sighed, hard, and handed me the joint. He said,

'Yeah, everyone was always in love with Elly. She had so many good offers in LA, but she'd end up in some car. All she'd ever do was drugs, and that was when she really murdered her arms. But in England, she blossomed, for real.'

'I blossomed here,' I said, stoned some, not realising what I was saying. Then I blushed in the dark and said, 'Whatever.' But Peter said seriously, taking the joint back,

'Sure you did, we all did. Cause it's – people are reliable here, it's not so, something.'

'Yeah, the difference between America and England.'

'Right? It's different. I would *never* be on the radio in New York, I'm too nuts.'

'Did you ever read Henry James?'

'Yeah, sure I did. Oh, Henry James? No.'

Then the Carnes came in, Sin and Con, they were black and forty, contrary to my preconception. Stringy, slow-limbed Texans, they looked like they'd had snaggle teeth before they hit the coast, and now they had those denture-style teeth of LA people. They turned on a couple of lights, sat down, spliffed up, said they'd had a hellatious Indian where the chicken tikka was the colour of a baboon's butt. Peter asked if they ever thought about Elly Jelly Rachelle, when they all met in Venice? Con said,

'Man,' and they rolled their eyes and laughed. Sin said,

'How we going to forget Elly Smelly Belly? After she stabbed that man,' in a high tight voice like a penny whistle.

Con said he and Elly used to make the run to Mexico to buy fireworks, did Peter ever remember that? Peter said, 'No, no way.' Sin said it wasn't fireworks, either, and Peter said he'd forgotten Elly had stabbed that dude, it was like it went out of his head. Con said damn, now

he was gonna have bad dreams. Peter said, 'I have bad dreams *every night*,' and

they were telling these stories while I lay staring, fucked up from

rum, hash, it being like 4 a.m., and events. Then without planning it I had got up; saying my stiff goodbyes. I felt like a narc, to be leaving, like you do when everybody's doing drugs, even hash. Peter got up upset. But he didn't try to

tell me to stay, and we went out side by side and down the dark stairs. He held the door open for me and tried to kiss me but I couldn't let him. I was just beginning to hate him. Oh, yeah, shit, I hate guys for fucking me, I was remembering while I wouldn't kiss him goodbye. He said,

'So you really won't do the photographs, really?' I was outside, at liberty, looking up where the stars still prickled in the greying night. I said, I was laughing and said, 'No, I'll sit for you with my clothes on, though. I don't care what body you give me. Get a Penthouse.'

He said, 'Wow. There's a lot you don't understand about me, that's for sure.'

I was looking down the street where it was moist and sparkling tar. I was ready to walk. He said,

'Goddamn. I need those pictures. But you think what you want.'

'I think I'll go back to the office and get my bike,' I said. He closed the door without saying goodbye. I walked on towards my office

through the City which at that hour is like bombed-out streets, an extinguished world overlooked by night clouds. Got into the office and I turned on the lights in each room as I walked through, until it was all light, my eyes hurt. I went to a window then. I leaned on my palms against the night in the chill glass, scared. I was realising I had been scared. The things I did, they were making me incredibly scared.

Thirty-Eight

Then I went into avoidance, kind of out of control. I didn't go home for two weeks.

I showered at the gym, slept mainly in the office. I sent Alan to my house for clothes.

I had work then, a lot of work that was a handy excuse, or an actual reason. There was the fertiliser catalogue and the new brochures to push our brochure business. The sex-toy mailing list got thorny. A bedding factory where I'd named the season's prints — *Jade River, Catnip, Nubia* — had queried some names on 'racial sensitivity' grounds, and that was a week's work losing the contract.

I had a bad lunch with the accountant, who kept repeating, 'Just tell me what I should do with these numbers.' I agreed the books looked exactly how they would look, if there was stealing going on, and the accountant and I sighed, he looked, I don't know, henpecked. We were eating noodles which are tough to eat under those circumstances.

It was Alan. Alan had embezzled before. Last time, he won the money back on a horse named Corporate Crime; it was easier then to accept Alan's logic that that made it all right, cause it was during his cancer. This time, he was robbing me, since I was a partner, which I guess ought to matter to me. But I wasn't getting heavy with Alan cause you have to have peace somewhere, you have to sleep somewhere.

For a while, I was always going to go home at night. It would be midnight and the draw of the train, how it's muggy and the people are drunk. At home, I had a Mars bar in the refrigerator. But El, 'You're coming up?' and (*It's like, Peter, Sin and Con had talked about El like she* wasn't *gorgeous; any old mate from SoCal who once cried cause they were playing keep-away with her stuffed lion, Boo. And they squabbled about what* drug she was on that day. Sin and Con described themselves as 'has-been wannabes' and their crowd with Peter had been kids who slept on the beach and called themselves musicians on the basis that, they had a guitar in pawn. 'Jelly Baby' turned tricks then, at parties. She had a denim jacket that said '$100' on the back in Magic Marker. In the summer, she wrote it on the skin of her cleavage. Then she flipped one night and came home painted in blood, she'd stabbed some poor nobody from Baltimore, because she had been carrying a knife, she had said. They laughed at that, it was something that was funny at the time. That was her whole reason that she gave: cause she'd been carrying a knife.

Peter was at college then, an aunt had come out of the woodwork to pay for him. El, who had dyed her hair lime green and wore goth make-up and dungarees as a disguise in case the Baltimore dude had died, stopped turning tricks. She used to audit Peter's classes cause she couldn't be alone; that was a whole time period. And it was fucked up Peter, Con and Sin didn't sweat it whether El was a killer, but I knew that from Vinnie, there were times in your life, if you were that kind of person, that, people stabbed people and they had to run away, they couldn't stand there waiting to see how it all turned out. And it wasn't on TV the next day, like in the movies. And it was not true you went back to the scene of the crime, it was the opposite of true. You never knew if you had killed anyone. Anyhow

all the UCLA professors loved her, the dudes did. Smelly Belly actually learned a lot, she was like a sponge, Peter said. They laughed at that, too, they had an image of her that made her being a sponge funny. And Peter said he had got better grades because of her skimpy tops, which was the only thing they said about her looks, and I was numbed her looks had no power over them, her looks that drove me insane, that sucked all my attention out of me.) you didn't have to live with that, not everybody whored and stabbed tricks. Though you did have to throw her out and say she didn't deserve your help, she'd gone beyond some human pale, was what I couldn't do. I couldn't speak to her. The thought made freezing crawl all over my skin. I didn't want to be in the same room with Eleanor.

And couldn't face Todd. I didn't feel the same about him, overnight. The helpless-puppy routine at thirty, his pricey skateboard, carp tattoo, organic cashew butter, when he couldn't make rent, were now incredible. I'd got fed up, Todd's rubbish on the floor, his paint all over the floor. He never got the plumber sorted so the toilet function petered out into the bucket method. And was never really thorough with the bucket method. It was fucking un fucking cool. Todd,

back in the day, when we were living in Holborn, in the Potemkin Squat with April, May and June the squatters' rights wimmin, right. This squat so established that you had to do two days' committee work a month to live there, and they introduced you to the advocate when you moved in. They had the telephone in Margaret Thatcher's name as an unfunny joke, that kind of people. So we moved in,

and April, May and June (not their real names) went to Mud Festival, Puddle Tribe Awakening and WOMAD or whatever, womanning a Druidburger stall so they were gone for two weeks when I was working in Leeds. The point is, Todd's alone. I got back first. He came out happily to make me tea, and I'm

like going up the stairs, looking. Place is a mess. But mostly: all the plants are dead. Flat out and brown.

At last I go, 'Todd. *What happened to the plants?*'

He stops dead on the stairs, nonplussed. Says, 'What plants?'

He says, 'I didn't know we had plants!'

So that was cute, back in the day. When it was someone

else's plants, but Todd thought it was because he was an *artist* (One autumn, Todd and I were fifteen, when we were boyfriend girlfriend, we were out in the woods. We grew up in New England so, all the psychedelic foliage. The forest floor was heaped with red, brown, yellow leaves like earth confetti. And Todd said,

'Wow, it looks like cat food.'

I said, '*Dry* cat food.' We laughed and sang the Meow Mix theme song; Todd said in all seriousness that we could see this, both of us saw the same thing cause we were *artists*. We were not artists.

Todd still hasn't got it. But it's easier, I totally accept, if you earn six digits, last year I earned six digits. My life doesn't have to have meaning. Todd's a bicycle courier at thirty-one. If you're from a middle-class family, that *means* you're an artist, or at least a writer, if you can spell. Todd can't spell. Todd can't draw. His art is garbage pasted on expensive materials on my dime. Like just a spoiled kid. It takes a petty little bourgeois to be *interested* still to *épater la bourgeoisie*, as if the bourgeoisie could matter less. And if he cleaned his own garbage up, maybe.) it was honestly a waste of life.

I should have bought a one-bed flat. Why hadn't I. It drove me crazy, why hadn't I. I flushed my whole life with that one decision. Now I had Todd *on me* for the rest of my life, like a corpse in the well and he would poison my life. How that could ever make sense, that I should buy a whole three-bedroom *house* to fill with *losers* and *incompetents*. Eleanor walking around in bloodstained knickers or designer gowns, two sides of the same shit coin. Todd and Eleanor, two sides.

I slept under my desk. I slept on the gym couch. I got caught sleeping on the Sofanet fold-out by their cleaning lady, who said I gave her 'ever such a turn', but *she'd* not tell. I got a pinched nerve from carrying the backpack. I got my first ever dandruff.

I started bringing rum and Coke into the office. I'd drink it underneath my desk and think of things other than. I read Nick Hornby, Sofanet Nick had all his books in a drawer. Time stopped, it was like more than two weeks, it was a phase like a marriage.

And under my desk in that den, safe, I sighed with the high of solitude, of alpine solitude. It was my new life. The building hummed and I would lie on my back

and coming down with flu, into that shivery privacy where

I never slept so well. I never liked, just a bag of Fritos, so well.

I'd shut my eyes in cabs, just ill enough to feel brave for never going home, like a rebel

hero in the Resistance outwitting the Nazis, freeing slaves from a plantation in the South, I was a cadre on a task of liberation

as the rain dashed left and right on the grimy town and clouds made the sky an

orange shroud that made the ducking crowds lurid.

Todd called, called and called, until I had to pick up. It was the Friday and we had had a kind of arrangement, we were going to a skating rink. There was no way. 'I've got to work until this is over,' I said, not making sense, my eyes were totally unfocused. I'd started taking calls from under my desk, though it was hard to think there. You didn't want to deal with anyone. Todd said how he'd missed me and

'Oh, yeah,' Todd added humbly, when I didn't say anything. 'I got that show. Lennie's letting me show there cause thingy pulled out on him. Not thingy, Sarah.'

'Oh, cool,' I said not hearing.

'In a week. I mean, you think you'll be home by then?'

'In a week,' I repeated, distantly, chewing at my broken fingernail. 'Yeah, count on it, that's a week from today. That's soon.'

Then I was telling him I had to make calls.

I told Sofanet Nick nothing was wrong. I said I couldn't go home now, I was snowed under. I was shamed when he believed me and bought multivitamins, concerned. 'I splashed out on the organic for you,' Nick said, and handled the bottle too much because I wasn't taking it. 'Thanks,' I said, inaudibly, and had to clear my throat and say it over. 'You're a mate.'

I told Alan nothing was wrong when I talked to him finally about his stealing. (He said it was never embezzling, he'd forgotten to falsify the books, was the simple answer, but he was on it and) 'Fuck all that, that's bollocks. You've been crap. You ought to learn to talk to your mates, cause I can tell.'

'I'm cool, I'm perfect.'

He said, 'Todd or the bitch?'

I told him this was like that other time I slept at work, that Christmas. That was glorious. I read all *Moby-Dick*, and on Boxing Day, Alan dropped in to fuck me, with a baggie of skunk. We always remember that, but he said, 'Bullshit, you're fucked up but you're not saying it.'

And, when I talked to Hutch

one time. I called Hutchinson, expectant, like to tell him big news. I talked and talked about I don't know what I talked about. Not Peter Rabbit, not El. Hutch said,

'I told you, I'm in love?'

My talking and my pleasure stopped.

I almost said, *you're* not in love, with scorn. *That* isn't love. My face was burning, I don't know.

I said, 'With that – nineteen-year-old? Or who?'

'Not Fran, no. It's graver than that. That seems an innocent time, now.' In his voice was tired misery. He added, 'Oh, well, she doesn't love me. Has that ever happened to you?'

'Yeah, of course it has. Of course.'

'When?'

'I don't know. It hasn't, then.'

'I thought you might have been in love with someone in the States. Unhappily. Without requitement – like me with Alex. That's her name.'

'Alex, right. She doesn't love you?'

'In love with someone else, you see. I fancy it's a woman; she avoids the pronoun. *The person I'm in love with*, sort of thing.'

'But she slept with you, right?'

'Oh, yes, once, and very beautifully. But she feels my love exerted a hypnotic influence. So that night was all me, there was none of her in it. She was infected by my personal emotion.'

'Oh, people are vicious to you when you're in love with them.'

There was a span of his tired, miserable breathing. I added, 'So I'm told. OK.'

He said, 'Well, it's hard when someone's so terribly young,

they don't articulate well. She claims I misunderstand her, but I don't see what there is to understand. I don't know why I love this person. Ha!' There was a pause, and he said, plaintive, 'Are you on your way to visit me?'

I said, 'No,' hastily, like dodging a projectile. I felt angry. Like he'd tried to corner me. I hated him. And while I hated him I thought, this is ridiculous. I hate Todd, I hate Hutch, what's happening to me.

But I was thinking he was such a cliché. The dirty old man, his teen girlfriends and the highbrow erotica he had on his shelves. And all that time I used to go to his house, when I was

desperate and alone
he took advantage of me
I was sick
he used me

and I didn't rate myself enough to care, to think it mattered, to be angry when it was abuse. It was abuse, from a decaying old man with just a prick animating his whole frame

I was thinking cause my friend was lonely. Wanted me to come and cheer him.

I said, 'I'm sorry. But I've got to work, you know what . . .'

'I know what you're like, yes. No, I understand,' he said, depressed. He said he could get someone else to come, that he had fancied making flan for someone. But not me, it seemed. 'I would have rather it was you.'

I said, 'Shucks,'

and cried obscurely in the night. Into the crook of my heated elbow. About my fever but about my loneliness I guess. As well, because I never had relationships and if I died of fever, who would oh, who cares. Hot tears and the sensation of the building rocking with my scared heartbeat. Like the building marching with me, off to the edge of the world, into a memory of Dad piggybacking me over frightening concrete, turning to a chaos of bad dreams.

In the morning, I woke up under my desk and it was afternoon. It was reality and I was that sick. For about an hour I lay there with the lights off, realising, feverish. It's when you've woken up but your life is over. You don't see any next step, but you woke up, putting you into a ridiculous position.

It was Friday. I had Todd's show in a couple of hours. I had to get to Lennie's and the risk of Peter being there, of El being there. People, anyway, asking how I was, as if that was an innocent question.

Finally I just had to change into some dirty clothes, dirty. Being too sick for the gym. So for the shower. Lifting one leg at a time was tricky. Then the panties didn't seem to have a front.

Forty

And Mark Keynes barges in the office while I'm changing. This is what happens. I am in my underwear I mean.

He goes 'Oh! Fuck! Excuse me!'

'Fuck! Don't walk in my – don't, Jesus!'

Keynes, with his back to me like lightning like a gentleman, says, 'I did knock,' in a voice stuffed up with anger.

I'm scrambling for my clothes. I'm aware now of the light in the venetian blinds, as if the world can see me. It's hard getting clothes on that fast, like you're trying to force them through your limbs.

'Yeah,' I go to his back, 'I haven't seen you in . . .'

Mark says, 'I didn't know you were here, I only came to leave some orders, we put through some new orders for February.'

'Cool. You can leave them. I'm just, cause I didn't feel well, I didn't go home and,'

'Cause I hadn't seen you.'

'Yeah, it's been real busy.'

I said, 'OK, I'm dressed.'

He turned and flinched. Longing filled his face like a bright colour. His nostrils pulsed where he was breathing too hard. He said, 'You do look ill,' gruff.

'I am.'

'Well. You look it.'

'I haven't been going out at all,' I blurted. 'With anyone,'

Mark inhaled rough.

(I hadn't answered Mark's voice messages, OK. It's why you shouldn't screw clients, cause you get this situation where their message is about the orders, but the voice is about you. And you're like, *fuck*.)

He started: 'I really had a good time with you the other night. I only wanted to explain I'm not available for a relationship. I'm not on the market.'

'All right.'

'I'm not saying that I meant it as a one-night stand, exactly.'

There was a pause. He searched my face.

I said, 'Yeah.'

I said, 'I don't know.'

I said, 'What's going on? You're just standing there, kind of. So, these orders, I don't know.'

Mark rubbed his forehead harshly. He said, 'Christ, you are a piece of work, the bloody *orders*.' He was raising his voice and stopped suddenly;

(And Mark Keynes was an intelligent, heartfelt person, he was everything you wanted in a boyfriend. All the secretaries raised their eyebrows when he divorced. '*He* won't last long in the wild,' said Sue Blue with her public-school assurance, knowing all about life; it was funnier cause Mark didn't know he was prey. It was a fucked-up metaphor for a sad guy who wanted ordinary love. To get in from the rain and a woman is incredibly glad. And he doesn't have time to fold the umbrella, she's there. The house bright with her, all the way home on the train he knows. I could never be her.

When I told Lennie once I had never had a boyfriend, since Todd when I was a kid, he said, 'You mean, Todd and you are still together.' 'But we're not lovers,' I said, 'we aren't in love.' We wondered aloud what the fuck was love then. We discounted everybody's love we could think of in turn until we needed a drink. I'd been helping him plaster that day. We were covered in it as we walked to the pub in our worst clothes. All the Turkish Dalston locals were eyeing us, the rain was blowing, and Lennie said,

'I think you ought to trade Todd in for someone you fuck,' which is why I remembered it.)

Forty-One

At fifteen, Todd and I were boyfriend and girlfriend. We lived together and we shared a bed. We had a routine I still use as a model when I think about being in love.

First thing every day, we played tennis. We shared a shower matter-of-factly, to save time. Sat together on the school bus; had geometry together and we had a lunch period. We'd get two cheeseburgers each and a shake and in the afternoons, we played tennis till the sun set.

Nights, we made love. Had sex, fucked, two-three times a night. Before the murder, that was our life.

It was a fantasy because his parents knew. There was this disbelief we all suspended till it was like grown couples sharing a house. Craig served wine at dinner for us all. We talked about the sixties, unselfconsciously, the sixties just kept coming up. Janet and Craig were McGovern Democrats who wished they'd done more in the sixties, but they missed the boat. Craig quoted French situationism to us, he taught French at Tufts and translated Guy Debord. Todd decided to be an anarcho-syndicalist. I pissed everyone off, defending Mao. We drank two bottles of red every night, cherished notions about our special life and

really we, all four, loved each other. Todd and I would mess around about it, call each other Craig and Janet, imitate them having sex when we were having sex. Because we got so close that you resented it. It made your hair stand on end when you went home. You hesitated on the doorstep, thinking, *what if, when I go in, it's gone.*

My mom was killed and it was gone.

Todd and I cut school to hitch-hike to Bert's trial. We missed four days of school because the trial kept being put off on technicalities, they wouldn't say what.

Once my father came up to us.

'They stopped having high school, or what?' he said. 'Those people let you play hooky?'

'Like you never kept me out of school?'

'I was a drunk,' Dad said. 'What's your excuse? You drinking?'

I said, 'This is my friend Todd. This is my dad.'

We stood there fucking dying. Then the lawyers came back in and we went back to sit at opposite ends. Todd and I were going to sneak out. Then, we looked and Dad was gone. We didn't have to sneak out after all.

I felt weird like I'd driven him away. I felt weird like I'd driven him *and my mom* away.

I hardly knew my mother cause she left us three or four times. My dad was always begging her, we kids were on his side. I remember one scene, she was standing at the door with all her luggage. Dad lay flat on his belly on the hallway carpet, mumbling, drunk, wet all over his face.

'I got an allergy to *your sickness*,' she said, 'I want as far as I can from this.' It had been going on for hours; it had been going on for hours every day then.

Me and my brothers were spying from the stairs, and at that point, Vinnie rebelled and chucked a fat *Child's Garden of Verses* at Mom. It cracked her good on the head, and we scrammed, laugh-screaming, like the ill-bred vandal crumb-snatchers we were,

to tell bedridden Dawn. (She had her chickenpox then.)

And I have just three pictures of my mother, all from one vacation. She has a cast on one leg, she's wearing a halter top and grinning like she's having this wonderful time. She looks exactly like me.

★

Bert Best broke my mother's skull with a hammer. He swore he didn't mean to break her skull. He meant to hit her with a hammer, not fatally. Then it was too late. He would do anything to take it back, he told his defence lawyer on the stand.

He seemed wan, dishonest, overwrought. It was tough to care what happened to him. Years later, when I got to know the ins and outs, I realised that Bert was wasted through that total trial on pills. That was why he looked wan, kept blowing his nose.

I was surprised he really had a Texan accent. I think once he killed my mother everything about him had changed for me. Then nothing really changed. He remained Texan. Likewise when he stated his profession, realtor, I was dis-believing. He had these appurtenances everyone has.

I don't know what I thought, but he was not a killer like the beasts they talk about, that need hanging. Bert just killed someone, Mom, in a fight. He had been drinking (taking pills although they got that declared inadmissible) and hit her with the wrong thing. Down she went. His life was over too.

They found him guilty cause he was. He got twenty years. And Todd and I walked out and when the wind hit our faces, we felt as if we'd been reprieved from serving twenty years. I said,

'I can't believe they buried that guy like that. It was an accident.'

'For real,' said Todd, nodding stupidly, not having heard. Then we walked down the road, in the ditch, a long way, not remembering to hitch-hike. And our silence was the same activity as tears. I couldn't cry.

The grass trembled and flattened itself in the wind. Bert was going to grow old in that cell. I didn't want anybody to suffer any more. I wouldn't step on ants all the way home, I couldn't stomach anything.

But that night in bed, when Todd tried to kiss me, I yelled,

'I got this *murder* on my mind, I'm fucking *sorry*,' and shoved him. I was out of bed and

suddenly raving how Bert should rot in prison. He should get butt-fucked there, never see the sun or the blue sky. Then I started on my mother. And my father should have been killed, too. I should have been. They ought to send exterminators to our house and clean us all out, we were a pestilence. And then I said *pestilence* over and over till I sweated.

Todd made that Swiss mocha coffee that's entirely sweetener. He said it was OK to feel that. It's natural to have those feelings. Sometimes you had feelings other people found hard to hear, because it would frighten them. Those people had to keep your whole pain in mind.

I got a weird headache in the spot my mother had been hit.

Todd tried to touch me and I hit him in the face. I hadn't meant to and was more scared than him. I said, 'I won't get over this, will I? I'm damaged goods.'

Then I swore, 'This will pass OK. It's like you said, I'm traumatised.'

Todd said, 'I got to be patient cause I'd do more damage to us,' and we shut up. Then it was as if we were small kids hiding from our parents fighting.

We looked up at the shelf at Todd's new pair of mounted antlers. He'd got them at a church sale for three bucks, we called them 'Ex-Bambi'. Now they seemed macabre and like my mother's antlers.

And Todd started saying what love meant to him, at fifteen.

He said that he was full of this pain, that was too heavy to bear. It was like a stone lion that he had to carry everywhere. Like those stone lions at the Harvard Library where we went that day we climbed John Harvard's statue.

And he *needed* someone to help him carry his lion. When he met me, I was strong and I seemed like I cared.

He broke off and started crying. I flinched but kept on looking at the antlers. I told myself that I would *love* to cry, if I could cry. I would give *anything* to cry.

Todd said, 'Jesus Christ, T.'

He never called me T again. That was our love nickname. I called him T too, but I had called him Todd for days.

I saw the stone lion in my mind. I felt its dead weight and its cold grain. I said bitterly,

'That's not a great proposition, I should carry your *pain*.'

He sobbed, 'I *meant*, I'm carrying yours. You *bitch*. I carried yours . . .'

Forty-Two

Todd lost his perfect grade-point average. I still played tennis but he stopped. I took it all the way, I got a tennis scholarship to Brown. Thanks to Todd's parents' tennis court. Thanks to my gear they bought. The coach who gave us lessons as a pair, till Todd wouldn't come to lessons any more and I just carried on as if.

Todd never went to college. Todd dropped out six months before the finals. He fucked off his GED.

Back then I made believe Todd gave up tennis cause I outclassed him. I was the star, and it demoralised him. In fact, Todd was always the better player. I don't know how conceit plays tricks like that. There was no question he was better. He was higher ranked.

And when he announced that he was dropping out – his grades were in the toilet, and he'd put on fifty pounds – in Todd's chubby phase of eating 'family' barrels of potato sticks and watching *M*A*S*H* reruns –

Janet quit her job at Raytheon to 'get Todd through'. Then they smoked dope together in the afternoons. I'd come home from school, the house reeked, they would be snacking. Janet fattened unbecomingly, like a short-haired dog.

The day I left for Brown, Craig came out on the lawn to stand with me and wait for my ride. Todd and Janet were still sleeping at noon. 'Well, I guess the kids will wake up in their own good time,' Craig said to me, with poison in his voice.

'Just say goodbye to them,' I said.

'Goodbye,' he said, perhaps misunderstanding. Then he leaned to me and kissed me on the lips

as my ride appeared and honked. So it was brief enough it could have meant nothing. I forgot it then and there. I didn't look back from the car.

Craig was at an academic conference in Montreal. It was on, like, 'Infidelity in Eighteenth-Century Discourse', some topic that would later seem heavy-handedly ironic. One night, very late, Janet called his hotel room and got his student, Pia. When Craig came to the phone, he just said, 'I'm so terribly sorry,' without preamble; Janet threw the phone against the wall so hard its guts came out, and it was saying 'Baby? Baby?' in an insect voice until she stamped it out.

Todd came stumbling down the stairs then, a marijuana zombie. He said, 'Mom? What?' and she fell in his arms sobbing.

He says he looked over her shoulder and just thought, '*It happened.*'

The hollowed-out Todd and Janet didn't leave the house for days. They watched Marx Brothers videos, smoked cartloads of dope, called for pizza. It was an idyll of its kind. They lay in wait for Craig who didn't come home from the airport, days after his flight, and when he did

Craig blustered at his wife and said he'd never leave his *family*. His *home*, and if she hadn't got *grossly overweight*. Some wives would thank their stars. He was shouty and defensive till he got his own wine habit. Then his sleeping pills. That turned the volume down and

it took all their might to swallow this new life.

I walked smack into this when I came back from freshman year. The high-achieving Amazon, you know. I put on ten pounds and hated them and their TV that never shut its fat mouth. When I bitched to Todd

he said, 'What do you want me to do about it?'

(For him to kill them and himself.) I said, 'Leave.'

And got him as a free gift a few years later when he took me at my word. It all turned out for, kind of for the best, for him. I guess.

The latest news of Craig and Janet, they became Republicans. They donate to Bush and have like haircuts for the blind. Another in a train of misfortunes! I thought painfully when I found out. Reverse karma, meaning life is unfair and plain fell
    like something tumbling like
    a Slinky in its perfect stair routine
    to hell.

Todd never mentioned the pain stone lion again, until I couldn't bring it up. Except I wanted to say, I would have carried it. That's all I was trying to do, that's all I wanted to do.

Forty-Three

On the way to Todd's show, I bought a big bunch of flowers idiotically as if Todd even liked flowers. My fever was like a companion as I walked, cause Lennie's is actually walking distance. There were kids playing football in turbans that I had to go around. Some places here, so near my house, I'd been already with Todd. A Turkish caff we'd had a fight in, about whether Kim Jong-Il was deluded or evil. I saw the homeless dude we gave our cigarettes to the day we tried to quit smoking. It made me feel like a shit; and like Mark had said before he left my office, slapping the orders down on the chair, 'Ciao,' snide like that's what bitches like me would say. I never say fucking 'ciao'.

The flowers began to cramp my hand. The fever was making my shoes feel heated. By the time I walked up to Lennie's, I was weaving. Then his stairs felt fucked. Like they were all different heights and

it was Lennie's same old scene with the unwashed, have-nots in their fluorescent tape. Nose rings, dirt, the lot who never take off their coats. They're like they're waiting for a bus. They were drinking wine from ribbed plastic cups. Then citizens in actual clothes were the buyers, the nouveau Dalston rich, and everybody tried to talk to them. They were things like barristers, slumming, and you felt they had personal problems to be there.

Todd spotted me and looked away. He was talking hard to Annette then, presenting his back, fluorescent tape too cause he cycles. He has an orange T for Todd on his coat that bugs me. It's supposed to be great *because* it's stupid, really this is just stupid twice. I started to think what I'd said wrong in our last conversation, but it was beyond that. I'd known coming here, I'd bought flowers idiotically.

I was at a loss what to do without Todd, and Peter Rabbit wasn't there. El thank God wasn't. I ended up putting the flowers on the mantelpiece. Then I alone looked at the art, feeling like the reject who ends up studying the spines of the host's books. They were charcoal drawings on canvas, using flattened Marlboro boxes instead of frames.

They were of a little girl and her lion. The girl was eight-ish, nude. The lion and the girl were pictured walking, the lion massively shadowing the child's introspective pose. They were drawn with a few lines and they were great. They were unbelievably pretty, absorbing, they made you feel a specific way no other thing in the world could make you feel. That's what I mean, I realised then, by Art.

The pictures were El's. They were identical to hers, I could tell. They were El's, signed TODD.

Three had sold. Lennie joined me to say.

'They're charming,' Lennie said. 'People like charming. Actually it's kind of shit.'

'They're great, though. Well, the drawings.'

'Todd's a nice guy,' Lennie said, and went off with Haiku or some Japanese girl, I didn't catch her real name. Then for a long eternal time I was staring at a drawing. Sin and Con had played keep-away with her stuffed lion till she burst into tears. Her stuffed lion Boo was something her mother, Rachelle's real mother before the foster-parents, had given her before she could remember, said Peter. She came home painted in blood. I shuddered, turned away

and went out back to Lennie's garden

which his ex-girlfriend had planted as a poison garden back in the day. It was tidy spurred beds like a medieval botanical drawing. Since, it had overgrown and gone to seed: I didn't know which plants were poisonous and which were weeds. There was a faint drizzle, like a rain too weakened by illness to robustly fall. I stood in the dark there rubbing my nose and feeling sorrowful.

Then Todd said from the darkness: 'Tanya?'

I spun to him, overwhelmed with feeling. I said, 'Todd? Yeah. I'm here. OK.'

He was at the bottom of the garden in his dumb coat, holding those flowers horizontally like someone who'd never held flowers. They sprang at both ends as he came. His face was guesswork in the dark. Still I smiled, I couldn't help liking seeing him.

I said, 'Hey.'

He said, 'I don't want these,' twitching the flowers.

I looked away at the fence, it was buckled, spaced like rotten teeth. And the poison smelled. You could smell it with the earth and traffic. 'Chuck them,' I said, and tried to laugh. 'I don't care about the flowers. Come on.'

'I wouldn't chuck them, really. It's only cause, El was talking?'

I got a burst of fever in my face. Then I was weak, I didn't know what to do. I said, 'What do you mean?'

'We did a lot of talking while you were away, that's all. You stayed away a long time.'

I cleared my throat and said, 'About – art?'

'No! No, she told me stuff you said about me. Pretty heavy stuff.' Todd ducked his head, looking at the bloom end of the flowers.

I said, 'That woman's so nuts you can *hear* the nuts rolling around in her head. I'm fucking serious.'

He met my eye. 'She said you said I peaked out at fourteen. And, you said I was too dumb for a best friend for you. Is that true?' He concentrated on my face as if it was a gun. He shimmered with the wet and grief.

I said, 'People say fucked-up things.'

'I'm going to move out.'

We had that moment of enormity. The garden seemed real like it was floodlit suddenly. I saw the long grass toss, rain flung off it in ghosts. There was scrap like rusted saws and bike wheels; a sink reclined, queen of the miscellanea, white as white skin. And it smelled like poison, like the poison you would put out for rats.

'No,' I said. 'Shit. Your feelings are hurt, and you?'

'No, even before, when you deserted me this whole month. It's like, you've got this life and if I don't fit in.'

'It wasn't a month.'

'Don't tell me! Tanya!'

Then he just unloaded, pacing in the poison grass which seemed to rock in dumb sympathy with his unravelling voice. It was a 'worm turns' script. I always treated him like some joke. I needed him to fail. I was so fucking pissed he wasn't failing now that it was obvious. That wasn't a friend.

My throat clenched, inclining to sob. My eyes were dry, it was a desolate span. Todd said the way I treated him, he lost all self-esteem. He was like Down's syndrome, how he felt, like a hopeless case. And he said, when I was listening again:

'What kills me is that now I did something, you act like, oh, cool, I'll buy flowers. Let's forget the past ten years. When all along. You could have just accepted I was . . . an artist. But it had to be, no, I was a fuck-up. I was sponging off you.'

'You *were* sponging off me,' I couldn't help saying.

'Here we go!'

'I didn't mind! It was cool! I hardly minded. I minded when I had money troubles of my own.'

'But then you smothered me. That was the deal, all along.' He said, painfully, 'And now it's too late. I'm *thirty-one.*'

'*I'm* thirty-one.'

'But you have a business. You have . . . Can't *I* want a house?'

'Of course you can! Who said you couldn't? But I never thought you *did* want a house!'

'Well, that shows what you know about me!'

His eyes flared open, galled. Then he took a deep breath and threw out:

'My art sucks!'

His face stopped; with a veiled, wary suspense, he watched me. Then his eyes went lost. Once it was over, I realised it was hope.

I said, way too late, 'It doesn't *suck.*'

He said, in a bogged-down voice: 'I know it sucks. I get it.'

And he said, 'I chickened out on this show, I kept looking at El's stuff on the walls.' And he wheezed in and out, and said,

'I get it.'

The poison stank in the dark. Now it would always be dark, and the world was poisoned. The stars were grains of poison above. I thought, this is what it's like to be psychotic.

Todd put one hand on his throat, as he had never done before in my presence. So he didn't look like Todd, saying, 'Yeah, you know El helped me out with those pictures.'

'I'm glad you sold some, yeah. They were saying, it's cool about that.'

'I know I did the wrong thing, don't talk *down* to me.'

Then his hand loosened on his neck and he swallowed. 'I totally tried to call you. It's been weird in the house.'

We looked at each other with our years between us, the history that might end. It stopped raining right then. So we found out how wet we were going to be, and shivered.

And when we had the fight about Kim Jong-Il, I was saying the guy was evil. I said, some people were evil, I was thinking of Vinnie's joint friends, one guy had tortured people who owed him money, burned out their eyes. I had got the bit between my teeth with memory. Todd had got the bit between his teeth; he was saying about Kim Jong-Il's operas and the mass card flipping where the cards made Kim Jong-Il's face, if anything deserved to be called insane. It was a narcissistic personality disorder. Then I said that Todd calling anyone a narcissist, anyway, was, pot kettle. 'What?' Todd said, scowling. 'What's that supposed to mean?'

'Pot calling the kettle black?'

'You're evil, then!' Todd said, and stormed out. I was stuck sitting there with both plates; I had to pay for the meal. Afterwards it was hilarious, until now.

Todd shrugged again and stretched his arms for an excuse to shut his eyes, the flowers flopping at one end. For a second he wasn't going to leave my house, it was stupid. It was bullshit you say in a fight. Then Todd said, not looking at me, 'Well, cool. I better get back.'

He turned without looking. Rain had beaded along his fluorescent tape, in a T. He walked self-consciously normally. I came dragging behind and

Peter Rabbit was right there, standing there in the hall, peeling bits off a big collage. He looked up

Forty-Five

When I got home it was 1 a.m. I stood in the street out front, hugging my carton of Tesco Economy orange juice Peter'd nicked from Lennie's fridge for me. A light was on in Eleanor's window. I stood there not feeling tired, feeling like I had been travelling here for two weeks to face El.

When I opened the door, there she was, coming down the stairs. She was wearing a white silk dress, so thin her nipples showed through as a colour. You could see the outline of her thighs. Her breasts would be soft like mine were, I couldn't remember before the plastic surgery. Not like fat. She stopped where the ceiling rose had been. I was aware of her clean bare feet in its plaster dust.

I said, 'How did you know I was coming?'

She said, 'God. I thought you'd never talk to me again.'

I held the orange juice against my belly. The cool of it now was sexual, it drew a cold line from my cunt to my mouth.

She said, 'Are you coming up?'

I caught my breath and looked back at the open door. Clumsy with the orange juice carton, I closed it, making the hall an intimate space, with the fraught air of under the covers. I turned the mortise lock, and said 'OK,' with my back to her.

The walk upstairs was one suspended, brightly lit, long breath, things get this way too late at night. Her calves worked up the stairs forever, with a kneading motion, they were El's one bad feature, thick, with red wrinkled dinosaur ankles. One wall was blacking up with dime-sized pictures of turtles, she'd been busy drawing while I was at work. I trailed my hand there, imagining being calm. And heard the shipping news from Todd's room, that chill voice eyedroppering its code words into silence that seemed broadcast from a ship doomed never to come to shore, which didn't mean Todd was home. He left the radio on a lot. I got to her bright-lit room (*And driving back in Peter's car, I had been feeling the orange juice nested cold between my thighs, and I was studying Peter's white eyes, white-blue eyes, kind of gingerly. The city was dusty and darkened round Hackney, like somebody's basement. Only car tail lights and kebab shops were a colour. And Peter told me Eleanor was sexually abused as a child.*

It wasn't the foster parents, but a friend of the family, Benjamin Cox. But the parents knew, though. And Peter talked non-stop, jittery, loud, about the paedophile, using his full name; the tolling name made it like a litany. Benjamin Cox had been a real good-looking dude, you would never know. Peter had never met Benjamin Cox, the Hortons stopped being friends with Benjamin Cox by then. But he'd seen Benjamin Cox; think Joaquin Phoenix looks, it was creepy.

At last I said, 'That's why you ran away.' I licked my lips, I was sick. I didn't want to know things.

'Sure. That's why we ran away.'

I said, 'That's why you ran away,' and laughed.

'That's why everything.' And Peter said, he was pulling up by my house, and he said, in a hoarse sweet hopeful voice, 'Don't tell Elly I told you, cool?'

I said, 'Hey, you're my only friend I got left, recently.' And, 'Thanks for the ride,' and I got

out of Peter Rabbit's car
got out into the night.)

out of breath. She hadn't cleaned and there was still broken glass among the heaped clothes.

I said, weak, 'Hey, I just saw Peter. Peter Rabbit? We were talking about you.'

She started chanting, 'No, no, no, no, no,' in a baby voice.

She chanted while she crawled into bed. Then she said, 'I never talk about Peter. But I will sometime, if you need to know. Not now.' She had one hand twisted round in her emerald necklace, like to tear it off. The other hand up in her hair. Her ruby earrings clashed with the emeralds, a thing you don't normally see. I said,

'Peter was funny, he was saying you all took stupid names in LA, cause it was punk days, and I asked him if he had one. And he goes, *for a smart girl, you sure can be dumb.* But he wouldn't tell me what his original name was.'

'*Roosevelt*,' Eleanor said in a strained and furious voice. 'Don't *talk* about it.' Then she let her necklace go, and hoisted her whole dress off. It went into the painting of her as Faith by *Roosevelt Horton*, I guessed. *RH.* She was naked. Her sleek, banana-type breasts, soft focus from trembling, were like somebody shouting in your face. It made my whole skin on my face tight, hot, I couldn't think. Her shaved cunt blazed with pink. And I don't know how anyone is cool about nudity. My stomach was knots. I was caught,

at the door, fuck, longing for Hutch or something safe. At last she pulled the sheet to her armpits, shivering. She said, tame, feeble, as if she too had been through that experience, 'Yeah, I wanted you to sleep in my bed tonight? But I was so scared to ask.'

I crossed my arms tight. My stomach was in me like a dagger. I said, 'I don't know if I can sleep in someone else's bed.'

'Yeah, really. I was frightened to ask.' She looked down at her lap, unhappy, trying to get a grip on one of her long hairs that had fallen there. Her neatly delineated freckles like drops of brown ink; in that light she was the beauty of the paintings, tense romantically. She started to talk in a bird-like, breathy clip about Schizo Mal, since staying with him she felt cold when she slept alone, without pills it was honestly murder. She realised she did sleep alone. That was actually pills.

I blurted, 'I sleep in my clothes, is that cool?' interrupting her, suddenly.

Her serious eyes changed. She drew a sharp deep scared thrilled breath. I felt hard in my throat.

'That's good because you won't catch cold,' she said. She tittered and said, 'That's a daft thing to say. You won't catch cold.'

I said, 'That's what my friend Hutch says. He's always giving me scarves. He puts these scarves on me whenever I leave his house, I've got a whole suitcase of them now,' as super-awkwardly I sat on the bed and took my shoes off. I slipped under the covers talking helplessly

about old Hutch's amours, unaware what I was saying, I was thinking about child sex abuse. If she talked to me about it, cleared the air about one thing, I had a slim chance I could sleep. She never would. I said that Hutch had women and he fell in love, short-lived. He'd fallen out of love for every reason, cause

one girl compared him to her father

one listened to opera with a faraway expression and made a fuss about his understanding the Italian

one sent a fax from his machine and wouldn't trust him that it sent, she kept expecting there to be 'more evidence'

one turned out to be Magnus Magnusson's ex

one was too Dutch.

'Oh, shit. Love is blind,' El said, and laughed, shrill. In her baby voice, she said, 'OK, let's sleep, OK? Hold me hold me?'

I lay down flat, blinking, and said, 'Oh, the light,' and turned off the light.

Then I was lying in her arms the way I lie in Hutch's arms. My heart leapt like a fish on deck. We didn't press together but. The bed was hot instantly.

I said, hoarse, 'Hey, why won't you talk about Peter? Peter Rabbit.'

'I'm sleepy now,' she said. She added, petulant and indistinct,

'I could talk about him, though. I said.'

'He told me how you grew up with those foster-parents. He was telling me. About the born-again Christians?'

'Yes,' she said. 'Really, the Hortons. I know.'

'Right, the Hortons.'

After a breath, she said, tentative, 'You were on a date with Peter?'

'No. We fucked, though. A while ago. That's . . . the kind of thing.'

'But,' she said, then paused, it was like she was turning something in her hands. At last she said, 'You had time to discuss the Hortons, though? That's nice,' and she added brightly, conversationally: 'Did he tell you that he murdered them?'

I had let go of her. The dark seethed the way it does before your eyes adjust. Like darkness made of flies, and it was four in the morning, to be dealing with this. *This lunacy*, I thought and said, 'You're kidding. I can't tell if you're kidding.'

'No. I'm going to sleep. Don't talk.'

'You can't *go to sleep.*'

'Please don't be mad at me. I *have to sleep.*'

'I'm not *mad*, but what does that mean? He murdered your foster-parents? When?'

'He didn't practically. But that's too much,' she said, with teen disdain, wrinkling her nose. 'I'm sorry I brought it up.'

'Practically? What does that mean?'

'*Don't push me.*'

'Just, did he murder someone, OK?'

'I can't do this right now, with this week and on no sleep. Now I'm sorry I even said anything now. It's a lie, OK? Let's leave it at that. I lie because I'm insecure, it's an actual Achilles heel for me, I know that. God, I should have killed myself, then, in the Hilton. That was Plan B, if you hadn't taken me, I'd bought the Nembutal. I've still got it.'

I said, through my tight throat, 'Fuck you, I thought we were friends. Don't give me any fucking suicidal threats. That's my pet hate.'

'Then let me sleep then and I won't.' She turned away. The sheets went with her with a feeling like a rug pulled out from under me. I lay in my exposed clothes.

Peter didn't mean enough to me to be a killer. I said, 'Why did he kill them?' too soft and not expecting her to answer. She didn't. Time was passing and I had to make her talk to me. Otherwise I should go straight to work, now, otherwise I would be up, lying here beside El all night, dying wondering.

Forty-Six

(And in LA, when I was living with Vinnie, Vinnie came home freaked once, to me where I was watching *Sixty Minutes* without watching it, and asked, did his eyes look white? I didn't know what he meant, I was disgusted. He said, are they kind of white? Some way?

They *were*.

'Fuck it, I don't know,' I lied. 'They're blue like they always were.' And Vinnie said

Paco, who had done time outside of Houston, that was one gnarly prison system there, told him murderers have white eyes, they get a white sort of sheen in their eyes. I said, 'Are you a murderer?'

Vinnie giggled, then we didn't talk about it for a week. He'd killed a dealer he owed ten thousand dollars to. They were in a vacant lot. The dude had a fix and went over hard, then Vinnie got the smart idea. He pinched the dude's nose shut first, and when he didn't wake, Vinnie found a plastic shopping bag and plastered it against his face. He waited ten minutes. Then he'd made ten thousand bucks. The day he told me, Vinnie was high and snickered through the story looking terrified. He said, 'I got way fucked up, when Paco told me the white eyes thing. I thought everybody could tell, cops, everybody. I was *frightened like a little girl*.'

I said, 'Yeah, damn,' and we were frightened like little girls without our parents. We stared at the window like shit might come through it after us. Vinnie said,

'Yeah, it's more Catholic bullshit spics think.')

Peter didn't mean enough to me to be a killer. It explained the white eyes, but that was all Vinnie's ignorant joint crap. I didn't want anybody being a killer tonight, it was too much in one night. Like the last, all-wrong pill you stupidly take.

Then Eleanor moved in the dark. She turned, her face appeared; I took a deep breath to say something, to say the wrong thing.

Her lips met mine. She kissed me deeply, insistently, like a man.

Forty-Seven

I never kissed a girl. It took a moment to remember that.

By then I was kissing El back.

Our breasts squoze together, pillowy. Her tongue flashed into my mouth. I was smelling her breath, whiskey breath like anyone's. My fingers were in her thick hair, cool hair, kind of without meaning it.

It was smaller. It was Eleanor. It was the wrong kind. Her hands traced my sides, tentative, impassioned. That kiss was something El knew how to do, like her drawing; arrogant, perfect, cavalier. The wolf just eats you, from too much strength, I was thinking and kissing her desperately. I was thinking hard ('Girls experiment, it's easier for girls,' Todd used to say, and Lennie used to say, most everybody said. I slept with hairy-assed greasy men you wouldn't shake their hand. I sucked their dicks and I swallowed. I got lice.

I couldn't. If Alan knew. My father, though my father was dead. Uncle Dominic, whose favourite word was 'flat-chested'. My Bengali dentist. But that didn't bother me when I gave my cousin Tony, who was fifteen, head. I mean, it bothered me if people knew. It didn't stop me.

I couldn't. Todd might come home. Cause of what had gone before, no way. It was homophobia cause I'm from Mass and working class. But I couldn't stop.) and then I wasn't thinking I was

kissing El hard with both hands on her face. I had loved her a long time, bad. I let my hand jump to her bare sweet foolishly sweet breast, a dizzying thing. God Jesus, I loved her to pain, to dying outright, fainting. I wanted to destroy her and die.

She felt my tough thick breast and winced. I almost

laughed. I almost said, explained, but then she slid her fingers into my cunt.

Her hand there, slick and gentle. I think I went as stiff as glass, as see-through. El said, 'Jesus.' I had my face pressed into her hair into the pillow, smelling old spilled booze, perfumes, and trying to breathe.

I came to the roots of my hair. I never came like that. I came so fast.

Then we were holding each other, like painted together with sweat. It's not like fucking a man. I don't know why that surprised me.

And Eleanor said, 'I'm in love with you, Tanya.' Evenly, like a precocious child reading aloud. I opened my eyes and saw blurred white, the moonlight seeming to hover above the white sheet.

I cleared my throat but said nothing. I tried to reach between her thighs, not meaning it, half assed. She trembled, pulling away. She said, 'No – not now. Sleep? Do you want to go to sleep?'

I said, 'I know. I have to sleep. I have to work tomorrow. Yeah, I guess we better.'

She said, 'I'm going to turn over now. I'm sorry you don't love me.' She turned her back, curling up. Then she was breathing too fast.

My eyes had adjusted and I could see Eleanor's hair, star-coloured and mussed. Her luminous shoulder pulsed with breath. Her drawings drooped and looked like a net in my peripheral vision. I put my index fingertip to the small of her back and said, 'I do love you. Don't be stupid.'

Her back tensed and released. After some small time, she said, 'Thank you.'

★

I thought for a long time, staring at the window which had paled already from dawn. Headlights swung over the ceiling and slipped down the wall. El had burrowed her face against the pillow, sleeping I guess. I couldn't think about what I had done;

    and shut my eyes to let her body fall into me. I was pressing to her like, way back when, in the Hilton, I had wanted to get in bed and hold her and forget. It was warm like melting sugar. And joy stole into me. Sleep was stealing into me where her long hair lay under my cheek. Its blonde came to my mind like a drink. I might have semi been dreaming

    as the first bird shut its eyes and sang and
    it was potently morning
    lit in corners, like a new house.

A couple hours later we woke. I didn't ever go to work, we went to Peter's

Forty-Eight

Rachelle Freespirit Lynch first had sex with Benjamin Cox when she was four.

It wasn't *sex*, *per se*. It wasn't penetration. He held her in his naked lap until he ejaculated, groaning and shushing her panicked cries.

Doug and Ruth Horton watched from the love seat, tense and motionless. They breathed shallowly, through their mouths. That is the simple movie of her bad dreams.

At some point, she was coached in how to stroke his erect penis. To mouth it, being careful with her teeth. At last the videos appeared, in which she saw the more violent acts, the *penetrations* she was spared.

While it was going on, they spoke to her only to coax or threaten. They talked as if she couldn't hear, they talked their macabre *shop*. She was alone as people seldom are, invisible enough to inadvertently be crushed.

On the drive to Benjamin's house, it might still be all right. She would ask and ask until they lied. Sometimes they only stopped in for a bite, they all went out to a picture. Sometimes, as the door closed, the fabric of the world would split, exposing the reality behind; adults turned to naked cannibals studded with gross eyes.

Then it was over and the crack in the world healed. A trip to the bathroom and everything popped back into shape. Ma combed her little girl's hair.

Rachelle began to wet her pants again, to wet the bed. In kindergarten, she punched and bit not only other kids, but teachers. She developed a nervous snort she made with every breath. For her behaviour, and because she had lost the ability to recognise letters, in second grade the school transferred her to special ed. She got eczema on her head, then, lost a patch of hair and looked the part.

No one wants to be the monster. Jesus Christ saved Doug and Ruth Horton, they were washed clean in the blood of the lamb. Jesus shouldered their crimes and bled them out again on a cross in a Baptist church off the interstate. Jesus loved Doug and Ruth. They thanked Him with all their might, their money and their fear of the light, their deep thirst for oblivion.

There were no more trips to Benjamin Cox.

Forty-Nine

Cox had been Doug Horton's old best buddy at Penn. They met at Orientation and that was it. They spent all their free time together. They hit the library together to study. Doug was a business major, Ben was pre-med, but any class they could, they took together.

They drove to Mardi Gras and spent the night in a Louisiana drunk tank together. They took up smoking together, and tried to kick it the New Year's Eve they crashed Ben's Cadillac. Police came out and made them walk straight lines. That was a hell of a tale, you had to see Ben ape the arresting officer, doing his Penn accent to a positive T, and the fellow had no idea. Doug had some time not to laugh.

Ben gave Doug that Cadillac, with the dents he called 'souvenirs', when he got the new Mustang. He was the rich kid of the two; he gave Doug his old shoes and ties; he would have given Doug suits if they'd have fit. The drinks were all on Ben, the tickets were on his credit card.

Ben was the looker as well, girls ate Ben up. Other men never took to him, outside of Doug, but the girls fell left and right. Ben had it all; talked circles around you, dressed like a page from a magazine, plus his cars were the tip of the iceberg of his money. Ben could fly a plane. Ben sailed competitively and spoke real French. He had fast girls he screwed, nice girls who baked him cookies. One lady professor gave him money the times he quarrelled with his folks. He never went steady: there were, as a rule, three women at his restaurant table. For whom he'd pick up all the tab; people at Penn called Ben 'Deep Pockets'.

Doug's nickname was 'Horton the Elephant'. Pudgy already at twenty-one, he never got the girl, he was the nice guy who finished last, everyone's sidekick. His people were

Baptist, and Doug was brought up worshipping Christ on his knees. It took two years of college to cure his belief in a God with a white beard sitting on a throne, for Doug to say, sure, that was hogwash. He didn't buy the Communist hogwash either, though, or any philosophic hogwash. As for Ben's French Sartre stuff, wow, he couldn't make head or tail. And you'd never confuse Penn State with Harvard, but it was queer to be there, still, and be from just plain-spoken working stock, from the sticks.

When his mother came to visit, Doug was silent and looked ill in her company. She was a lumbering woman in a thin print dress, with rumpled fat magenta arms, her grey hair thick with spray and bobby pins, who peppered her talk about coupons with the mention of Jesus – at Penn State, Doug's mom drew stares. Slick Ben became her darling. He squired her through the campus, remarking (after hours, to his girl claque at Ollie's) it was like absurdist drama.

Doug tried to shush his mom, but nothing doing. 'I'm having the time of my life,' she said. She said it was a balm to see he had such nice respectful friends. She'd take that comfort. Well, a fellow didn't back-talk parents in the flock of Karten Baptist Church, where Doug's godfather, Douglas Pill, was pastor. Doug just had to bite his tongue, and there were tears in his eyes at one point, of despair.

When Doug and Ben were driving back from dropping her off at the Greyhound bus, Doug turned on Ben. He didn't know why Ben wasted his time with some fat fool, some nobody, who didn't read any birdist drama and would never dream of reading it. He could take his lousy car. His charity car. As soon as Doug got home, he was clearing his closet of all Ben's stuff, it stank. Just cause people didn't have any money, or Ben's big hotshot brains, didn't mean they'd be laughed at – Doug unloaded his heart.

Ben turned white, his jaw set. He was watching the road to drive. The car lit and went dark as they took curves, trees ran their shadows over them. Finally Ben said, low, 'Well, you know me so well. You think you know me so well.'

Fifty

At twenty-one, Ben and Doug met Ruth, Doug's wife-to-be, together.

She was walking on the beaten-down grass beside a two-lane highway, coming from school. A cute thing, Ruth was dawdling to coax a stray dog who jogged after her, but backed off, if ever she stopped, his ruffed neck stretched to sniff. The two boys stopped the car. Because she wouldn't get in, they left it parked there on the shoulder, and walked her to Marguerite's, the ice-cream parlour, where she had two pistachio cones in a row. They played gin rummy until the sun went down. The dog sat at their feet at last; Ben had that skittish mongrel, called Joe College, for years. Then they drove Ruth home and Ruth's mother ran down the driveway barefoot, weeping, and dragged Ruth out of the car, saying 'Baby, you're all right! Baby, are you all right?' cause it was eight at night and Ruth was ten years old.

She made Ruth cry. She repeated, sobbing, that she'd memorised their licence plate number until Ben quit protesting, he lit a cigarette and looked off at the woods. Doug was raving about Annie-Beth, his little sister who was Ruth's same age, and the spitting image. It took five minutes for Ruth's mom, Gladys, to understand nothing was wrong. Then she went dumb and stiff, like she might faint. Turned and went to the house again, staggering, dragging bawling Ruth.

Ben got white chocolates delivered to Gladys the next day. The delivery man had a uniform; that impressed Gladys most of all, and she was shame-faced, giggly, when Ben came by. She made him admit that it looked fishy, they should have known better, that a silly mother wasn't to know. Ben countered that anyone would think it was a miracle people liked her kid. Then she offered she would bake them her blue-ribbon lasagna, as an olive branch.

Gladys became fast friends with Ben and Doug, soon enough. Her husband was in the Navy, half the time at sea, or more than half, cripes knew she wasn't any priority. She liked to have a man around, even 'man-cubs' like she called Ben and Doug. Doug and she both liked to shoot at bottles; he'd bring his rifle along cause Gladys had a whole state park out her back door. Ben brought her flowers, a knick-knack, some apt tribute whenever he came. He called her 'Beauty', and 'Heartbreaker', till Gladys said, *if she didn't know any better*, and *if she wasn't a married woman*, testing the waters.

Ruth was small for her age, a serene imp with a narrow rosy face who always looked like she was sucking on something, like she had a secret she was sucking on while she listened and ducked her head. Ruth hardly spoke; she would clown with you, though. She'd tie your shoes together, stick her hand in your pockets to steal, saying only 'No fair', 'Dummy', 'OK', kind of monosyllables, in a dim and inward voice, like she was talking to herself. An oddball with that foxy beauty particular to children, that is not a first stage of adult good looks, she charmed especially Ben; Ben was crazy for little kids.

Fifty-One

That started from Ben's strife with his family. He was always at war with his family, therefore with his wealth. At Penn, came times, Doug even supported him. Ben had an erratic and histrionic mother who drank, who had been Miss Florida before she married. She held the purse strings cause Ben's father was eighty and not a father. Well, the old man had seven sons from previous marriages, two among them Bens – his favourite name. Sharp as a razor when it came to the equity market but he didn't recognise Ben once when Ben grew a beard. So it was, keep Miss Florida sweet (Ben always called his mom Miss Florida, making Doug start, making Doug purse his lips) and Ben wouldn't bow before Miss Florida, the tramp, she could burn in hell.

When he was eighteen, Ben fled to the south of France, where he lived by the shore, making a bed of papers and old bean sacks in a cave he called the Grotto. There were assorted homeless people around: an Austrian lady with long grey braids who hiked to town to dance at street cafés for change; a gaunt man with no tongue. An alcoholic couple who had eight dogs had been living there since the war, and were rumoured to be secretly rich. In the daytime, sometimes, too, kids came from the village.

There was a gypsy brother and sister who came out crabbing, who became Ben's friends. The trio spent a whimsical, insular autumn on the beach together. Brother and sister could both build expert fires, and fish, and cook the fresh fish in the fire. The boy once brought his fiddle; they traded French, American, German songs, the Austrian woman dancing, singing in a dark, destroyed alto that grew and dwindled in the sea wind. All day in the water, where the girl, Thalie, swam seriously, in lines, her bay arms sure as a strong pulse; Hervé only dived. Seen from the waves, the land seemed to unwind, to sprinkle with silver light and grass. Far away were dogs barking, and at night the lights of boats.

Ben taught the kids to play poker. By the time the winter came, they both spoke English with his Midwestern accent. He promised to take them up in a plane some day, 'to complain to the angels'. Then one day, they didn't come back, and they never came back. Ben waited two weeks, then walked into town to make his phone call home. Next day he was on a jet to New York.

'I'd like to take ten kids, five kids, and teach them half those gypsy brats could do,' Ben lectured Doug and Gladys, pacing her crabgrass lawn. 'You could dump Thalie in the Gobi Desert and she'd have a hut built and a square meal on the fire inside an hour. They were smarter than any adults, they were smarter than Einstein. *Kids* are. We lock them in schools, it's sensory deprivation, it's a slow lobotomy. You, me, we're all retarded from it, brain damaged.' Ben worked himself into a lather, gesturing with fists. Meantime, Ruth rode his shoulders, pretending to pick nits from his hair.

Gladys called from the sidelines, 'She doesn't look smarter than Einstein from where I sit,' so Doug could belly-laugh with relief. Ben then swept Ruth off, making her cartwheel and come down, so often he did this that she landed pat like a gymnast and walked off unmoved. And Ben said quietly, '*Damn* you.'

For four years, Ben and Doug spent every weekend they could with Ruth and Gladys. It got harder. Doug started his first store, a gift store that folded in six months. His second enterprise was a Christian-interest store, seeded with his uncle Naldo's money. He was bound and determined not to fail, this time, he went to a different church each Sunday, glad-handing, drumming up business. Ben was working as a resident, crazy hours. The boys saw less of each other, and Ruth complained that when they came, they weren't as 'interesting' – meaning, they weren't interested in her. In the tearful postscript to a screaming match with Ben, Gladys said, 'It's that, the bloom is off the rose. Don't lie to me otherwise: the bloom is off the rose.' At last Ben got his research job at Duke, and left town, on a sour note.

Ben closed the book. On Doug too: there was no word from Ben for twelve years.

Fifty-Two

And four years after Ben's departure, Ruth becomes Ruth Horton, at a heartfelt ceremony at the Karten Baptist Church, in pretty nowheresville. The church, the parking lot, the town are packed with all Doug's family. They're so God-fearing, Ruth and Doug have to sneak their celebration champagne in their bridal suite, and use mouthwash. At the reception, it's nothing but wineless punch. Ruth wants to laugh her head off. When she has Gladys alone, they two will laugh their heads off. Doug was the one who taught Ruth to believe in a life force, a spirit that moves, like mathematics in business. But these people are all, Jesus Jesus Jesus. Doug warned Ruth but she could never imagine.

She comes up to him when he's standing alone, daydreaming by the punch bowl with the ladle poised in his hand. She's feeling beautiful, wild, like a movie star with bold manners. She says in his ear, 'Bet you can't say "Christ child" five times fast.' He jerks and the ladle clatters into the punch bowl; people look. He says, with a tightened expression,

'That's something Ben Cox would have said.'

She stands breathing hard. Her eyes fill with tears and they don't mention Ben again for two years.

She's twenty-one years old, a bottle redhead three months pregnant, fidgety under her first fat that feels like layers of dirt. She will keep plucking at her tightening clothes. The sun is going down and she's trying out one of the new lawn-chairs while Doug tries to fix his fishing pole. It's probably the line somewhere, so he's reeling it out. Out of nowhere, as she's under the spell of the failing sun, her senses following it along the round of earth to what you can't see, Doug says in his hapless boom, like the voice of a cartoon steer,

'You figure old Ben Cox has gotten married?'

She snaps, 'Ben will *never* get married,' instantly. She's sitting forward then, like crouched on her pregnancy, with the bitter scowl of the harpy she will never become. They meet each other's eyes, uncertain, hot. Then Doug throws down the pole and walks off, setting his bare feet gingerly in the pebbly grass.

Isaiah is three when Ben's first book comes out. Doug sees it in the paper, where they did a 'Penn Alum Hits Big' type interview. It doesn't sound like Ben, but Doug figures that's the editor. He's going to tell Ruth, he'll explain how the editors change what you say to suit their usual style. He comes in through the screen door, hearing its springs, is aware of the sounds and the look of his home now, through Ben's eyes. Doug always liked that Sears furniture. The rust shag carpet, the panelling, it was all good value, smart buys. Doug likes things average, and he was getting used to seeing that as a nice thing, people feel at home with him, the secret ingredient to business success.

Isaiah comes running up; Doug clouts him on the head lightly with the rolled-up paper. Ruth looks up and Doug can't say a word. He was nuts, thinking she would be excited. He was out of his mind. He says, 'Traffic out there!' and she smiles her inward, doubting smile, Ruth sucking on something private. A candy so sour, bitter maybe, she can't talk about liking it. He comes up, longing to hold her for the first time in, how long. There's a fine cruel keening in his heart, as if he'd sold his one love, sold his birthright for a mess of pottage. He wants her to be that one love, for one minute. But Ruth is restive in his arms, not understanding, almost panicked.

★

The week they get Rachelle, Ben Cox is in town. They stay home with the baby. Never crosses their minds to try to see Ben. But they stay up all one night and fight. They fight for the first time about Doug's impotence, why they couldn't have a second child of their own. Ruth says the trite, poisonous things, Doug isn't a man, he must have another woman – things incongruous from her mouth. They drink, and both shed tears, they do the things married couples are supposed to do. They seem to be fighting a third party, arguing against some thing or some event; which is *going to defeat them*. They fight to make a point, how helpless they are, and it is going to defeat them.

Ruth says, 'Well, we really both married Ben, I don't know what we expected,' as if that's what they have always agreed.

The next day is Sunday. For the first time in months, they dress up and go to church. Usually getting up on Sunday makes Ruth feel clean, venturesome like a child on an outing. This time they're both exhausted and full of the badness of not sleeping.

At the church, they can't talk to anyone. They sneak out one minute after the service, not caring who feels snubbed. They're like two people who have gone to church in desperation, the night before committing a murder, and can find no reason there, no respite.

Rachelle is a difficult child. She's a charming child, a beautiful child that strangers dote on: you try walking in Center City with her; the ladies stop you every block. But she won't eat, she fights and kicks when you dress her. Every itty-bitty little thing is a tantrum. Mild Ruth never complains, no weeping fits, not like some wives. But she gains so much weight she has to buy all new clothes twice, in a year.

Isaiah puts on weight too. His grades suffer; he was always a loner, but not like now, not so you'd say he had no friends. Everything has changed, the day Rachelle came, or else it happened over time. You can't tell when it happened.

Rachelle screams, breaks things, requires care twenty-four hours no one can give. They lock her in her room. At first it's punishment. Then, it may have happened overnight, she's not allowed downstairs except for meals.

Ruth has become a dishevelled and fat wife, beating a path from the kitchen to the television set, she has her shows and nibbles. Her face is blank. It's as if all the features were erased although they're physically there. Isaiah sleeps both day and night like no little boy you ever saw. When he's awake, he eats. No one hardly speaks.

There's bound to be tough times, raising a family. Doug spends more time at home, he calls it rallying the troops although he ends up, sleepy like them, camped in front of the TV. He can't tell anyone, even his folks, he wouldn't know how to start. He thinks, from nowhere, 'Ruth is my *wife*' or 'Zay's my *son*,' defensively, as if some viper was pressuring him to abandon them.

They go to see Cox. They get a sitter one night Ben's giving a talk to promote a new book. He's been back in Philly a year, but they haven't seen hide nor hair. Although neither one mentions Ben's return, it's as if they had. It's like they talked about it every night, while they were watching TV, all night. It's like they wore out their voices.

When Doug suggests they go, Ruth says, 'Oh, sure! We'd better,' and titters.

They get dressed up. Ruth changes her clothes ten times before they can leave. There's no hiding they're fat. Doug thinks the whole drive there about a snot-nose nephew who called him, Ruth and Isaiah 'Tweedledum and Tweedledee and Tweedlethree'. You have to laugh at yourself, he mainly thinks. Now it weighs on his mind, he doesn't know how it feels, it feels so bad.

They get there late, they have to sit in the back. Ben is stunning at the microphone, even when he steps out of the spotlight, he walks in a spotlight. He's more than they remembered. When he speaks, they hardly hear a word. It's stuff like Dr Spock you wouldn't listen to anyway.

At the end, they almost leave without going up. Ben came with people, they hadn't figured on that. Ben's group are several women and a man, dressed Manhattan-style, what you might call socialites. Even their laughter sounds classy. Doug has been a businessman, a millionaire, even a council-man, for years without becoming close to that. Ben is rich in his flesh. Ben is rich buck naked if you took all his money.

They're going to leave, but they don't. They're still there, staring and needing to be recognised. At last Doug's afraid what it will be like in the car with her if he doesn't, and he strides up. When Ben knows who it is, he stills. He's unwilling, shaken. Doug feels like walking bad news.

'Well, well, well!' says Doug. 'You're doing a great job, a great job.'

Then Ruth flanks him, grinning, and begins to talk as Doug has not heard her ever, maybe at their wedding. Ruth is bold like a woman speaking on behalf of the puckish, pretty child she once was.

'Oh, wow, seeing you again, I don't know what to say. You can't be a stranger any more, you think we don't read the newspaper? Try and get away from me! You'll find out you can't! You didn't even know we got a little girl. We've had two, but I know you. Don't tell me you've changed, I

won't believe it. And Rachelle – Dougy, wouldn't he?
Wouldn't Ben love Rachelle? Well, she's just like you. You
have to come out and meet her. I won't take no for an answer.
Will I? Dougy, tell him, I won't take no for an answer. I won't
take no for an answer.'

Fifty-Three

'Yeah, they were gross people, for real,' Peter said. 'The Porky Hortons! Yikes. It's good I didn't kill them, though, I'd feel bad. I would have killed Cox, *no problem*. I've seen too much on the streets, dudes like that prey on runaways. I was stoked to do it, I was raring to go. But, no no.' He grimaced. 'Do you hate me now?'

'No,' I said, and let my eyes unfocus on my drink. 'Hate isn't the word.'

We'd got to Peter's at around nine, and he was up, he was at the door with a paperback *Goldfinger* open in his hand, bleary-eyed. When he saw us, he said, 'I've got the kettle on, cool,' and led us in like, natural. Soon as El had gone to sleep (I couldn't sleep, I guess I'd slept till 5 p.m. the day before) I asked. Peter said, as far as murder went, I could think whatever I liked, El killed them.

He'd been there, but Elly performed the deed. Stabbed Ma and Pa, and Cox she shot in the ear; gore blew out his opposite ear, intense. But if Elly Belly needed to say he'd done it, hey, it was cool, though. It had been a long time ago.

Now we'd been there long enough, we'd already fucked. I was on the couch, I was drinking vodka and orange with mostly orange. Peter sat on the floor beside, his boxers on with blue toy soldiers on them. Every other soldier had a drum. I kept looking at the shorts, I mean, when I was trying to think. And I cleared my throat and said,

'But you were supposed to do it?'

'Yes, ma'am, I was planning to. That was the master plan. But Elly just nutted up and, boom! She's stabbing old Pa in the gullet. It was a bloodbath. Both of us had to change clothes. That's pretty bad, right? We left town in all Ben Cox's stuff.'

'El could stab a man to death? At thirteen, physically?'

'Aw, they were such *rotund* people, Ma had to walk with a cane. Gross. And they were sleeping, sure. Oh, you still think I did it? That's OK. There's nothing I can do about that. That's great.' And he said, 'That's funny you were willing to bone me, then. That's significant.'

'Hey, you would have done it, what the fuck.'

'Whatever!' He wrinkled his nose, he was stubbing his roll-up out. He said, 'Cox had his after-school programme then at his house, it was fucked. He needed to be *slain*, for real.'

'Look, sweetie, my dad was a cop, so I'm not pro-cop fundamentally. But, you can send child molesters to prison, that's one thing cops are good for.'

'That's what Sin says. Sin *hates* Elly. Sin was all over me for that, she thinks poor Elly's a *sociopath*, and all that bullshit. Chicks hate Elly for being good-looking, I know chicks are like that.'

'I don't hate her.'

'Yeah, I know about you and her. She told me about your hanky-panky. While you were in the *toilet*. She couldn't *wait*.'

'OK, murder's wrong, full stop. It's wrong.'

Peter Rabbit wound himself up, inhaled big like he was going to shout – but shut his mouth, seemed suddenly bright with sweat. We were looking at the stairs, where El was sleeping upstairs. The shadow on the steps looked quiet. And Peter said low,

'But you don't know, though, what Elly went through. People get cops to do their dirty work cause they're afraid. Elly *never* did that. To me, she's a hero. Elly tore her *fingernails* off for months after that, she hated herself. She cut herself to smithereens. So, Sin to call her a sociopath, that's weak.' He put one hand to his cheek and spread the fingers, kneading and thinking. Then he said, 'My temper is *horrible, fuck*. I'm getting a beer.'

Peter went probing his face to the fridge. I watched his back, he had a tattoo there a friend made when she was learning to tattoo. It was a blue traditional swallow with wobbling lines, shaded outside the lines like a small child's colouring book. From a distance, it looked like dirt. And I said, I couldn't stop now,

'Hey. You didn't go to prison?'

Peter froze, his back tensed so it was like his back listening. Then he went ahead and opened the fridge and turned back, holding beers. It was a pecked-at six-pack dangling three cans. 'What's your point?'

'Is that why the stupid names?'

'Sure, we were trying to hide. Sure.'

I almost couldn't speak. I felt sick, cold, wired, fingernails down a blackboard bad. Finally I said, 'They were looking for you?'

'No,' said Peter, in a blank, unforgiving voice, 'Or, yeah, they were digging up the lawn at Cox's. They found his magazines, his child porn? They looked for us under the dirt in his backyard. What's your point?'

'The Baltimore guy El stabbed?'

'Is this some kind of threat? That's fucked.'

'No. You just got a lot of dead people behind you.' I shrugged. I drank the last of my vodka and orange. It went down like bile. I was going to be living with murderers the rest of my life, and I had to stop and realise I'd never killed anyone. Somehow I'd been thinking I had murdered my mother. I almost said, do you have bad dreams? It was something a shitty uptight Swiss chick asked me once, when I was drunk and telling the story of Vinnie killing that drug dealer. I'd said to her, *you're a bitch. You need to do something about that.* Now I felt like a bitch, scratchy inside, because I needed, and

Peter said, 'That's horrible.'

I said, 'I'm in love with you.'

His strong body froze and was startlingly real. He put both hands to his mouth. He said, '*No way.* I'm in love with *you.*'

I said, I was dropping off a cliff into saying, 'I'm in love with you and El.'

Then El ran down the stairs in a scarlet nightie, tripping with haste, and with her wonderful hair in both hands, cried,

'Tanya, love! I heard you!'

My heart made one big fist. Peter said, 'Come here,' holding out his arms.

Fifty-Four

In the weeks I lived at Peter's, I read several hours a day. The books were cloth-bound classics of adventure that Peter was given by an ex-girlfriend in publishing. They were about young men who gambled their lives, who died for romance, for glory. I had sort of pneumonia, I could read that pirate bullshit fine. I'd be there reading *Treasure Island* until it was suddenly dark.

I used to lie full-length on the dirty wood floor. The room was hot, the floor was cool, so flattening myself itself felt good. When it rained, the glass wall streamed, and it was like being an aquarium fish, above the fray. Then Eleanor would come lie against me. Peter would.

I didn't leave the studio, most days. At first I was sick. I lost track, how much time passed.

The first day was the one time we had sex all three. It was trippy Peter fucking El in front of me; she had her hand in me and I was coming during. We were in and out of each other. It was like love as a different animal, snakes. Like a fantasy about

her white hand going in, Peter Rabbit fucking me hard and needy. I'd run away with the beautiful artist killers, I was actually thinking like a teenaged kid. Then we woke up the following morning. When I'd had my coffee, it felt OK again.

At first, El had me wear her clothes because I didn't bring any. I would wear gowns of hers, or good as gowns, that smelled of lavendar spray the laundry used. We got posh groceries sent from Carluccio's, that we never ate. We ate takeaway. El played the same Nick Cave CDs all day, his dirges about sex crimes, and we all three smoked, we smoked tons then and stayed up till literal dawn. We'd fall asleep with the whole world coming to work in the street downstairs.

We never used the upstairs bedroom. We all three slept down on the studio rugs, on blankets heaped like a dog bed. We slept meshed like dogs. I woke at night sometimes with both of them holding me. I'd be dressed while their nude bodies gleamed in the dark. Then I'd get a feeling of safety so pure, it was drug rush. I'd listen to traffic, far away in the normal world, to calm me down.

Daytimes Peter Rabbit was making those phantasmagorical frames, he worked ten hours a day. He had a mitre saw so posh it was like US military hardware; chisels and gouges down to toothpick size. And he hand-made the fabric roses that he stuck on, he'd started doing needlepoint, too, that he'd cut up and glue amid newsprint snipped minute, into individual letters. It was obsessive work Peter did with the TV on. El painted.

The paintings that were best of Peter Rabbit's, that were known as Peter Rabbit's own work, were all El's. He still had two guys, good commercial artists, who worked for him. But El's were the rock-star stuff; people saw them and got their chequebook out. They were like, *how much will you let me pay you?* Saying they were his work happened, Peter Rabbit said, cause they were poor when they were making decisions.

Now they were rich. It was freaky how Peter and Eleanor just had cash. One night we got a Hilton suite, room service Maker's Mark, and Peter bought El a silver comb from a Mayfair shop, it cost my mortgage for three months. El would buy five dresses and throw them away, she had suddenly loathed them. When I went out to eat alone once, cause they were smoking dope and paranoid, Peter just gave me a ball of cash. I counted it over the meal, £260.

I'd always had to work for money painstakingly consciously, I knew what each task paid. Sitting with the ball of cash, I'd shed that. I hadn't been to work in a week. I had stepped off the roof and I could fly.

I'd rung Alan, early on, and said I wasn't coming in, I had TB. I meant pneumonia, but tuberculosis came out. Then I laughed like a girl, like I don't. I was sitting on the floor, caped up in a quilt, and I had at least bronchitis.

He said, 'Fuck off, I know you're getting shagged. It's not like I give a toss, it never stopped you working though. I reckon you're in love.'

'OK,' I said, out of honesty or cause I was angry.

Then there was fucked-up silence.

In a minute, I heard walking, then the phone dropped scatteringly on the toilet floor. I could picture the toilet floor. The lino had a pattern of black-and-white tiles, with paint spots where the decorators were useless. Alan started to puke.

Alan has a delicate, girlish puke, like a cat scratching to be let in. He's been a puker since his chemo, puking got like second nature. He does it on demand now at parties. Some guy gets him to, to piss his girlfriend off. I don't go to parties any more with Alan. And Alan had puked in my wastebasket once at work, when I said Tony Blair was all right. You could puke at me all you wanted, it was sticks and stones.

Then Alan picked up the phone and was saying I was forcing his hand to steal more, the fertilizer cunts had sacked us, and even the Sofanet cunts were being cunts; I was coming in tonight, right?

I said, 'I'm basically ill.'

Todd I called ten times a day. My first messages were, 'Call me, dude. Come off it.' Then the long-message phase, where I hashed out reasons he might not be calling back, what he was thinking, why he'd got me wrong. I told him I loved his art, *loved*. Once he got a girlfriend, things would be cool, I said, we'd got claustrophobic after Jennie went. At last I hung up as soon as the voicemail started. Then I'd sit with the phone in my hand like it was glued to my hand. I could sit for twenty minutes.

But El would be in the background, drawing something on the floor and singing in whisper voice. Peter Rabbit was in the background. I'd have a leg of lamb in the oven, and the smell of roast and turps and fresh-cut wood was timeless sufficiency, like staying home with a newborn baby.

And it was like home, if my family had loved me. It made me see, if my family had loved me, things might have been worse. But it would have been what I wanted. I was ironing Peter's shirts, and he'd put them on with a stunned expression, unmanned that anyone cared. When I made dinner from scratch, the cooking smells were nothing they had ever had before. Whenever I told El I loved her, she said, with delighted confidence, 'Nothing like as much as I love you, though.'

I was always gorgeous. Everything I said was insightful. They laughed at my jokes. Peter said he would lay down his life for me, that El would. Of course I was the one who didn't need anybody to lay down their life.

Fifty-Five

Peter would have left for the day, he would be at the BBC for a radio thing. Or he had some friends, who were on the Turner longlist when he was, he met for darts. He went to the cat refuge in Tottenham, too; there was a girl he liked there. He had to be out, anyway.

El would get to her feet while he was still on the stairs. She would stand and watch the place in the floor, the sound of his feet going down. When the front door opened and shut, she trembled like a bow when the arrow goes.

Sometimes she ran to me. It was her clothes, she could, she ripped the pink gauze to get at me, all shining like she did in her eyes, she kissed my throat with her madwoman's certainty and

her frank and hungering fingers in me, hunting for my sounds. Her pink feeding mouth, her pale hair spread and shifting around my thighs. She'd stroke me with a sane attentiveness El never otherwise had.

I got, I felt demeaned and scared. It was feeling used, and I would know she was a girl. It was like being nude in the high street in a dream, that happening, then

I came so hard, I saw stars.

Eleanor couldn't be touched. After that first day with Peter, our sex was one way. When I put my hand on her breast, she quivered with aversion like a dog being given a bath. She squirmed, tears came to her eyes. She laughed sharp, going, 'Don't, oh shit, sorry.' If I touched her knee, her thighs tweezed decidedly together, I couldn't make love to her.

And I didn't want to lick her cunt, exactly. I didn't want to touch her cunt, that much, but my palms would yearn and stiffen, my lips, sometimes my skin all over me. Her body was

173

a bright repeating pattern on the walls of my mind, it was a lust that was a phobia.

Once I thrust two fingers in her pussy, to feel it, finally, and finger-fucked her, speeding and angry. I didn't care how well. I felt maybe what men feel, *getting what they want*. El was holding still with sweat running down. I had to stop. She got up, stiff-kneed, clumsy, pressing her knuckles to her mouth and went to bathe, we never talked about that. I never did it again.

Peter and I would fuck when she went shopping, or some whole days El disappeared, and came back saying her old lies. Sometimes she must have been scoring drugs, she'd be home late, and stoned. It wasn't how it was with El, Peter didn't jump on me the second the door closed. We'd just be talking, then be fucking, then be talking again. Our talk was El.

Peter's theme was, El was getting better. She'd got out of bed and dressed. She cried, but the *way* she cried was different. She'd gone to a yoga class. She walked out, sure, because the teacher wouldn't look at her. The point was, it was a step. When she ate carrot salad, was a step. The day the gallery lady came by, and Eleanor made the tea, it was. When she wore shoes.

It got to be a bone of contention, when I started going back to work. Even Peter had to say she got worse. My first week back, El ate just jelly beans and rum. She got migraines where she couldn't talk, Peter had to get her medication on the Internet. She wore the same dress five days running, and slept in it, it looked worse than it was.

And she said *no one* she'd *ever known* had worked all day. She guessed people *did*, she wasn't saying they didn't. It was only. Then she would well with tears, her face would go bright red.

★

The day she OD'd, I was struggling to get out the door to work while Eleanor was crying and scratching her breasts. Then she fell to her knees, her side, and passed out with her eyes half open, on whites. In her sleep, she puked blue slime; the 999 guy said to 'keep her passages clear' and the ambulance took an hour. By night-time Eleanor was beatific in a hospital bed, chatting animatedly about other times she had her stomach pumped, and laughing at anything because I'd stayed home from work for her. Because I'd bought her peonies.

She said: 'I'm going to turn this around, you don't have confidence that I can turn this around? You don't know me, though, I have to remember.'

She said: 'You should go back to your house, you have a good life. I can only drag you down with me, I'm never getting better. Don't lie to yourself.'

She said, 'As long as I've got you. Have I?'

I said, 'I'm here,' and held her hand. The light in the ward looked false, fluorescent light on people in bed. It was like a soap set of a hospital. For some reason I kept thinking of throwing away those peonies, as if they were old. I'd zone out on the balled petals, that looked like they would crumble at a touch, too pastel to be solid, and almost reach to get rid of them.

Fifty-Six

When I started back at work, I'd been away ten days, eight working days. Alan wasn't there.

The office was like it had been empty a month, the mess left, milk spoiled in the mini-fridge. Sue Blue was off at Cannes because her brother was running some part of Cannes that year, he was something at Paramount. I had eight working days of messages. Alan had six. At first at work I sat on the floor and smoked and read a month-old *Sun*, and at one point I was rocking back and forth, like I was getting retarded.

The accountant wouldn't return my calls, and Alan wouldn't. I quizzed the mail guy, who first said he 'kept himself to himself', but then admitted, when last seen, Alan was passed out pissed on the floor. He couldn't swear when that had been.

When I checked the accounts, Alan hadn't stolen more: probably he hadn't fucked off to Bangkok, like we always talked. I tried his dealer, but even Basher hadn't seen hide nor hair.

The business was gone, overnight. The fertiliser deal was dead, they'd decided to 'spend more money with a more established firm'. The diet dog food lot regretted they could not continue working with us, as the quality of our work was not in question, and it had been a pleasure. The sex-toy cheque bounced. There was some dry spell with the direct-mail business; people had apparently noticed people threw it away.

Nobody returned my calls, it was like being blacklisted. When I talked to clients, they acted embarrassed, I'd hear my voice ring false. It was like the whole world seeing through you at once, being in that silent office. My eyes were dark, my hands were cold, I moved slow with bereavement. It was like LA. (When I was living with Vinnie in LA, he'd wake me to rant. When he came in late, he'd barge in my room and he

told me I was wasting my time, policing him, he never got better when he was policed.

'You remember I used to use Crisco when I fucked you? Are you still that dry?'

He said, 'I fucking begged you not to come here. You had to come, and now it's my fault.'

Then he'd sit on the edge of my bed and cry and Vinnie actually tore his hair. He'd pull his hair as if he wanted to pull it out. 'I fucking hate myself. I'm cursed.'

I'd say, 'You got to get back on that detox. Go on methadone. I don't care what you do, I'm only saying.'

He said, 'Yeah, but I got to get some money first, get straight, I can't do anything unless.'

I was working as a marketing support, I had this crap job. No one would talk to me there, I had a vibe. Weekends I'd watch TV two days straight. My body language then was 'shapeless, defeated'. I reminded me of Craig and Janet's housekeeper, Consuelo, a dumpy Salvadorean. Our friend Nathan Pederson used to think her name meant Tired, he called her that. 'How's Tired?' 'Dude, you're making work for Tired!' She used to wear an apron stencilled with the slogan: *I've Got More Time for Lovin' Since I Got My Microwave Oven*, and the joke was, she didn't know what the words meant.

So I turned into Consuelo, Vinnie's drudge, Vinnie's joke. That's when I got my plastic surgery. First the tits that weren't so bad, but then the liposuction felt as if I'd had my body amputated, all the world hurt. I was beat on the couch on painkillers for days. In our building, every week exterminators used to go through the halls offering their wares. 'Ex-ter-minator! Ex-ter-minator!' It used to make me cry, how much I wanted them to stop.

So that's how I took time out from my career. I put energy into my family, the things that matter. I put my money up Vinnie's arm.

One day, I was at the mall with my one friend from work, Ann from Mass who lifted weights. And some dumb fuck from our office saw us and waved, but I got in my head he thought Ann and I were *dykes*. Then everything Ann did grated. I picked a fight with her, saying male bodybuilders were all fags. I was a mess with shame, and that was when I decided.

I said that night, 'Vinnie, I can't *be* here stating the obvious while you *perish*.'

He said, 'Don't be hurt, but what I more could use is if you got some *money*.'

That week Alan called. I left, and left Vinnie a hundred dollars and change, for which he never forgave me. I haven't been back to America since.

And living with Peter and El was nothing like that stretch at Vinnie's. It was like that because of the work, no other reason. Because I felt shame but it was only my shit upbringing. What if anybody knew I was a *dyke,* right.)

Sue Blue never came back from Cannes, she had met someone. Alan never came back. I would have called the cops, but he'd specially sworn me never to call the cops. It was cause he grew plants in his flat, and he'd never thrown his angel dust away, which he had since the eighties – no one wanted to take it, but it cost 700 French francs in 1980s money. He had enough drugs there, anyway, to open a store.

I worked from Alan's computer some days, sending emails in his name, writing letters. We'd always signed each other's name, that wasn't new. Signing his letters, though, then, could be like lifting two hundred pounds, I felt so shit in that empty office.

And, a few weeks in, when I went down to Sofanet, to check where the artwork was for spring, I came out of the lift, and all the open-plan tarts looked up in alarm. One said 'Hello', in the wrong tone of voice. The fat girl looked at the door to Mark's office. I got to Nick already freaked, and he said, 'Tanya, they told me this morning, I'm so awfully sorry,' as I got in the door.

I stood in the door. He was playing with his stapler, wedging one finger into its jaws and tugging it out. He'd cut his hair, so you could see his hot-pink ears, part of the general decline.

He said, 'It's not you, truly, they've been moving all these various things in-house. It's not at all about you.'

I sat on his desk. At last I said, 'Bad news.'

Nick started to babble; the higher-ups at Sofanet were now consolidating the business, they'd had a consultant in on 'four walls management' where everything was between the same four walls, I could imagine. It was the new bandwagon that followed the old outsourcing bandwagon. They were even getting rid of the consultancy, itself, and wasn't that poetic justice? Pure ideology, it had no place. At last Nick ran out of steam. I couldn't say anything but, 'That sucks.'

I sat there staring at Nick's sister in the poster playing Desdemona. I was thinking of Mark Keynes; I was so far gone, in my mind I had been in a tragedy nightgown when we fucked. He'd got revenge, I guessed. It could be four walls management. Except I made my main client hate me by using the CFO for sex, which was not good business.

At last Nick said, 'I know you must need to get back.'

I said, 'Yeah, yeah; I won't keep you.' I went back

where the empty office had no work to do. And when the Sofanet contract came to an end, I didn't know how to pay the rent on the office, my mortgage. It would be, begging money from Peter. I was buying magazines for the first time in years, bringing rum into the office. I phoned insanely, it wasn't even drumming up work, it was loneliness. When I wasn't on the phone, I played Lou Reed and Radiohead, perversely, adding to the mood of the end of days.

Then I'd go home to El.

She'd be at the door when I got up the stairs, looking taut, like she'd been holding her breath. The rum and Coke would be ready in a glass, with ice. Those Nick Cave songs that sounded lovelorn, spectral, from out in the street. I'd lie on the cool wood, spent.

And she told me stories

Fifty-Seven

about the good years in London, at first. She was painting and Peter was selling them. They had pots of money, there was never an end of money. It was like you had a magic wand.

She met Mick Jagger, she guessed she'd told me. She had two blokes with private planes, all the people they met were rich, or dealers. She had eight blokes at a time, she didn't mind fucking then. 'That was what people wanted from me.' So, she needed a good time after that time in America, sleeping in cars. If what she wanted was diamonds, that was just what she wanted. If what she wanted was smack, she'd earned the right.

She was the only person she knew who had actually swung from a chandelier, in the lobby of a Brighton hotel. It held, but women screamed, there was a glorious rumpus. The lady desk clerk said, 'You gave me a heart attack, you're a grown woman.' She'd drunk absinthe and had a time when she was able to read, on absinthe, that didn't last, when she read French poetry. She'd sailed from Bora-Bora up the coast with a sweet depressive Spaniard who was an egg collector. Photos existed of Eleanor cradling a hand grenade; with Carlos the Jackal; trying to fuck a Labrador that wouldn't have it. 'Everyone fell about, but the dog was hit by a car that week and I feel responsible, the owner said I was, you know? He said that Zeke was cursed.'

Peter was the one enrolled at the Royal College. She had got them in: the portfolio work, the good portfolio work, was hers. I should see Peter's old work sometime, his painted air conditioners and painted bikes she didn't understand. She liked art, beautiful art. Everybody did, she believed.

They'd started making money before the graduation

show. Someone El was fucking saw the pictures, they'd had their fortune made, it was a laugh. The other students hated Peter then. A boy came up to him in the hall once and said, 'I'd love to cut out your *eyes*,' that was the atmosphere. Peter finished, though, he was a very determined man.

The first fortune they got, it was £20,000 in a go. Peter got it in cash, he didn't have a bank account, at first. Ginger Bear was crashing at theirs, then, with her infant; they had photographs of Ginny in her knickers, all rolling in banknotes, the baby stuffing money in its mouth. It was fine times, probably. Eleanor had blacked out a lot, she wasn't sure.

In those days, when it rained, she would go in the streets to give money to homeless people. She was a good person then, if that was good. She was compassionate. She couldn't think of people being out in winter. God, she didn't know how one slept, knowing that was going on. The homeless men said she was mad, they were her greatest critics. Still, when she got the flat in Battersea, she got the keys copied twenty times and had all winos bedded down in the sitting room.

Most of those men were there for the drugs. They had beds somewhere, she later realised. But she was very free-handed then, she shared her drugs and had pizza delivered. They weren't respectful. They robbed her diamonds, too. They robbed the neighbours. None of them raped her, though; everyone assumed they would. She had got past worrying whether the homeless suffered, now. Probably the drugs did something to her brain, she felt utterly different.

But it was that; and the time she had taken the pigeon to the posh veterinarian. The bird had been got at by a cat, it was so frightened you could see fear in the way it breathed. The vet girl didn't want to take the pigeon, she said it would have *diseases*. The *veterinarian* said — well, it was funny. El guessed she had made a scene, they threw her out, and she had ruined the pigeon's one chance. She sat on the pavement in front of the vet until the pigeon had finally died. That was the week Ginger Bear died. And Ginger Bear's brother died the following month; they all died then. Everyone was dying.

And she said half the people she knew those years died. It didn't seem unusual, then. It was the nineties, she supposed that people died. She didn't know what she meant by that. That there were a lot of drugs. 'It's actually normal, if you look at other cultures. People don't live so monumentally long, we're not designed to live long, I believe.' But she'd survived. She was the one who lived.

And her very old boyfriend, Hank, he was a cocaine dealer from Baton Rouge, he'd done forty-five of his seventy years in the pen; the time Peter met Hank, he told El, 'Fuck, this dude's been *through the mill*.' Hank had one eye, burns up both arms and a bullet hole in his thigh; he was like a piece of sorrowful gristle, chewed, tough, and ugly. Hank was crazy as hell, as El. He'd beaten a grass to death with a fireplace poker, that was one example. He told El, 'People like us can't never go back, we ain't real people, sugar, we're trolls.' He'd had an X-ray in prison that showed a huge, boxy, inhuman heart.

Hank had a plane. He had flown her down to Africa, she never found out what country, somewhere people still had slaves. His house was on the shore. There was a ten-foot fence, and she had to be led through the yard, cause it was mined.

One day they drove his army jeep in zigzags down the empty beach, sand spraying, and the shore birds rising in clouds. The sea and the whole brown coast was theirs. Sunlight tipped on the glassy waves. They fired guns over the water, Hank emptied his machine gun over the water. Eleanor danced in the shallows, on coke, and remembered that she was a *murderess*. And not like other people, she would kill the other people if she wanted. She was frightened of nothing.

Fifty-Eight

It was the year Rachelle Freespirit Lynch turned eleven years old. She had white fragile features more beautiful than any adult good looks, she had white-blonde hair. She was pedalling her bike downtown, where she wasn't allowed.

She was going to get a *Teen Beat* magazine, which she wasn't allowed until she turned twelve. The day was hot; Rachelle felt woozy but she couldn't call from town for a ride. If she got in any trouble again, they wouldn't let her have a cat.

Where the road began to wind, the sidewalk ended. The cars all swept too close. Their wake tugged, warping her into the road. By the time she got to Landry's, the general store, her legs felt thin from fear and effort. Getting down was like she'd been saved from a storm at sea. There was sunlight as if the whole woods and houses around were on the floor of an ocean of sunlight. The smell was gasoline from the Exxon station over the road.

On the porch of the store, Ben Cox stood, holding a bakery cake. A Seven-Up was set on top of the box, and a red pack of Marlboros. At first Rachelle didn't know who it was. Ben recognised her first and looked away sharp. Then she was frozen, blind with wanting and fearing him. She forgot to lock her bike. She went up to Ben with her blood pounding, words storming, overlapping in her temples. It was like bearding God in person with your puny human desire to live.

Ben was a tall, athletic man in his early forties, with thick blond hair he got cut in New York. He dressed like a page from a magazine; moved with edgy, powerful grace. On the step of the weather-beaten general store, in the mundane scene of roads and signs, he looked like a mirage of light.

Rachelle confronted him, both hands wound in her long hair. He smiled, glib.

'I guess you want my cake,' he said.

Somehow the right thing came to her. She said, 'You're Ben. No, I want a cigarette.'

She only went every couple of days, at first. He had his after-school programme, but no way the Hortons were sending her to that. She had mentioned it, leaving out Ben's name, but Pa turned white with fury. He had to walk out of the room and come back to deliver his absolute, positive no.

She would say she was going to Maggie's house, cause Maggie had no phone. Maggie's mom was on welfare, they lived in one of the summer cabins by the pond. Pa always believed Rachelle would go there, because there was a playground used by campers in the summer. They knew she loved the roundabout.

In his after-school programme, Ben taught French. The children had to speak French the whole time they were there. Apart from that, apart from the lessons supervised by French exchange students, it was like camp all year round. The house was in ten acres of land, a Victorian house with a balcony. You climbed the cherry tree to pick the cherries, and Ben didn't make you wash them, you could sit there in the tree and eat. Ben had computer games in French, and skateboards, stilts, a treehouse with a roof and shuttered windows. The pony, Mignon, was too old to ride, but you could feed her corn and grass. There was an in-the-ground pool.

The food was hot dogs, cheeseburgers, and every day, Ben bought a chocolate cake. It was frosted with the *mot du jour*. Three o'clock was cake hour. You got it on paper plates Ben had printed with the children's photos; everyone was served their own face.

At her middle school, the kids threw spitballs in Rachelle's hair. Someone wrote PIG in Magic Marker on her locker, and Rachelle was too ashamed to wash it off; they'd see you washing it off, and laugh. Girls dumped her books, and boys barked when she passed. She was called Ra-Smell, or Smelly Snorton.

But at La Petite École, all because Ben favoured her, she was queen. Kids picked cherries for her. She decided when she was It. One of the same girls who threw spitballs in her hair at school had given her a valentine signed *Your best? friend.* When Rachelle rode in on her bike, a cry rose up and she saw the bright clothes move in the shadows of trees. Then they were running to greet her.

He made her stand very still while he stripped her clothes. The nightstand lamp was a green-shaded study lamp that left the room its shadows, and the windows were open. The room was charged with night. There was a fan going on the floor, its wind was the first thing, prying in her damp corners, fingering. Then Ben's fingers.

She knew his naked body. It was there beneath anything in her mind. He had come walking out of her lost self, gorgeous, clothed in the power of nightmare. When she was the beautiful child strangers stopped to dote on, she was Ben's. As long as he was naked, she was part of that power, and when she bent to lick his cock, fear went through her like an electrocution, but the fear was no longer hers.

They drank real champagne together when the others had gone. They sat on the balcony, Rachelle in her swimsuit, still wet, with the clear alien harshness of chlorinated water in her nose. His hand curled over her thigh, restless, toying with what came next. He said, 'You were always my little love.'

They sat perched over the world and they had conquered the world. Crickets squalled in the pitch dark, everywhere; crickets sang the world. The stars were dreams only they could interpret, and love was bigger than the coursing air and stars, Ben was to her.

He told her his problems, like he did with no one else. He needed Rachelle to help him with his philosophy; Ben was writing a book of philosophy that would free the world. He said he was the brains, but Rachelle was the 'newborn soul', his oracle. She would shut her eyes and he would lean by her, close, while she reported the movements of her soul. It stirred to the left when she thought about school; it flowed up out of the top of her head when she tried to imagine God. When she thought about Ben, it filled her body, avidly pressing her skin.

Whenever he touched Rachelle, her body rang like a frightened bell. She didn't know what the feelings were, each was a spasm with the potency of loss. Sometimes she held a bright living leaf in her hand, pulled it lightly down so its branch stretched to her, and felt the same force, what Ben called *the spectacle*. And what she was living was *epiphany*, an invasion of the flesh by God. All true love was, but nobody had that love; only one couple on Earth at any one time. She walked up and down his hall sometimes when the kids were there, the jabbering nonsensical day outside; stunned that she was the chosen. All other lovers were monkeys play-acting what she knew as burning reality.

He prepared her for the time when they would have *true sex*. When he entered her, the world would begin to change. It was a cycle that worlds went through, and on every world, the true lovers would enter each other at the same moment. Then a single spectacular cycle would begin, and imperceptibly, all that was coarse and false before would fill with grace. For Rachelle, it might be painful. From her pain and her spotless love, the world would spark into beating anew.

At school, she had new friends, girls and boys who called her, as she now insisted, *Sheba*. She told them she could hear the demons in the earth; she pressed her ear to the playground grass and reported the business in hell. She had stolen a pornographic novel she found in Pa's drawer, and doled out individual pages to her favourites. Each day, Rachelle elected someone to carry her lunch tray. Ben gave her money, impossible princely sums like fifty dollars, which she spent on cigarettes and gifts for her friends. Sometimes, when she got a specially coveted item – the dog-shaped radio, the pocket knife, the scorpion preserved in resin – she would make the children fight to see who won the prize.

One day she had dressed at home in an outfit Ben had bought her – a scaled-down version of the classic little black dress, cut low in the back, that went with a set of plastic pearls – when Ma walked in. Ma made her undress and took the clothes away; she barricaded Rachelle in her bedroom while she hid the wicked clothes. The fight went on for hours, Rachelle weeping, swearing that she would run away. She felt her real life soiled by Ma, the gross adult eyes seeing filth into her purity. When Pa came home, there was a search of her room. The remaining pages of the porn novel, *One-Night-Stand Girl*, were unearthed; her cigarettes; tarot cards; a diary of masturbation fantasies that Ben had prompted her to keep. At last, beneath her copy of *All-Time Best Horse Stories*, a Polaroid of Benjamin Cox was found. In the picture he was wearing a suit, but barefoot, with an electric razor in his hand. He'd shaved a stripe into his beard of shaving foam, and his smile at the camera was tomcat-tish, joyful.

There was a stark frozen moment; then something flipped in Rachelle's chest. She burst into a little girl's tears. Ma and Pa were going to save her now. She was scared to even think about that house, and Ben, and what they did. The *spectacle* was a contaminating lie, and the other children were like a chorus singing as she was staked and sacrificed.

Then Ma began to weep. Pa put his arm around his wife and helped her out of the room. He gave Rachelle a final, hateful, trivial glance, and slammed the door.

For a long time she sat on her bed with nothing in her head but white. Her stuffed lion, with its back to her, was potently inanimate. The things in her room looked at her with their silence, their impotence. At last she went and opened the door; she listened to the nothing in the corridor. She tiptoed through the aching house, she couldn't find Isaiah anywhere. In his room, she said to Sauron, the oldest parakeet, who looked shredded and bleached; who had a chronic eye infection and always winked: 'Don't be afraid. I love you.'

Sauron twisted his head to gape his single round hyster-ical mindless eye. She flinched. She said, 'But I don't love you any more, now.' She opened the cage and the parakeet flut-tered and shrank as she put her hand in. It took a second; the worst was the crunching bones. Then she looked around, exhilarated, brave. She was panting. She imagined she could see through the walls of the dead house, straight to the ardent, stainless sky.

The pain was intense and went through her in rings. She felt no change in the world, just intimate, physical pain, a descrip-tion of tissues. She was staring at the shape of the windowsill, noticing the moulded wood again and again. When it was over, it hurt differently, like an opened blister.

Ben said, 'Now you're going to be mine. If you ever tell anyone that this happened, our love is over.' He said he wouldn't be able to change it; if she broke her vow, the love would die that instant, burn to ash. She would slowly die thereafter, he concluded, with an air of having discovered a curious fact, and stood up getting his pants.

At last he turned, dressed up and a different person in his clothes, his face deliciously intent on something very far from her, and said, 'You doing all right?'

She said, for the first time, 'You don't care about me.'

He said, unruffled, 'You're the only thing I care about. You don't understand me at all.'

For a second, she saw it plain; like seeing to the back of the television set, with the pictures gone, the glass transparent, the mystery reduced to dusty tubes and a plastic backing. He had fucked her like a *one-night-stand girl*. There was no spectacle, no epiphany. He was *shooting his cum in her snatch*.

While he was in the bathroom, splashing his face, she cried – a little, hardly knowing. She was never going to trust anyone again; she thought that might be true. People were possessed by demons. Maybe the demons ate them; there was good in people, fighting the demons, but the demons always won. The bird she'd killed, it was something in her *evil*. She thought of making her school friends fight for toys, cruel, and imagined a ballerina, ghosted round by lewd, snapping mouths. She tried to recapture what the demons in the earth had said; it had been pretend, but there was something real, a prompting. Then Ben came back, an instance of human sunlight, a hero people paid twenty bucks a piece to hear speak. He said, 'You can stay here tonight.'

She'd begun to stay overnight the day of the black dress incident. She'd arrived at Ben's house after dark, ready to hide in the woods behind his house if he wouldn't let her. But he was prepared. Ben was always prepared. He got Pa Horton on the phone.

He made her go in the other room, she couldn't hear the conversation. But after that, Ma and Pa steered clear of her. She could come and go. She lived in the house like an adult, making her own food, hot dogs and frozen chicken cutlets. She had developed a habit of peeling wallpaper off the walls and eating it, but if they caught her at it, all they said was, 'Cut that out, honey,' gently, ready to be cowed. They no longer spanked her. Once, when Ma came in, Rachelle distinctly, without meaning to, pronounced, 'Fat bitch.' Ma started but kept walking, shielding her panicked face with both hands.

Ben wanted her. That was the tide of her days, it drew from waking to night, the moment of her walking up to him when his stance changed. The press of his hard body never left her mind. All day in school she waited to go to him, she had stopped doing homework or listening. When called upon, she would say, 'I don't know,' in a routine, angry undertone that made the other kids laugh and shift in their seats.

At La Petite École, the mood was overheated. They had a new game of mobbing Ben, pummelling him while he yelped in mock-fear. They were jealous of his attention; he would be dragged to watch a softball game, then dragged to play He-Man, then dragged to read to a little girl who would not be consoled without him. One of the French exchange students declared her love for Ben and was gently encouraged to leave.

Rachelle sat apart and would sometimes openly smoke until the others left. There was a leather chair she owned; when she got up, she left a piece of red construction paper on the seat with the words: 'Reservée – Rachelle.' She ate chocolate cake, all she liked, without the rules of having one, her own, plate; some days she ate nothing else. Ben had bought her sketch pads, and she filled them with drawings of Mignon, of imaginary beasts, of Ben. If she didn't get the drawing right, she had to eat the page. Then the parents' cars came. All the voices moved to one side of the house. There was a slamming of doors; the final voice went on a long time, a mother seizing the chance to talk to Ben alone.

At last he came to her from outside, intent, unbuttoning his shirt. She had learned how to go to him and put her hands up on his bare chest, finding the scarce hairs there. When she felt his penis, half hard in his pants, she had to look the other way. She had to blank her mind. But her shyness made him want her more, he would lift her up and, fucking didn't hurt the way it had. She was going to feel the things he felt, Ben said, when she relaxed. Already she *came* when he licked her, although she felt soiled and wrong, then. She had to have brandy. She didn't see why people wanted to come.

She would ask him, 'Will you marry me, when we can?'

He promised and crossed his heart. He said, 'You're part of my soul.'

Now at night they snorted cocaine together. That made her talk and race through the house, getting Ben to chase her. It made her understand the epiphany was real. Otherwise she wouldn't be able to draw the way she did; Rachelle had always been the dummy at school, but now she drew Mignon *perfect*. She saw the changes in the grass, it looked more tentative and slender, it was conscious. She could see the change in her own hands against his darker skin. Even the least things – a spider dead in its own web, a stretched-out ponytail holder, a greening penny – had a lurid, beckoning significance. She would watch the shadow of a branch moving in the wind, groping the shape of the wooden steps as it ran up and down, and know things no one had ever known before.

One day Pa lost his temper. He snatched Rachelle from where she sat, where she had shredded a manuscript of his; she was intending to put it in the parakeet cage for Azrael. Pa got the ping-pong paddle and was looking around for his wife to witness this, for his accomplice. Then Rachelle began to speak in a dull, throbbing voice. She was sobbing, gasping, without tears.

'You sold me to that man. You're a pig, you pigs abused me. You're sick child abusers, you make me sick. You sold me, you can't hit me. You can't hit me any more, you *killed me.*'

She clung to his cold, sweaty shins as if a wind might sweep her off. It had said itself, it wasn't her. It was something you don't mean.

'You're a witch,' Pa said, in a quiet, convinced voice. 'I'm wasting my time, disciplining you, there's no good in you. I only thank God you're not my child.'

Then Ma burst in and made a frightened yelp, a parakeet sound. She said, 'Don't – *honey,*' and Pa stood, shovelling Rachelle from his lap with both hands. She dropped hard on her hands and knees, startled, half expecting Ma to come kiss her hurt knees better. Pa said, 'Leave her alone.' The parents left; she heard their laboured, excited breathing shrink down the hall.

Ben had new favourites. There was a girl called Lisa, an eight-year-old with short cream-coloured hair. Rachelle heard Ben tell Lisa's parents their child had a *gift for languages*, offering them a rate on private tutoring. The black girl, Tilly, was let to take naps with Ben; she slept while he held still like a stalking animal, feeling her form relax against him. Both had the clean plump bodies of even younger children; the fumbling ecstatic way they handled things was like a toddler.

Rachelle had hit five three already, she weighed the same as some grown women at twelve. A friend of Ma's had said she was an *early developer*, meaning the breasts that showed even in loose T-shirts and lumberjack shirts. She had pubic hair, and new hair under her arms, she was hairy as a hog. She tried not eating, but Rachelle was starving hungry all the time and her body changed implacably, bearing her away despite her diets, despite her prayers and oaths.

When she got to La Petite École each day, she had to hunt Ben down. Her heart would be beating all over, that he not be with Lisa or Tilly. He would be with them and a gang of children, singing *La Marseillaise*, or prodding a turtle someone had found. His eyes would move to her and move away.

Now he gave her her own foil packages of cocaine to take away. He remarked that you started with an elf, and she became a teen drug addict overnight. He supposed he had himself to blame. Sex still worked when he'd had a couple of lines, she could get him started with her mouth.

But the day came, he was saying, 'Enough, enough,' for a minute before he pulled her off by the hair. He said it again, into her face: 'Enough.'

She said, 'I love you.'

The crickets squalled outside. It was a mechanical noise about nothing, she needed more coke. Ben was looking at the bookshelf, scratching his chin. He let go of her hair.

He said, 'I lied to you. There's no such thing as the *epiphany*.

It's time you grew out of this, I can't play make-believe with you any more, I have real work to do.'

And he said, 'I haven't been fair to you. Next time round, I won't make promises, that was selfish, I admit it.'

He said, 'You should look for a boyfriend your own age,' thoughtfully, as if it had come to him what was best for everyone.

Then Rachelle said, with the world falling out of her, turning to fear, 'I could send you to jail.'

He said, 'Go home.'

Fifty-Nine

And at the time Peter came, Ben Cox was paying Rachelle two hundred dollars a week hush money. Ben gave her coke, and she bought more from a high school junior girl in Philly. She got pills from a neighbourhood man, for blow jobs. She'd tried to stop, she'd *been* through that phase, when she went to church on weekdays, that was purest shit. Twice she'd cut her wrists, but she was only a coward, she couldn't do pain. She'd make it, one of these days, she must. She knew where Pa kept his gun. She couldn't live with Benjamin Cox in the world, she couldn't be.

Peter was crouched by her bed, with the magazine crumpled in his hands. She had kept it in the cellar, buried under Sears catalogues in a carton. They'd had to wait until Ma and Pa were asleep. It was flimsy, stapled, printed on thin paper like a local catalogue. It was just children having sex with adults, that was all it was. It was just pictures.

He trembled like a leaf as he crushed it. Then he couldn't touch it any more, he dropped it. It seemed like an artefact smuggled out of hell. He started crying, blubbering, like a little boy.

He sobbed, 'Kill *him*. Don't you die, Elly, Christ's sake. Let's kill the bastard.'

She said 'Are you on my side?'

And Peter fought lions and dragons for his Elly. He walked through blood and fire. He gave his life.

Sixty

'Yeah, Elly can be a pain,' said Peter Rabbit, winding his camera to put in another roll of film. 'Before you came, she was tripping, she was in Elly outer space. She's got her demons, bad.'

We were in the studio, taking those photographs Peter had asked for at the start. I was being OK, so far. I was doing it. That was my version of a personal triumph, if you thought that people change. I had stripped to the waist.

I said, 'Yeah, she's hard work. I can deal with another ten minutes, I guess. No, I'm OK, go on, what you were saying?'

'That she's *way* better, she's *so much* better. She's just a little rescue dog.'

'She burned down buildings, though?'

'*No way.* You believed my shit? Don't listen to me. She *tried*. She never burned down shit. Elly couldn't light a *match*. That was in California, anyway, that's old history. That's like the Roman Empire.'

'She won't burn my house down. OK.'

'Whoa. Elly adores you. Elly's going to burn your house down? Elly wouldn't harm your hair on your head, dummy. Look at the window.'

I'd been naked with them, Peter and Eleanor both, already. El first; one day when the quilt fell off, I held still for it. El, not seeming to notice, went on with her story about the time she gave the fur coat to the prostitute. 'I wouldn't even wear that rubbish. I don't believe in cruelty, it ought to be sold for crack.' I was laughing and thinking of myself as a woman who walked around easily naked. I was thinking I hadn't ever done it since Todd, before the Frankenstein scene in LA with Dr Wagamama, his nickname because he was

Japanese and everybody went to him for breast augmentation like fast food. I don't remember his real name.

I said, 'I wouldn't wear a fur coat.' I was smiling like an idiot. I said, 'You could really put a gun to my head.'

She said, 'Honestly,' and smiled at my loins and thought, and said, 'But – you would look beautiful in one.'

Peter Rabbit came after, but I told him I was doing it. I said, 'I'm going to try to be naked now, don't wonder or anything if I freak out.'

He said, 'I saw you naked before, dodo. We bone.'

'You didn't notice, I guess that's cool.'

I took off all my clothes in front of him. Peter was watching, being nice, right.

'Do you think my scars are hot?' I said, trying hard. 'Or does it give you a surgery phobia? I think about films of operations, my problem is.'

Peter said, 'Can we do those photographs now?'

I have big mismatched breasts that stand still when I walk. The left one got infected, that's what the main scar is. The thighs are scrawny. Other people can't see, to me they look like they belong to two different people. One time only, I wore a bathing suit with Vinnie, and asked him when we got to the beach. He was in some shitty mood and said, 'Surgeons have bad days, too. They're human.'

And maybe it helped to have boundaries, if you were fucking everybody on Earth, for instance. Maybe it felt like they didn't get a piece of me that way. I don't know. I still don't feel like I know what it was like, to live my life.

Peter crouched down with the camera. He was doing photographer poses from a movie about a doomed model and a serial killer. I was aware of his clothes, how it would feel to wear his clothes. I was going to put my big Clash T-shirt of Todd's on, when we finished. I was going to stop it now.

He said, 'In French, she's worse. If you ever see her talking to French people, look out. Uh-oh, Elly in French. When she was with Abdul, she was a *night mare.*'

Sixty-One

They'd split from LA cause, OK, the Baltimore dude did die. Sin and Con didn't know, but there was no, *was the Baltimore dude all right*, about it. Elly got him smack in the heart. She was covered in blood like a *newborn* when she made it home. 'It was yucky.'

It had been Abdul that saved their ass big time that time, his passports. Abdul was a sweet Moroccan boy El met from blundering into a Hardee's men's room, stoned. He took her straight home. They spoke French together, Ab maybe wanted Elly more for that. He was just a little sawed-off runt, but it turned out he was a member of a passport ring. He was a forger. He had all space-age equipment in the kitchen in his house.

Abdul was fifteen. He got obsessed by El. He made her passports after passports, he made one for Peter Rabbit. (Peter Rabbit said he'd show me his passport in the name of Peter Rabbit some day, it was *just like* the real thing, it was *smoking*. He was *living on it now*.)

But when they found out he was creaming passports off the top, Abdul's partners in crime eviscerated him and shoved his guts down his throat. 'Elly *found* him. It was gnarly.'

That's when Elly went on the streets and the Baltimore dude and all. Poor Elly was jonesing bad once she couldn't turn tricks, she was hooked like a research monkey. The cops came by the house one day she was with Book Fletcher, their neighbour who had lung cancer. Book got his cancer when he was doing time for grand theft auto, and he always believed he was a government experiment. He was one of these really good-looking black dudes, Peter said, but old.

Book went out to the cops in his bathrobe, playing

'worried neighbour'. It was Baltimore boy all right. It had been two months of Elly sweating it, now she flipped and cut her throat real bad. Almost hospital bad, which would be like, *hello, slammer.*

Peter got their shit together. They split to France, to friends of Ab's in Nice, but she was psycho talking French all day, in France. They couldn't go back to the US, Elly didn't dare. So, England was right on the doorstep.

'She got us in the Royal College, yeah, you know about that. It was fun at first. Whee-hee!' said Peter Rabbit, weakly, putting the camera back in its case.

I said, 'It's fun now. Hey.'

Peter said, not meeting my eye, 'You'll move on soon. You're way too healthy for us. It's good.'

'What if I don't want to move on?' I made a face. I had my t-shirt on, I was feeling pretty good again. But my voice sounded childish, waspish, almost like Eleanor's.

Sixty-Two

This day, it had started as one of our good days. It was a dry clean autumn afternoon where the air felt candid, real. The sex-toy people had paid the week before, I was wearing new blue jeans. Sunday so, I didn't work Sundays always, even back when. El was dressed in satin and working on a sketch of a cabbage you could tell was a cabbage. I decided we should go to the Café Flo.

Peter didn't come cause it was our thing. For old times' sake, El walked there barefoot, even though she took real sandals, suede with heels. A little boy walking behind us with his mother noticed El's bare feet, and whined he couldn't go barefoot too.

We got steak frites and a bottle of cheap champagne. El had her sketch pad on the table, drawing while she talked in her mannered, good-girl voice. She'd sharpened her pencils that morning, the No. 1 draughting pencils for fine lines. The pencils lay in a neat raft on the fresh tablecloth.

'I'm actually optimistic now,' she was saying. 'It's good. I have to hold on to this feeling.' And she started, as she did sometimes, on Peter's 'getting better' spiel.

She'd cut her opiates down, and smack. She'd quit Benzos ever since the presciption ran out, and E wasn't really a drug. Ketamine, yeah, except she disliked ketamine, that was no real danger. Possibly she'd quit smoking first, since that was in fact the hardest.

'This is like in Van Nuys,' she said, beginning to draw a room around her cabbage. The cabbage was in an armchair. 'I never had my bad side then, I have to hold on to that.'

'But that was when you —' I said, and stopped. The waiter loomed with champagne. I had to taste it, nod, he poured it into glasses, and the time it took to wait out the foam. Then he was gone and we were drinking. I said, 'When you stabbed that dude?'

El changed. She pressed the pencil to her lip, making two halves of a frown.

I said, 'Peter said. I don't know, maybe he was kidding.'

For a moment she looked out at the street, her face startled, betrayed. She said, 'That was different. That's not what I meant.'

Then she looked at me, relieved, and said, 'So this is better than Van Nuys.'

I said, 'You got to give me more space.'

For a long time, she was drawing. We each had another glass of champagne, I'd forgotten and was watching the street. The confident feeling of blue skies through clean glass; there was a sheltie tied to a lamp post who stood up, expectant, wagging, every time someone passed. An Indian girl stooped to pet him, looking guiltily back at the restaurant. Then

El said, 'So, you're leaving me? That's good you decided to tell me.'

I said, from the calm place I had gone, 'No. I can't promise I'll never leave you, though. And I meant it about the space.'

She said, 'You're so cold-hearted. God, you're cruel.'

I coughed, at first I was laughing. I said, 'El. What are you talking about?'

She said, 'It's not funny,' she was raising her voice, intense. Her knuckles had whitened on the pencil.

'You knew I want more space,' I said. 'I never said that?'

'So you're leaving me,' she said louder.

The voices at the tables around changed, the room stiffening as the volume all went down. Of course you couldn't even go out for lunch. I looked at the sheltie, ashamed like we might scare him.

I said, 'We're in a restaurant. Come on.'

'Fuck the restaurant.'

I reached forward, trying to snag her hand. She jerked it back, I was saying, 'We're not going to do this here, don't.'

'You don't want to touch me. I see through you. I see it now.'

'OK, I don't want to touch you,' I said, feeling the anger now, my knees gone tense. 'You ruined my life, my work. What more do you need, Christ's sake.'

'I never needed you. You make me sick, you're sick.' Her eyes were squinted tight. El was baring her teeth. It was a face like a kung fu movie villain's, unbelievable in real life.

I said, 'Look, this is fucked. Calm down,' and reached for her hand again.

She speared my hand with the sharpened pencil. She used all her weight, and sprang up, her chair flying into the passing waiter.

I was stupid at first, looking up with reproach. She'd intended to break my hand. She'd gone deep into the muscle, past pain to numb. Now she would be sorry, I would have to comfort her. Then she went for my eye.

I flinched back, but she hit the socket, sending sprays of hurt, fright, into my head. My vision splayed. Standing up, I was half blind, high on rage, like the nerves breaking out of my skin.

I grabbed the pencil but she pulled it free and stabbed my throat. Then I slammed her with my good fist, all the knowledge coming back from Dad. She staggered back into another table, where the dude stood up. He had both hands raised like he knew a man should do something. Everyone had hushed like animals reacting, shrinking. Everyone was animals.

El shrieked, 'You can't! You can't play with me any more! Cunts like you!'

I said, 'Don't,' in a strange, dull voice. 'El. Are you trying to kill me?'

Then her face fell apart. It went into red and grimaces as the tears began, and she was turning the pencil at her heart. And she was already stabbing herself, with the most power anyone has ever done anything in front of me.

The maître d' appeared from nowhere, grabbing her arm, there was a brief dance till she dropped the pencil. He was yelling to the busboy about calling 999. El tensed against his arm once more, then weakened and seemed to trickle off into a waif.

I said, 'No, it's OK. I know — she's going to be cool. Don't call,' and cause it's all I could think, 'She has to have her medication.'

El stilled then, both hands up holding the maître d's arm, bewildered. Her face cleared. El seemed to look out of it at me, with fragile recognition. She mumbled, 'I need my medication.'

We got back in a cab I barely remember. I remember realising belatedly I could see from both eyes, and being scared all over again. The girl sous-chef had given me ice in a dishcloth to put on the eye, but I'd been sitting with it wet in my lap, not thinking. Once I realised I could see, I started using the ice.

As we got to our door, El muttered, 'My sketch pad,' and started to cry. I said, hating myself, 'Don't cry; I'll go back and get the sketch pad tomorrow.'

Then we were in. The familiar room was like landing in a soft place. You wanted to shut the door forever. Peter stood up from his Xbox, saying, 'Oh, no. Oh, no,' as Eleanor ran to his arms. I went up, blundering with that ice to my eye. Peter reached towards me over El.

And I had a clear thought of getting a cab to my house, a flash of the solitude in a black cab, the dusty shade on the seat, a scene from adult life that I knew wasn't going to happen.

That night Eleanor held me in her arms, concentrating every second on me in her arms. And I dreamed that we were going to hell together, I was tearing the old tags off my suitcase. Outside, all the people were dead. The world had come to an end, and we had to get out on the plane to hell.

I was too late for the plane. The dead stood in the street and swayed, they were going to rape me, giving me death.

When I woke up, only El was there. I was still preparing to go to hell; then I remembered Café Flo. There was sunlight, watery as if it was stirred by breeze, on the tawny floorboards. She held my good hand.

She smelled like oranges she'd been eating while I was asleep. She was wearing a sapphire pendant, nothing else. I tried, but I couldn't imagine her spearing my hand, the kung fu villain face. It was something from a dream about hell.

She said, 'I had to wake you up, you had a nightmare.' Then she thought, pursing her lips, intent like children who haven't learned yet how to net thoughts easily, and said, 'I'm not going to give you nightmares any more. I've figured out how I'm going to be good.'

I said, 'You're good.' Then I said, 'You don't have to be good.'

Sixty-Three

That was the last week my business made money. I was going to work to get away from the house. When I got there, I read papers. I'd stopped bringing rum, cause the mail guy's words about Alan, 'passed out pissed', got close for comfort.

For a while, it was cool to see no one. I didn't want clients to see the black eye. The lid was swollen yellow and black, with a scratch that went down to my cheek. I had a broken blood vessel on the white itself, a crimson speck. Within a week, with ice I used compulsively, you could say, I was going to say, it was a sty.

The hand was bruised, but people hurt their hands. The neck hurt worst, that at first I'd hardly noticed. That got a green bulge that was perfectly round, it looked like a bite from an insect from outer space. I got these electric shocks when I turned my head.

One day, when the eye was better, I tried seeing Nick for lunch. We went to that Cuban that was not the same. It's never the same. The tables were empty, the manager was in the back shouting in Chinese, no parrot. A drunk kept banging on the window outside. The food was luke-warm, grey, like wet with the wrong thing.

Nick talked. Nick was in a good place, because he'd 'taken the plunge' and moved out from his sister's to a shared flat, living with a 'female barrister', Amy. She was overweight like him and they were on the Atkins diet. When they'd lost a stone each, they got to buy a cat. He loved his sister, but he knew he couldn't do it for her. He'd stopped taking her calls. 'I'm going to a film with some Al-Anons next week, and I'm really quite looking forward to it.'

I was dying in my gut, I couldn't tell Nick anything.

You couldn't talk about my life, to a Nick. Lesbians were gynaecological. The Café Flo scene, murder, paedophilia, you might as well shit on the floor.

I said I'd been good, too. The house was really coming together. Todd was moving out; he'd sold some art, which was a turn-up for the books. I was having to rethink the business, which was probably a healthy thing. We'd got too stuck in our groove. And I'd even been 'seeing someone', the artist Peter Rabbit, sort of.

Then Nick looked concerned. I guess I'd talked about Peter before, and the chick who jumped out of a cake.

'What?' I said. 'It's only dating, it's not . . . What?'

'I'm cautious by nature,' he temporised. 'You're far more experienced than me.'

'It's cool. Say it.'

'No, part of my programme is not second-guessing. It's not that I think you would need second-guessing.'

We stared at the waitress for a while. She was playing some game on her mobile phone. When she scored a point, we sat back.

And I said, 'Shit, is that the time?'

I finally tracked down Alan at his sister's in Stoke-on-Trent. It wasn't what I'd guessed, it was the cancer. It wasn't that bad, they'd caught it in time. It was only bad that it had come back, at all, reported his sister Jules. He might be impotent, too, which I wanted her to turn into a joke, but she didn't, so I couldn't. She said, 'I had *sworn* him to tell you. He's such a bloody fibber.'

He was planning to be in the city next week, for tests, he would probably see me then. Right now he was flat out with drugs. Whatever worked, was her philosophy, but they were rough. He'd not been able to stand.

I said, I couldn't help myself, 'Do you know whether he's planning to come back?'

She sighed. 'No, I shouldn't imagine so. He was set on shutting it down, but I had understood that to be your joint decision, so Alan is a piece of work, is all I know.'

I said, 'Whatever he wants.' I'd turned to wood. 'Just tell him, whatever he wants.'

I spent the next morning in the office, crying. I'd found some pictures of us in Star and Garter days with Forter and the beautiful temp who hated us. We looked young. They weren't such great times, at the time. Now they were the best times. Alan and his old friend Ian and me dropped acid once and went to Alton Towers, the three of us waving cotton candy and watching the trails, and the roller-coaster trails, then Alan was my now age. We would fuck for lunch. I never cry.

At last I hid the pictures in a drawer, and went and stood at my nondescript window. It overlooks the windows of the tenth-storey opposite. The offices on that side were empty suddenly. You could see prints on the carpet where the furniture went. The workmen had tracked dirt there in paths, and you could only see inside because a builder there had turned on lights. He was smoking, looking like a barbarian loafing in the ruins of a high culture.

I didn't know when that office shut. I never looked out much. Now I felt like a neighbour had died, and I'd walked past, concerned with my problems, never realising I was going to die. I said, 'No, dammit,' and went and splashed my face in the ladies' room we share with a hepatitis charity, and you always think you're going to get hep C from the seats. I went down

to see Mark Keynes. The CFO, for which you have to get past the secretary. I was going to say there was an invoice issue he'd asked me to stop in about, at about this time, he might not remember. Mark was there, though, at the secretary's desk, conversing, with a plastic goblet of wine.

Someone must have left, cause it wasn't Christmas. They were drinking red wine in the best of spirits, as if the person leaving was a pain in the ass. When they saw me, they instantly sobered.

'Oh, yes, Tanya, right,' said Mark. 'You will have got my message?'

The secretary said, 'Hello. Hi,' and looked at my breasts.

I said, 'No, I hadn't, but. Could I have a word?' I was halfway to crying. But I wasn't going to cry, I was angry. Mark looked concerned like people like him do and opened the door of his office. As I went through, he drained his cup. The secretary said, 'Ta-ra for now.'

Mark shut the door behind me. I was looking at the guest chair, smiling wrong, and I wasn't really cool to sit. But I did sit. You'd hang yourself by crying. Fucking the client and crying, two rules. Mark said,

'Yes, I'd wanted to speak to you about an opportunity that's come up.'

I nodded, our eyes met. Then we said nothing.

Mark's office was my office, one floor down. It took a minute to notice that, because it was furnished. He had a fat therapy armchair, one office chair I'd sat in, and plants. The carpet was brand new, blue, the kind that looks like it grew on the floor. The oak bookshelves had management tomes and Grisham-type books in hardcover.

Mark cleared his throat and said, 'It shouldn't come from me, but I'd said, and Liam agreed, that as we know each other,' and I'd started crying.

There was a blurry minute, he had turned to the window. If I'd gone out with Mark when I had the chance, I wouldn't have to be afraid of Eleanor. Somehow I would still have a business, and Todd. I would have got fucking plants. I said suddenly,

'Alan's got cancer. He's got cancer again.'

Mark came back to life. He said, 'I don't have tissues, of course. Would you like me to go and ask Jasmine?'

'No, sorry. Damn, I'm sorry. Just say what you were going to say. This isn't normal for me, it's been a mad week.'

'Of course. The thing – it's Head of Marketing. We wanted to ask you to be our Head of Marketing.'

For a second I didn't know what he had said. Then I laughed, the way crying people do, aware of the tears. I said, 'I'm sorry. That's not funny.'

He said, apologetically, 'Mainly it's what you're already doing. So I put it to Liam, and everybody knows you, is the point. I realise – is Alan all right? Am I being a prat?'

'He's all right. He's selling the company.'

'Oh, that's good. I mean, from my point of view. As I'm stealing you from him, or trying to.'

He crossed his arms. He looked tender, unhappy. I was no longer crying, I was thinking of working in a company. I never had a real job, only Burger King kind of jobs and Alan. That LA marketing gig could count. I said, 'I don't know, working at Sofanet.'

'It's not like a blue-chip company,' Mark said. Both of us laughed, because whatever the company you work at, everyone treats it as a joke.

I said, 'I should think about it. *Yes, of course.* But I also should think about it, you know what I mean. Let's talk tomorrow.' I got up uncomfortably and looked at him. I mean, I looked down at him.

And Mark was a solidly built man who did karate, he was good-looking in a beaky way. You noticed the hair on his wrists where they came out of the cuffs. In a meeting, everyone addressed him, even when Mark wasn't the senior person. Once he had called the CEO a 'golem', and in Mark, even that seemed boyish. It was disproportionately funny.

Now his big hands were clenched on his biceps. He had a white shirt on that had had a jacket over it, that pattern of wrinkles. Even his fucking dress shirt was poignant and Mark said, looking down,

'Perhaps this is obvious, but I apologise if I came off too harsh, at our last conversation. Don't panic, I'm not – that's not what this is about.'

I said, 'Are you up for a drink?'

Sixty-Four

The last weeks I lived at Peter's, I saw Mark Keynes a dozen times. He was my new Hutch, though we didn't fuck. And Mark supported Tottenham and knew about house prices, Mark would never call you at work with a problem from a passage in Kant, like Hutch did. But it was somewhere to go when I couldn't go home. And, that thing of hitting a low point, and people who are kind to you seem larger than life. I'd sit in his place, with his nothing furniture that made it like sitting in an airport, safe. We'd watch some crap like football, then

I talked.

I told him about my mother, and the end with Vinnie. I talked about being promiscuous, all the waking up in the morning with a bad head. I talked about tennis, how tennis was the real-life part of my life once. Then one day you woke up and you weren't an athlete, you were one of those lames you'd despised. You couldn't even walk on your hands.

I talked about my friends in college, they were all rich kids who sailed. They had novelty licence plates and parents who had Martin Scorsese over for dinner and they generally never had broken a sweat yet. All of them told me, when we were still in touch, how to live. I should have a relationship. Todd should go. I should tell my family where to get off. I should face the issues that made me compulsive around sex. There was a subtext, they wouldn't be my friend if I proved *dysfunctional*. It made me feel, even when I was the one who stopped returning their calls, they'd dumped me.

I told him Vinnie's wolf story, how, when he was fifteen, Vinnie's friends and him broke into a zoo, and Vinnie played with the wolves. He scaled the fence to the wolf enclosure and wrestled with them, rolling on the ground, throwing sticks. All his friends were holding their breath. The wolves would fetch, Vinnie said, but they weren't so hot at bringing back the stick. You didn't want to go in their mouths, getting into some grief about the stick. And he was that kind of great brother, then, for a while. Then I said

I didn't know why the bad guys had to die at the end, when they were people you loved. In my opinion, life was too fair. And I told him I'd been sleeping with El.

We were on his bed that night with a bottle of red. We'd been trying to read some Proust, to see how far we got, we flipped for who got *Swann's Way.* I won. Then I just spilled my guts before I got to the madeleine.

Mark said Eleanor sounded like a lot. He wouldn't ever try to compare that to his troubles with Jan, who was going to marry a mutual friend, a much older banker, in April. He hoped I didn't mind, but my situation made him feel better. 'There was some madness, at the end with Jan. Including El, was one mad thing I did.'

I cleared my throat. I said, 'So, what did you make of her?'

'At the time? I know that I thought her a bit of a waif.' He said, with a remembering grin, 'She stole from me.'

'She nicks things, yeah. She stole my Palm, I'm pretty sure. What did she take from you?'

'Twenty pounds.'

We laughed about, how little. He said, 'Yes. What's the point, at that point?'

'She wanted your mojo. Fuck knows.'

We went into our separate worlds. Mark was playing with his watch, shutting and opening the latch, absent. I looked at that *Pulp Fiction* poster; Uma Thurman looked like

Eleanor the way all beautiful women did, some. El would be watching *Big Brother* now, drinking her chocolate milk. She'd be waiting for me, chewing the corner of the quilt, wound up and sad. And Mark said,

'I always fancied you. You certainly made it hard work.'

'I don't know why you'd fancy me. I thought you were a masochist.'

'Fucking hell.'

'Well, I shagged everyone, that's all I mean. I am the office slapper.'

Mark reached forward and took my hand, the first time he'd touched me since. I guess I flinched, he got a humorous look. He said, 'If you want the true answer, I saw you had a kind heart. It was your gentleness I saw in you, I hope that's not the worst thing to say. It's been a time for me, I look for gentle people.'

Then kissed me. He put his hand to my cheek. I caught it in my hand, pressing the palm with my thumb.

'I don't see it,' I said. 'But, thanks.'

That was the night we slept together. I stayed overnight. I didn't call El or Peter; when it got to be twelve, I let it be the whole house of cards. I'd been thinking about the phone, and El cutting herself, and then it got to be twelve.

And it was like I could let the whole thing disappear by shutting my eyes. I could see why Mark had the Sofanet furniture, the bland, anonymous, showroom furniture. No one even knew I was there. I slept straight through the night, sleep I drank like I was dying of thirst, and woke not frightened that El was dead.

Sixty-Five

The next morning I went to my house, my good investment I'd bought thinking life could be different. It was the first time since I'd been at Peter's. I'd thought I didn't want to barge in on Todd. Of course, more, I was in flight from my life.

It was weird walking up to it, like unexpectedly spotting an old flame. It looked so fucking the same. The curtains hadn't moved. The blue paint was flaking in the same place on the door, baring old psychedelic layers of paint. I used the wrong key at first, and laughed like there was someone to hear me. As I stepped in, I called for Todd, and called again, my voice was actually shaking.

Todd wasn't home. The walls were covered from ceiling to floor with drawings.

They carried on up the stairs and the first-floor rooms. They made the house dark. In the front room were actual paintings, of Todd, in polished, Titian sort of oils. The background was intricate pencil on gesso or primer white. That was a miniature scene of wilderness/indoors mixed, like a furnished wood, and sitting in the chairs were lions. It was possibly better than the old Peter Rabbit stuff. But I just looked at the pictures of Todd, like he'd been waiting for me.

Todd with his arms up, doing a crossless Christ, Todd smoking his Judge Dredd hash pipe. In one, he was on his bed, nude, just like Todd, brown eyes saucered in Todd awe. It was what had happened in my absence. For a minute I thought Todd painted it. He was the one, all along, my Todd was the real *Peter Rabbit*.

El had been coming here while I was at work. I got that hot-cold failing down my spine. For the first time I knew

217

she was a *murderer*. She could be here in the house. I'd just betrayed her with Mark.

I went upstairs, my feet hollow and light, and up the stairs, she had added to the turtles with a drawing of herself. She was on a horse, Godiva naked, breasts semi-erased, amid a crowd of gawping children. In the hall upstairs were more of Todd, nude, that made me want Todd safe, with me. They'd been fucking. She was probably why he wouldn't answer my calls.

I got to my room and it was me, in colour. I was frowning, my arms crossed under my inflated tits, ungainly with fear and misery. That's how I looked when I looked at El. She'd painted the same thing five times, larger than life, and they were scarily alike. Looking around was like hearing a deep drumbeat repeating. I went to

the bathroom, which had not been painted, and her room had the same old drawings. Todd's room was clean. I went back down to the kitchen, sick and wanting a spray-paint can, and I wanted to hide.

On the kitchen walls, the pictures were a nude obese man. She'd given him an empty circle instead of a head. He stood with his hands out stiffly, presenting his palms. The detail varied; the focus on the shy, humped genitalia was searing, photographically keen. And the genitals were mottled with dried blood, what I could recognise easily, since these weeks with El, as real dried blood.

That was all the pictures. I went back through the rooms, expecting to find a companion fat woman, find Ma Horton, right, and I was calm enough to want to know what Ben Cox looked like. By the time I was finished, I was starting to be OK. I was thinking of coffee. I could drink it outside, on the steps

when the door went. I even wet myself, a drop. I was

thinking, *that's what it's like, to wet yourself from fear.* And Todd walked in.

He was in his cycling gear, with his blue rucksack still on, bright-faced from the ride. He looked impossibly normal, like a movie star in person. When he saw me, his jaw dropped.

'Tanya, no!' he said. 'No way!'

He felt solid and alive in my arms, like a real live puppy, too great to be true. I went, 'Oh, God, I've been missing you crazily. Don't ever do that to me.'

He let me go, he was bashful and glad. He said, 'OK, I threw the phone away? I'm an asshole. *You* could have come home, sometime.'

'Don't try it.'

'I was being immature. But you should have come home. Uh-oh. You saw the house?'

'El trashed my place, you let her trash the place, dude.'

Todd laughed merrily, and that was all it meant. El had made a great big mess. 'Yeah,' he said. 'I did the primer, too. I'm an asshole. Wow, you're here. You want to come upstairs? I got a six-pack.'

We went up to his room. The plain walls looked unspeakably sweet, fresh. We sat on the floor where you saw his matchbox cars underneath the bed, he'd lined them up like they were parked in a lot. I was getting that pure intense happiness thing, when you were ready to die, and then. I never loved beer like that. Todd was going on happily

how El shagged him twice, and then she got neurosis, he was pretty heartbroken at first. But you had to give people their space to be neurotic. Oh! He was giving up art. No! It was a good thing, because he came to lots of good realisations.

He could kick himself he didn't be a tennis player. Layla and him met a tennis player while I was away, at a Rachel Stamp gig. Todd was so bummed out. The guy said it wasn't too late for Todd, but he was lying.

Todd guessed I was going to be mad, when I saw my room. He swore he didn't know El was doing that. El was really upset with me, she told Todd a lot of messed-up stuff, about me being a lesbian. She wasn't such a great friend. He guessed I wasn't seeing her anyway. He thought she was a special person, but maybe the bad stuff was probably drugs, she could put you off drugs big time.

He talked to El lots, though, cause they were lonely together. Did she tell me about the Russian spy she knew? Only he was a fat spy. *And* she met Mick Jagger, but he stole her matches, he was kind of a dick. She was a total raconteur, she'd taught him that word. Did I ever know El spoke French? She wasn't dumb.

And El was such a talented artist, he couldn't *believe* she wasn't famous. It had to be because she couldn't cope with the stresses. That's what she kind of said. El offered that Todd could be her public face for her art, it was an awesome opportunity, but he hadn't made up his mind.

'No,' I said, hard, suddenly.

Todd rolled his eyes. 'Tannie. I got to make up my own mind. El said I could do it for a while, I'd get some money and start my own gallery? It's more for her, though. She didn't even do any canvases yet, don't have a cow. Anyway, she asked me.'

I took a deep breath. I said, 'Cool. Are you going to stay here?'

'Right! I was going to leave. I got a room at Lennie's, but I don't know if I'm going to go.' He bit his lip and searched my face a little. He admitted, 'It's that cool attic.'

I reached under the bed and pulled out the matchbox school bus. It still had the red American price tag on its belly, it was 99 cents. I started to peel the tag off, it was my turn to talk. I think I'd believed I would tell Todd *everything* and he would tell me what to do, like a big brother.

Todd had let his hair grow out; it was moppy and the ends were blonder from summer. In his T-shirt, he looked like somebody's kid. While I was gone, he'd tacked up a Gwen Stefani poster, and he had the old street sign up from our street in Mass, Apache Road.

And Todd was a person who still believed in Santa Claus when he was twelve. He'd told me that in confidence, and added, looking daring and stubborn, 'Kind of, I still do. I don't think it's as stupid as the Pope.'

I said, 'Remember that guy who climbed Mount Greyback with a violin and stripped himself naked and he'd never played a violin before, but he thought, at the peak of the mountain, naked, he'd be able to play it?'

'I was kidding about that. I wasn't really going to try it.'

'It didn't work even for him.'

'Oh, no. You're saying this thing with El is like *that*? No way is it like that. I wanted you to beg me to stay here, anyway, duh. You're so not being *any* manipulated.'

There was a pause, then he said, 'You're going to wreck my bus.'

'I was taking the sticker off.'

'You broke that wheel that time.'

I gave him the bus. He pressed it against his lip.

I said, 'What will you do, if you don't do art?'

'I thought I'd be a vet, but it's a lot of school. I mean an animal vet.' Then he said, 'Hey, where have you been? At work?'

'Mostly.' And I said, while I still had the guts, 'Todd, look, I love you but I think you should move to Lennie's, for real.'

He sat up straight. His face changed and changed. Then he leaned down and put the bus carefully back in its place. He said, 'OK. I was *going* to go yesterday.'

'Yeah. I'm glad you didn't go without seeing me.'

'I couldn't do that. That's dumb. But you mean I've got to get my own life, right? You're trying to help me.'

'I'd rather go with you, shit. I wish I could leave with you.'

Sixty-Six

And I could have said, I came to lots of good realisations, that you let a crazy person into your life, it's not just your life on the line. And when you've moved, I'll maybe tell you things, when it's too late for you to be here when it all hits the fan. I could have said, you talk to that psycho bitch again, and I'll wring your neck. I could have shared my feeling of being the hero cop who moves his wife and kids to a cheap hotel while he pursues the big mob boss. I could have said, *I would lay down my life, for you.*

I said, 'I'll come and visit you, lots.'

I helped Todd pack and carried stuff out to the cab. I waved but Todd was sulking, ducking his head away in the back seat. He had his hair all in his face, and I was like a mom sending her kid off to his first day at school, too much for comfort.

Then it took five minutes to walk and buy a set of new locks.

Sixty-Seven

Once I fucked this cameraman. He'd been a cameraman in the Vietnam War. He worked for something now, *The Big Breakfast* kind of thing with celebrities playing mud hopscotch. For the money cause he had kids, etc. But when he was young

he filmed in Vietnam. And I got like some *fan* about it, like I never get. I had to hear about it. It was like my all-time one-night stand, his stories.

Until, at 3 a.m., he got this video out. He'd been getting all his footage on video for getting work. This was one he'd done for himself at the same time. This film never aired. It was

several US soldiers in a shaggy little village. The villagers were South Vietnamese, friendly people who were telling the soldiers something through an interpreter. They were two women and a man with a broken arm. The broken-arm man kept staring around him, not concentrating on the conversation. He eyeballed the trees.

The interpreter kept laughing though the people talking through him didn't. Then hell broke loose.

The camera filmed the ground bouncing towards the lens as the cameraman ran. It showed scrambled foliage. You heard shrieks, cursing and popping gunfire.

Then you saw one of the US soldiers, bouncing in and out of frame, he was carrying a Vietnamese woman in his arms. She was all blood down her leg, clinging to him for dear life, wild-eyed. He ran best he could, with a look of self-conscious heroism on his face. Determination in the face of odds, he ran fiercely then

another shot came. There was a burst of red. The shot

had blown off half the woman's head. The soldier's running tailed

off, he was jogging. He was struggling but his energy was gone. He clutched the headless body which now flapped in his arms. And his mates were cursing him to run.

He ran clutching that loose corpse with an expression of stunned humour on his face. Embarrassed, like he'd done a pratfall. He turned to the camera and panted,

'Shit. I don't know how to put it down.'

Sixty-Eight

It was after I'd put the locks in I called Hutch. I was sitting in the kitchen with the headless men, one on each wall so you didn't have anywhere to face. I'd been trying to make myself call El. Then I thought of this other thing I should do. Maybe Hutch could give me pointers on the El thing, I wouldn't get too specific.

I hadn't phoned in so long, Hutch didn't recognise my voice at first. He sounded fearful, happy, on a good knife edge and

not like Hutch.

Before, whatever black dogs attended him inwardly, Hutchinson had floated beyond the real world. He worked at the bank as an attenuated inside joke about the bank. His lady-loves caused him chagrin for existential reasons. He'd use the word 'epiphenomenal' in a sentence, to the cab driver.

At his first interview at Lloyd's, Hutch was asked where he saw himself in ten years' time. He thought about this profoundly, beetling his brow. At length, he replied:

'I think I'd like to be very fat, and have a lot of cats.'

And got the job. That is the Hutchinson keynote: he *got the job*.

Now Hutch was talking thirteen to the dozen, of a sudden engaged, real, here. The tone was, racing to keep up with his thoughts. And he was shamed and euphoric; he had fallen in love.

'I'm joyful, Tanya, do you hear it? How I'm at last joyful?'

I said, 'Yeah. It's weird.'

'Are you coming to see me?'

'Well, I wasn't. I had something to do,' I said. And I said, cause that's what I was counting on saying, 'I'm sorry I fell out of touch.'

'Oh, no, I shouldn't fret about that. I would have been more persistent, I take it upon myself. I had had a faint sense the women I had slept with before were interlopers. I didn't want to see white Patricia, in the main. But Patricia still fancies me. It's foul when one has to be fancied by . . . Patricia, I suppose. Can you hear that I'm not thinking clearly?'

'So tell me.'

'I'm going to be married, it seems.'

There was a pause, I listened to the street outside. An ice-cream van was passing, it was playing the *Dr Zhivago* theme. I was trying not to think about being in love. Finally I said, choked up with my fucked-up nerves, 'Congratulations. To that – Alex?'

'Yes. To that Alex. She proposed to me. I think that's good, because proposing is a sign of weakness, isn't it? One does try not to propose.'

'But then you have to say yes.'

'You really are . . . oh, I feel terrible. Is that supposed to happen? I suppose it is.'

'Is she British?' I said, because Hutchinson was famous for his hatred of British women, whom he found cold and mercenary, who defined feminism as, they should never make the tea but they should always choose the film. But I had a side bet Hutchinson would marry one.

He said, 'No, she's American.'

He added, 'Like you,' as if I might have forgotten, and he added,

'But she doesn't remind me of you.'

'Oh, God forbid!' I said, laughing though I was a bit hurt. He added,

'She's very blonde, I think that has an effect. I feel like a sexist saying that, I don't know why. The beautiful blonde, one feels clichéd. She is rather beautiful, embarrassingly.'

My stomach went light to dark. I knew. I knew *like that*. Hutch was going on,

'You don't know how we met, do you? I suppressed this because you'd think me mad, not that you were ever misled I'm sane. Alex came to my door for shoes.'

'Oh, shit,' I said, exhausted. I was standing up. My feet felt like they weren't screwed on tight enough, I went to the doorway and leaned. I said, 'Go on.'

'It just so happened I had shoes in her size, that Laura left behind, my sister Laura. So I let her try the shoes on and she walked back and forth in them. I was in love like that.' He laughed uncomfortably, added, 'I don't know. Perhaps I'm fooling myself? I'm getting married, though, so I'd better not be. Why "Oh, shit"?'

'She came to your door barefoot –'

'– asking for shoes, that's right. She is a mad wee thing.'

'Did you ever . . . you never met my lodger, Eleanor?'

'The ex-Dutch girl? I never did meet her, no; not invited, you see. You haven't had me to the house. That is a hint.'

I said, 'Oh, come and bring your fiancée!' which was such a funny joke he couldn't get. I felt unhinged and started heading to the stairs. I said,

'I'm coming over, after all, if you have time. I want to talk.'

I spent that day and night telling Hutch his beloved was a murderess who took so many drugs, both illegal and prescription, that her brains had been fried, she couldn't *read*. She had slept with a thousand men, and women. She wasn't going to stop cause she was mad as the proverbial box of frogs. *Don't flush your life down the toilet* — was implicit.

Hutch chose not to understand. He kept saying, 'Oh, I knew. I did realise. I had guessed. That seemed probable.'

His antiseptically clean flat had little sprinklings of El. When I went to the bathroom, her shampoos were there, with the tops all open and crusty. There was a near-empty bag of jelly beans on the couch I couldn't stand to see, that I threw away behind his back. She'd drawn herself in lipstick on the refrigerator, with the caption 'DIFFICULT'.

Hutch was thinner, which shouldn't be possible. He'd developed a nervous blink that was totally new. Pouring wine, he used both hands, like an old man.

At one point he said distractedly, 'Who are you in love with? I am such a wretch, I never asked.'

'I never said I was in love,' I said, fast, shook up.

'I could have sworn you did. I am sorry, though I know you have the best of it. I shouldn't like to sacrifice it now.'

'But, Hutch —'

'There's no fool like an old fool. Or is it: the heart has reasons reason cannot know? At any rate, I hope you won't judge your old fool too severely, as I'm happy. I should be wroth at you for soiling my happiness, you see. But I had counted on you, finally, to eat my flan tonight, I hope you won't disappoint.'

Eleanor had told him that she was a student at UCLA, taking time off to choose her major. She successfully concealed her age, her near-illiteracy, and her prodigious drug use. He'd thought her affected in the manner of American rich girls, nothing more. 'The lesbian infatuation: classic.'

At last I told Hutch that infatuation probably was me.

That was why she stole my PalmPilot, tracked down my ex-lover, introduced herself: 'I'm sorry, but I came out bare-foot and I reckoned someone might have shoes?' And I told him the bare bones of my affair with El.

He said, 'Do you know, marriage *par dépit*? What's quite ironical is two of my friends from university, Harold and Zack, were married *par dépit* by women I had treated rather callously. Both divorced now, you know, they're all divorced, my friends.'

I said, 'But she was never in love with me, she was insane.'

'Oh, I know that I oughtn't to make myself feel worse, it is unsightly. I'm sorry to compel you to witness this, poor brave Tanya.'

The wedding would be his family only in their local church. He'd talked about his family before, they sounded that sort of *absolutely lovely* middle class from Wiltshire who would take an El on faith. His sister was already planning flowers. There was going to be a sit-down dinner with the vicar and his wife, cause Hutch was an intensely conservative eccentric, that is, an *absolutely lovely* middle-class person.

After the wedding, they would move to Brittany. Hutch was semi-retired, he could commute for what he needed to do. 'I rather fancy a helicopter, if I can go in with some other braying drunken ex-pats, that's how I shall proceed.' El would mellow in the nurturing countryside. Hutch speculated that she needed time and space away from everything, that all psychiatry could be dispensed with if the mad could be removed to eighteenth-century cottages in Brittany, that gardening was possibly the ticket. He was wondering if Eleanor might like an Old English sheepdog, he'd spoken to a breeder in Dorset.

Because he knew it wasn't going to happen, all these things were like medicines prescribed to the terminally ill.

He talked them up excitedly, avoiding my eye. Slyly, he prompted me to agree.

I kept saying, 'I'll stand by you whatever you do.' He'd press my hand. We put off going to bed as if something would happen, we'd see the one obvious solution, a sheriff would arrive at the door to rescue us at the eleventh hour.

Sixty-Nine

I woke on Hutchinson's couch at noon. I'd been up till dawn, after he went to bed, just lying staring at the dull light off the defaced refrigerator. At one point I'd got up to squint at his framed photo of me with a milk moustache. I was trying to see who I was. Waking up, I went back to it, as if it might have changed in the night.

Hutchinson had left a note.

> DEAR GIRL,
>   DON'T FEEL YOU MUST GO. I SHALL
> BE BACK BASICALLY NOW, I AM AT THE
> ESTATE AGENT. RING IF NOT,
>   HUTCH

I almost went to work, it was my typical avoidance. I could just leave them to it, El and Peter were actually adults. Hutch was an adult. Todd was, you can walk away. I took a whole shower before I was sure.

I called El from Hutch's kitchen. I had opened the fridge and was staring inside, not aware that I'd opened the fridge. When Peter picked up I would have just talked to him, I was still all ready to let shit happen. But he said, 'Elly's right here,' and that was all he said.

She got the phone. I heard her excited breathing. At last I had to say 'Hello?'

El said, in a polite, clipped voice, 'Tanya, yes. You were out. You don't owe me any explanation.'

'I went to my house.'

'I was out last night as well.'

'I went to my house.'

'I heard you. I thought you wouldn't like those drawings.

I know you never liked my work.'

'I don't like what you suggested to Todd.'

There was a pause. I was staring at Hutch's condiments, trying to clear my head.

Then El said, 'I knew this day would come. It's a relief, in fact.'

We waited through the time when I should ask what she meant. At last she said, 'People dispense with me. It happens. That's why I don't try fidelity, I cheat all I can. No one's ever faithful to me.'

I shut the fridge door hard. I said, 'Don't bother. I know about your boyfriend.'

She said, impertinent, cool, 'The trouble is, I've grown to hate you.'

The word hate filled my head. I had a flash of punching Dad. You could go to her house. You could just say *Kill me, bitch* and go.

Then the stale, familiar tune of Eleanor crying. It sounded weird over the phone, biological. She said, 'I don't mean this. It's not me.'

'It sounds just like you.'

'It's not me.'

'Don't go to my house any more.'

'Are you coming home?'

There was a pause like vaulting a chasm, a gap of nothing when I shut my eyes. I said, 'I'm not.'

She was wheezing now with tears. I told myself Peter was there. There wouldn't be a pool of blood. You couldn't become the slave of a person because she threatened to die, you couldn't keep her alive forever.

At last, I said, 'I'm here.'

She said, shrill, 'I should come get my furniture. You won't want all my garbage in your house.'

And I said, as if this was planned, 'Yeah, I can't hang onto your stuff. I could rent that room. I don't want to be insensitive.'

'No,' she said. 'No, I don't find that insensitive.'

'A clean break,' I said. Saying that was like cool water through my body. I got light-headed. I put my finger on the lipstick drawing of El and smudged her mouth.

'I'll do it today,' she was saying, waspish. 'I can get a van, don't worry what I'll do. I know someone who can get me a van. Not Peter, it's someone who'll do it, don't worry.'

'I'll pack stuff,' I said, flat. 'It'll save time.'

'I wouldn't want to spend more time there than absolutely necessary. I can't stick being unwanted.'

We made it for four o'clock.

When I rang off, I was covered in sweat. I had immediate remorse. Eleanor hadn't done anything. She was sleeping with my friend, the adult. She said to my friend, the other adult, he could be her public face for her art. Her murders were ancient history, it was like Peter said, it was the Roman Empire.

Then I thought of Hutchinson buying the Old English sheepdog, his pinched and helpless face as he said, 'The heart has reasons reason cannot know,' and I started for the door.

Seventy

It's a ten-minute walk. Part of it, when I bought the house, I thought I'd see more of Hutch. I had the whole fantasy going, of walking there with a bottle of wine. I'd never got to walk it before, though; I had to stop and ask directions. I was coasting on the cool, sick energy I had from the phone call. I'd already thought, how I'd put all her stuff on the pavement, if she didn't get the van.

I blurred straight into the house when I got there. I wasn't going to look at the pictures. Then, when I opened her door, I jumped. There was nothing to jump at. The room was quiet and cluttered, it was only a room.

I was smelling her perfume. I almost sat on the floor. Now that I was there, I was full of the last few months, my body cluttered with the ways she'd touched me. I heard her halting, saccharine voice, louder than the real world.

I started by folding clothes, I wasn't thinking too clearly. After a while I had to go back and throw stuff out, El never cleaned much. There were Tic Tac boxes sown everywhere. I found a syringe underneath a book and got chills; it was like finding centipedes under a rock. I threw out an old T-shirt of mine that had been there all this time.

For a while I just gave up and watched TV. I pretended El would do it, it wasn't my stuff to pack. It was a documentary on the illegal trade in rare beetles, a masterpiece of unintentional humour under other circumstances. But the sofa I was sitting on was hers, a big yellow sofa that wouldn't fit in her room. It made me think about everything that had to go, and I had to go back.

I spent an hour cleaning, clearing the dead wood. I had to go out and buy new garbage bags, she'd never thrown anything out. Then I was back with clothes. Her gowns and gauze were too her, it was like folding her empty skin. Every object seemed not inanimate but dead.

I couldn't go on living in this house. I began to rehearse in my mind, some speech where I'd say to Mark it was just for a week, till I got a short-term let. I could afford a hotel. There must be a hundred hotels near work. Mark would know what the house would bring on the market.

Sometimes I'd stall and stare at the drawings. I could almost remember loving these drawings. It was like a smell that clings to something, almost, so you sniff deep, trying to remember the smell. I'd loved El. I'd seen her as something damned and gorgeous, dancing in the ruins, kissing the spy. She'd been my depraved but valiant princess, almost, I could almost remember a day.

Finally I got her suitcases down from the top of the wardrobe. I got a sprinkling of dust in my face. There were only three now, she must have stashed the others at Peter's. There was already stuff in one. I thought small things might fit, you can always fit more, and I opened it.

It was full of little girl's clothes. They were old, they had that defeated appearance, a gloom in the fabric. They were a kind of American clothes I'd worn too, stretch polyester slacks. In the middle was a beat-up copy of *Zazie dans le Métro*. I had to, so I opened it up. It was signed, *To my Zazie – Bent Socks*. Underneath was a gilt-framed photograph of a leonine blond man, shaving, barefoot in an immaculate suit. He was even better-looking than I had imagined, the way real gorgeous people are, and he grinned with El's shy, longing delight. Then I saw the trophy.

It was lodged in a corner, wrapped in an old pink *Charlie's Angels* T-shirt. At some point, she had kept candy in it, a couple of wrappers spilled out. She must have tucked it away in a hurry, not bothering to empty it out.

It was a bronze cup for *Most Valuable Player* in a grammar-school football team. The soccer ball was welded to the figurine's foot with a visible lump of solder. On the base was engraved the valuable player's name, *Andrew Short*, and I'd seen it before, I'd heard the story behind it, at Curt Short's Fourth of July bash. I could even picture where it went, in the upper shelf of Curt Short's trophy case.

I was crawling skin all over. I was saying, 'Shit, shit,' looking over my shoulder, my heart pumped ice-cold water. It was three forty-five, El never came early. It was fifteen minutes, I could get out of the house.

Then I thought of Hutch.

Seventy-One

I called three times in a row and couldn't get Hutch to answer. I had to go and open a beer, I was cruelly aware of the fucking clock ticking. I drank it so fast I hurt my gullet. I took my cellphone up to Todd's room, needing a safe place.

I would tell El not to come. I was going to say I'd meet her at theirs. I'd hint I was missing her, that I'd been thinking. I needed to have a serious talk. The next call would be the cops.

On the third ring, Peter Rabbit answered.

I said, fucked up, uneven, 'Is she there?'

He said, 'Elly? Elly left *hours* ago. I think she went to see her boyfriend, she was mad after talking to you.'

Then the doorbell rang.

Seventy-Two

The silence of the hallway means time's up. Cause Isaiah is away, it's a silence you know well from other times Isaiah was away. This is your family home, you know its sounds, and you will never sleep here again.

She sets foot on the hallway carpet, nursing that knife. The knife indents her breast and her look is inward, burn-ingly inward. She remembers and can find no point of rest.

Cause before, and between the regular horrors, Ma squirted Bactine on her skinned knee, kissing the 'boo-boo' better. Ma pulled out a teddy-bear-printed hanky for Elly to blow her nose. Ma cooked her meals, Pa Horton took her fishing on the boat. They caught a blowfish that threw up its own gut and Elly had bad dreams and Pa crooned nonsense to her until she slept again

with Pa at the foot of the bed to guard her. She had no parents. She had already killed them, in a way.

Rosie put his arms around her from behind and said, sounding scared, unwilling, making it a question, 'It's not too late?'

'You're hurting my . . . tit,' she said. He sprang away, she had five stitches where she tried to, it was stabbing herself in the heart. She wouldn't try to stab her parents in the heart, it was too difficult. There seemed to be bones between the bones, and she stepped forward.

She wasn't scared of anything. She smiled suddenly.

Pa and Ma Horton slept in separate bedrooms. They would do Pa first because the second person to be done might wake. It would be that much easier if it were Ma. You never knew how strong Pa might be, in a pinch. Ma was good as crippled with arthritis; to talk about it that way made it seem like a logic problem, like the fox, the goose, and the corn, and they'd only talked about it that way. It was just last night, they had. Now it was as if someone switched the job on them at the last minute, now they were expected to murder people.

Then Elly walked forward briskly and turned the door-knob and

Rosie wasn't with her. No, it was better if he didn't see her

walk up to Pa and aim. She stepped back and couldn't. Pa spluttered, snoring again. He lay on his side, he made a messy target, it was nothing like she had pictured.

She thought about nothing and stabbed just below his jaw with all her might. Blood covered her arms, so warm. Pa Horton was making a noise that could have been pleasure. You had to get through his throat good, you had to make certain. She pulled the knife out, it was surprisingly phys-ical, like digging, she stabbed badly so she had to do it again.

Rosie stood behind her and made a sound like an unhappy moo. She laughed nervously and caught her breath.

They watched in the prosaic darkness while the blood slowed. The light of a passing car filled the shades and fell away. A clock was ticking on the nightstand. A numb incomprehen-sion crept through her mind. That man was dead. It was like breath had risen out of him and melted into dead air.

Wet, she began to shiver. That prodded her. She whis-pered to Rosie, 'Do you still love me?'

He said, 'Yes,' frightened, unwilling. She couldn't think about that and went ahead.

Your blood is warm in you and I'm so cold. I'll have your life over me like a blanket, I ought to kill you. What you did to me. Ma lay on her back in the centre of the king-sized bed. You'd have to get up on the bed to reach. And Elly clambered up on Ruth Horton, straddled her girth like a lover. She even snuggled, she had lost her balance. Then as Ma began to stir and see and made that first odd cheep, roused by the scent of blood, its musk, its innuendo, Elly reared back and plunged the blade into her throat. The blood poked Elly in the eye, the eye. There was a plopping sound effect and a separate gurgle till the breath stopped trying. Enjoying her arm's strength now, aware of nothing but her arm, Elly grabbed the knife back, unplugged Ma's gory hole. The smell this time was strong.

She saw the person lying there again, what she had done. The broad face made stupid by death. It looked past Elly at something niggling, a pinpoint. Sorry for herself and feeling like the only person in the world, Elly started crying, bawling. She howled because the people were dead. No one could hear her.

Rosie's hand shocked her, patting her back. He said, 'Elly, please, you gotta wash.'

She said, panicking, 'Cox. No, Cox.' She didn't know if she could do it. If she didn't go now, she couldn't do it. 'Cox,' she said again, but let herself be led to the shower. She stood, mutely staring past Rosie at something specific, a niggling pinpoint, while he stripped her.

He was staring too as he turned the water on. They both moved like zombies, the warm jet of water seemed to go on in a different world, in the world an hour ago, where people still were alive. It was happening, she had to move her arms, clutch slippery soap.

He said, 'I'll do it, it's OK. You did, you did good.' It turned out he meant that he would dry her. The towel was warm from being hung by the vent. She cried again because the sweet towel was warm.

Then she was going where Pa kept the .38, wedged against the wall behind the leg of his bed.

★

241

They drove to Cox's house in Ma's car. They had thought that was a weak point of the plan, they'd never driven before, not for a second, never ever. Rosie did it cause he hadn't done the other thing. It turned out it was easy and they talked about that. They laughed when the oncoming lights scared them. When they got to Cox's, he drove around the block three times, saying they should 'scope the place out'.

At last he parked across the street. There were no lights on at Cox's, the way it was set back you could barely see. Rosie put his hand on Elly's wet hair and said, choked up, 'I love you like a star in heaven.'

She said, 'I'll never go to heaven now. That's hysterical.'

He kissed her on the cheek, although his kiss had no potency. It felt like something tapping her by mistake. She said, 'No one really believes in heaven, but I do.'

'If there's a heaven —' He stopped. They sat in the car and heard crickets. The crickets seemed to scream at the top of their lungs to warn Cox. At last Elly opened the door.

Rosie made a point of staying abreast of her, as if this time he wasn't going to let her do it herself. But she had the gun. She held it pressed to her buttock. And she was angry by the time they reached the top of the steps. The scent of autumn was compelling and young, and she pressed the doorbell with a stabbing gesture, ravenous.

She pressed the doorbell again and again. She started muttering, *Come on, Come on.*

A window overhead opened. Cox stuck his head out and both kids jumped.

'What are you doing at this hour of the night?'

'Come on!' Elly shouted. 'Come on!'

The window slammed shut. Elly pressed the doorbell, she held the bell down. At last a light showed in the pebble glass set in the door. Elly nodded at Rosie, she was breathing oddly, through her mouth.

The door flew open hard. 'If you want to come in, I'm sorry, but the answer is no. I know you're very upset, but other people have responsibilities and I have class at nine. Other people are depending –'

Rosie made a forced noise like a seal's bark and shoved Cox suddenly, bowling him over. Cox slipped, fell on his ass, and cursed. Then Rosie fell on him, punching him again and again, frenzied. He shouted, 'You shit, you evil shit!' and put his body into it, coming down like falling from his full height.

Then Elly kneeled beside him and Rosie cried out, 'No! Elly, don't!'

But leapt to his feet. He pressed his face to the wall while the sound wiped out his thoughts.

When it was over, he went and shut the front door carefully, it closed with a savouring noise like smacking lips. He leaned against the door and stared.

She sat on the corpse's thigh, looking up with nothing and time in her eyes. It was done, they had time for the rest of their lives. If they could stop the time coming; but Rosie said,

'I can't stand around. Goddamn. We got to split, this is awful.'

She said, with a new, half-stupid daze, in a candied voice, 'But, no. Only look at my clothes.'

He stood outside to listen for police while Elly used Ben's shower. He was almost hoping for sirens, as if the police would come and rescue them, but they never came. Rosie only had a little blood on the back of his jeans, but he had to shower too. Elly didn't ask why, she was good.

She spent the time he was washing digging through Ben

Cox's clothes. When Rosie was finished, she'd set out shorts and a belt for him.

Elly was dressed in baggy clothes, a grown man's clothes. She looked ridiculous in a way that would never be funny. The shoes wouldn't fit, she had to put her sodden loafers back on. They stuck to her feet uncomfortably, and by the time they got to the empty summer cabin Elly knew, by the pond by her old friend Maggie's, Elly's feet had gained a bloody patina. She had to go out to the pond, in the dark, to scrub them. She went barefoot for a long time, even in city streets, after that.

Seventy-Three

'I didn't know for definite,' Peter Rabbit said unwillingly. 'Elly makes up some gnarly stuff. You know she's a big fat liar.'

'She bludgeoned Curt, for Christ's sake. You let her live with me and Todd, you knew that.'

'She never did anything like that for *years*. Twelve *years*. I was watching her like a hawk after that. I think she got a bad lot of heroin, she said.'

'Did she get him off my Palm? I know she stole my PalmPilot.'

'No way! Elly knew Curt *before* you. That's how she met Keynes. He was like some fucked-up father figure, Elly's always finding dudes like that. He took her to church. It was bad news.'

'Why would anyone kill Curt?'

'Yeah, she put the moves on him, just being Elly. Elly thinks everybody's all about pussy. And he boned her, first mistake. Then he freaked and laid his Jesus trip on her. "You need to be saved through Christ, you fallen woman." That's the *wrong* thing to say to her, you know that. Elly nutted up and, boom! She took that dude *apart*. I got her set for counselling, but Elly wouldn't go. Elly's stubborn.'

'You're insane. You got her counselling?'

'*Twelve years.* Twelve, since the Baltimore guy, and that was different. She was hooking in the street.'

'Two months, three months since Curt died. Christ.'

'What am I supposed to do? Oh, Elly doesn't know any better. I can't do that to her. You could do that to her, send Elly to prison?'

'No problem.'

There was a silence. I heard my laboured breathing. The doorbell went again, and she was leaning on the bell. Peter said,

'Poor Elly. Elly never gets a break.'

I said, 'You let people die. You let her kill people.' I was hanging up without knowing it. I went downstairs, insane with energy, clutching the cellphone hard. I felt it like the bones of my hand.

I opened the door. El was there, in a white dress with a bow. She had a Sainsbury's bag with her, nearly empty, I was thinking of what it would hold, in packing mode. I stepped back with the same momentum, saying, 'Good, great. Come in.'

She stepped in, fearful, keeping her eyes on my face. When I shut the door, her shoulders relaxed. She said, 'I didn't get the van.'

'Oh, why did you come, then?' I was leading her to the front room.

Both of us looked at her yellow sofa. For a long, light-headed second, I was back in reality, in which it was all about moving her stuff. We would have to have men to move that couch. Her bed had to go down stairs. But that wasn't reality.

El said, 'It was a trick, I know. I needed to see you.' Her voice was stretched, unclear. She sat on the couch, already crying.

She was a beautiful woman with the webby beginning of crow's feet, with new dark circles. She'd lost weight, she looked like an adult now. Her skin was still unblemished, white white, like something fresh from the box. She was the prettiest girl you ever saw, still, if you didn't know her.

I said, cause I had to, 'Look. Is Hutch all right?'

She took a deep breath. She said, 'Jamie?'

'The one you found off my PalmPilot, yes. Jamie Hutchinson.'

'He's all right,' she said, wanly, as if sharing a joke. Then she said, 'You took forever to come to the door.'

'I was on the phone.'

'I'm not upset, no. I just must say before it's too late, I think I've had an overdose.' She grimaced, and smiled, it was her same triumph. The tears kept going like something pumped by a machine. I had a stale, familiar anger, I could feel the whole script she'd written, tugging at me.

I said, 'I guess you think I'm going to call an ambulance.'

'I don't think you're going to do anything. I may as well die. I know I took an overdose, actually. I did it right there.' She pointed at the door. 'I rang the bell and started taking pills.'

'I'm going to call the cops.'

She looked at me, quizzical. She rubbed her eyes and was infantile, saying, 'What? What did I do? I haven't done anything. I have the PalmPilot, God, you're so cruel.'

'You killed Curt Short.'

She frowned. She looked at the floor intently. At last she said, 'I don't have time to discuss that, actually. I'm going to sleep soon. You have to know I wouldn't kill anyone, normally. But I know you'll think I'm lying.'

'Did you get him off my PalmPilot, too? Or my address book? Peter said you didn't.'

She stood up. I flinched away, but she kept coming towards me, trembling and all the old tears. When she was close, she suddenly laughed and grabbed the cellphone out of my hand.

She pelted it against the wall with all her might. Then I ran, and she ran to get it. She was laughing like this was a game. She got there first and beat it on the floor a few times before I got a good grip on her wrist.

Then she said, 'Don't!' cross, and let the phone go.

I picked up the phone, she was rubbing her wrist, put out.

The cellphone screen was black. I was there pressing buttons, my head felt weird and tight. The motion of her throwing the phone kept passing before me.

She stood up, saying, 'Of course, it's ridiculous for me to be angry. I *was* breaking it, I shouldn't feel hurt.'

'What was the point of that?'

'You haven't got another phone. Did you get a new phone?'

She had walked to the couch and sat down, with a pointed weariness. I stayed crouched on the floor.

I said, 'You want to die? You want me to let you die?'

'I wasn't thinking about it.' She lay back touching her face as if curious at the sensation. She said, 'I love you. I'm going to lie down on the floor. If you want, you can go to a payphone.'

I watched her arrange herself. She shifted to avoid what I guess was a nail in the floorboard. Then she tugged her skirt out at both sides, looking down to observe the effect.

She commented, 'Yes, I'd rather die than go to prison, I think. It's for the best.'

'I'll wait for you to fall asleep, then I'll go to a payphone.'

'Perhaps I'm lying, of course. My God, I'm such a cunt. But I could be lying, you can't believe what I say. I'm a liar.'

'What kind of pills did you take? Most people don't die from pills.'

Then she leaned up on an elbow, looking at me. She said, 'Don't worry. I do want to die. I'm not afraid now. Being with you was all it needed. I would like it if you held my hand, but I know you won't want to do that.' She lay back again, shutting her eyes. Now I noticed a few stains on the skirt, crisp stains like ink, like her freckles. In the soiled dress, stiff on the floor, she looked like an abandoned doll.

My mind was uncoordinated, jumping, I couldn't make

it think what to do. If you had to choose between a whole life in prison and death. If you had to choose for someone else.

They would take her to the hospital and pump her stomach. There would be that good patch, the nurses were always kind. If it was Nembutal, she'd be prison-ready by the following day. They would take her in cuffs, but she would charm them, they wouldn't be rough, it would just be a ride in a car. It would be walking down some halls and changing clothes. In prison, she'd get her drugs, she could draw all she wanted. I'd send her jelly beans, I'd set up a standing order, she'd have jelly beans for life.

I got up, my legs were barely working. I almost went to the door, but I went to El. I was praying now she'd leap up, turn out to be faking it. She could even get away, it wouldn't be my fault.

She lay with her hair swept over her throat. Her hands were at her sides, upturned, cupped. I bent near, remembering kissing her so many times. She was vividly human, her breathing was like thinking. She was Eleanor who sang to me in French when I was feverish. It was my lover lying there, a woman who shut her eyes at scary movies but killed in cold blood.

Then abruptly she peaked her shoulders up and her head came following and she puked. She vomited a liquid starred with eroding pills. It instantly darkened her hair and spread, she dropped her head back into it. There were more than twenty pills there. I started to cry

cursing her. I reached for the Sainsbury's bag. It would say on the vial how many there were. I might not even need an ambulance.

There wasn't any vial in the bag. There was a carving knife. There were slight traces on the blade, at first I thought it was the discoloration you get on expensive knives. When I touched the blade, though, red came off on my hand.

It wasn't one of her hyper-sharp knives, it was one of Hutch's. It was one of his set with the iron handles he'd had time out of mind. I got fear like a stroke. I got rage as spots in my vision.

I don't know if you get over killing someone. Killing somebody makes you know there's a hell. I went to the kitchen. I put the knife away in a drawer, and I was weeping like a sentimental woman. On all the walls, Curt Short posed, headless, brindled with her blood.

It was the Sainsbury's bag. I crouched down gingerly and moulded it to her face. You do these things when you have to, when you're having a nightmare, in a war. It dimpled with her breath. I held it snug. I held her still when she tried to move, she was jerking her head like a newborn trying to feed.

The plastic strained on her open mouth. It throbbed like a heart. I don't believe in capital punishment.

Eleanor died with her face in my hands. I wasn't crying then and the dried tears made my face feel paralysed. I didn't know if I'd be able to stand. But I did, I stood, and felt like I'd broken out from a cave into painful sunlight.

I put the battered cellphone, that might be evidence, in my pocket. I went outside and I was a murderer walking to the phone.

Seventy-Four

I called Hutch's ambulance first. I said there'd been an accident, crying again. I got the address out right. The guy was
asking where the injuries were, had I applied a tourniquet,
stuff I couldn't listen. I hung up the phone and I was paralysed, thinking of the wait. They would have to break down
the door.

I called back 999. It was someone different, if it wasn't
I was going to hang up. I gave my own address and said a
friend had threatened an overdose. When he asked what pills,
I said the address again and hung up.

Then I was running to Hutchinson's. That ten minutes
on foot, I don't know how long it took.

She'd left the door ajar. I found him in the bedroom,
finally. He was sitting on the floor, in tears, alive, whole,
absolutely whole. As I came in, his whole body perked; then
he saw it was me. He sank and swallowed and said,

'Oh, I thought you were her. How embarrassing. The
state of me, Tanya – I think she's left me, you see.'

Seventy-Five

She'd gone straight to his house from talking to me on the phone. When she got in the door, she accused him of seeing me. There was no reason he shouldn't, of course. But he felt like a criminal, sadly. He said she ought to forget about me, it would all be water under the bridge, when they got to France, those were his ill-chosen words.

She went and got the knife then. He was afraid he had laughed. She looked such an urchin, the knife too big for her. One does laugh when one ought not.

She had got the pills in the Sainsbury's bag, loose. She swallowed a handful without water, with her eyes on his face, she was swallowing *at* him. Then she began to tear off her dress.

She raved about cooking. She had never been able to cook. He would be better off with a normal girl, he must be actually crazy. What did he think it would be like? He was crazy, she couldn't even cook. He had seen her take pills now, he could guess what she'd be like.

'No, no, dear beautiful girl, there's no need to marry me if you'd rather not,' he said, at which she slashed her stomach end to end. He had screamed, one screams apparently. It hadn't bled much, what concerned him was that she had the knife when she left. She had the presence of mind to dress, did I suppose that meant she would be all right? He had tried to catch her, but he felt he was an old man. He was an old and useless man.

I sat on the floor beside him, crying at the sight of his life, his movement. I was holding him in my arms when the ambulance came.

Seventy-Six

Eleanor was dead as dead. They broke my front-door locks, finding Eleanor dead. I had stuff stolen, in between the time the door got broken down and I got home. It figures they can't leave a paramedic there to guard your stuff. It was mostly Eleanor's jewellery, and the VCR. Of course, I wished they'd taken everything, I would have torched the place with everything inside it. But it's a terrace, it's impossible, you can't torch just your place.

She'd had sixty Nembutal. That was the cause of death on paper. I got the death certificate; El had no real next of kin. Of course I felt like it was a certificate of murder, something to hang on the wall, a black diploma. I put it in an old suitcase before I thought of her suitcase, with the cup.

Hutch paid for her gravestone. It was a fancy thing El would have liked, white marble. It had a quote from Shelley: 'Our sweetest songs are those that tell of saddest thought', and the name she had told him, Alexis Lovechild. It was so much hassle to get her identity straight for the death certificate, I thought somebody would step in. No one polices tombstones, though, you could be buried as Genghis Khan.

It was Hutch and me at the graveside. Her ashes were in a fancy box, like we were burying perfume. That box made it intensely present, that people end. The box was like 'I had a dream about you, only you were a box'.

Hutch threw the first clod of earth. He was clumsy with his new-found age, I had to help him up. The gravedigger looked away. Then we walked out of the graveyard and stood on the grass by the main road. I missed El like a rib extracted from my chest. I kept picturing her in her scarlet nightie when I went to Peter Rabbit's, wild with joy to see me. I know I had no right.

Then Hutch said, 'I'm better off without her, I realise.' He compressed his lips, looked ashen and fierce. The traffic wind was blowing his hair to one side.

I said, 'That's not important.'

Peter Rabbit didn't come. I'd left a message for him, but he never called back.

When I sold El's paintings from the house, Peter Rabbit's dealer phoned him to check their authenticity. The authentication came back, nothing else. I wanted to talk about El, of course. I wanted Peter to know. The dealer only knew it was OK to sell the pictures, and he wasn't authorised to tell me Peter's whereabouts; he had left London. I thought then Peter Rabbit would turn up, eventually. I never saw Peter again.

I never told Hutch I'd killed her. I told Todd and Alan and Mark.

I told them separately, but it felt creepily the same. They made excuses for me, to my face. The knife and Hutch got emphasised, the pills might have killed her anyway. There was no time, I'd had to make up my mind. They said fuck knew how many people Eleanor had killed. She was a *serial killer.*

With Todd, I broke down, angry, and said that I'd wanted her dead, and I wanted to rot in prison, you could never go back. I didn't want any of his shit forgiveness. I could be a serial killer, it was shit. We were in a pub, and I talked too loud, hoping some good citizen would call the police. I said I knew why El got the way she was, this was like having venom for blood.

When I said I was a troll, Todd burst out laughing. I was stopped, bewildered, then I said, 'Fuck you.' I was looking around for cops to tell, then, I was that kind of drunk. I said, 'I'm like El, now. She's taken me over.'

He said, 'Tannie. You're so not like El at all. I'm sorry I laughed. It's just, you looked like a total troll, when you said that. It was pretty funny.'

When I told Alan, Alan told me stories of people he knew who'd murdered people; two drug dealers, and a female jockey who garrotted her 'wife'. The old girl did ten years, but the dealers walked away. The trick was to not tell a soul for a year, so I'd just fucked up.

'I'll keep your secret, but you have to put out, now,' Alan said, rubbing his hands, and: 'Joke.'

I said, 'You don't get it. No one gets it, this is so depressing.' What I'd said was depressing, too, I had to say, 'And I don't get it. No one's angry, I don't understand.'

Alan said, 'What if we just love you?'

When I told Mark, he felt sorry for me. He got withdrawn for a while. We used to spend nights watching football. He watched, I stared through the screen seeing the past. El dancing on an African beach, the scarlet nightie, her hand in me and the way her words came from me, sometimes, nowadays. 'I'm no good. You ought to stay away from me. You could never understand.' The footballers might as well have been swarming gnats.

One time I caught Mark frowning at me, and said, insanely gratified, 'You're looking at me like I'm a murderer.'

That made him sorry, again. He rubbed his eyes and said, 'I was thinking what I would do, in your shoes. I'd got as far as giving my money to charity, but that's crap.'

'It didn't help me. I could sell the house too.'

'I know, I was thinking of that.'

'It is crap.'

What I had given away was the money from Eleanor's

paintings I'd sold as Peter Rabbit's. I couldn't paint over the pictures but I couldn't keep the money. By the time I had the place replastered, it was only £20,000. I was going to hand it to beggars in the street like El, was my original taste-less plan.

When I wrote the cheque, it was like a story you hear and don't believe. I only felt I'd done it when I had to sort out the tax. I gave it to Oxfam because, who cares who. Oxfam hounded me, of course, after that, I had to change all my numbers. At the same time, journalists called, the paint-ings got this brief attention. With the journalists, I got rabid. I told some girl from the *Telegraph* to fuck herself to death with a broken bottle. Todd said she wrote it up, and all the people at Lennie's were in awe.

Now I was crying again, my new trick. Mark laughed, he said, 'I am sorry Tottenham's losing.'

Then he put his hand on my head and said, 'This doesn't change a bit of what I said about you being gentle.'

I said, 'You're mad,' though it was what I needed to hear. And I said, 'I killed someone. You need better than this.'

'I don't know anyone else who could go through what you did, and show up for work next day.'

'I'm a sociopath,' I suggested, and both of us laughed.

He said, 'What you are, is daft.'

I never moved back to my house. I was living with Mark, though we never said so up front. At last he bought me a chest of drawers. And we were something that could maybe not last forever. He would find Jan Two, it was a matter of time. It was more than enough.

The day Mark said he loved me, I made him a cake. He said it to me in the morning, before he went to work.

Mark had his coat on, saying goodbye, and the words 'I

love you' came out, out of habit. We stepped back from each other. Then he said, 'I stand by that,' and we laughed.

I was taking a sick day, so I had time on my hands. I got flu all the time then. So I decided to bake a cake, even though I would spend the whole day deciding what baking cake meant in a relationship, thinking of Jan.

It was the same yellow cake I'd tried to make at that party, when El first came to my house. I didn't remember till I had the batter. It's just my cake I make without a recipe, that and coconut which you never have the coconut for. I finished cause I do, I shut my eyes and do things. That's why I'm here at all.

And I thought it would have turned out different if she'd eaten that cake. If she hadn't been busy fucking Mark in my bedroom, if she could have stopped being that person for one night. And when people eat cake, they're doing all right, but when they start fucking strangers in strangers' houses when they should be eating cake —

I don't have any answers.

By the time the cake was done, I was happy for the first time, since. And no one ever sent me to prison for murdering El. I guess that was a good thing. We just went on; Todd started at culinary school; Alan quit working and moved two Thai massage girls into his flat; his cancer didn't come back. Hutch got an Old English sheepdog, and the real puppy blotted out the memory of why he'd got that breed. His new girlfriends accused him of loving the dog more than he loved them, correctly. Mark loved me like people love girlfriends they keep two years. He loved me more than enough.

Acknowledgements

Thanks first and foremost to my exceptionally loyal, gifted, and thoughtful editor, Rebecca Carter, whose dedication has transformed this book. I would also like to thank my agent, the ever-charming and brilliant Victoria Hobbs.

For his help when funds were low, thanks to my father Richard Grossman; and thanks again to him and to his wife, Lisa Lyons, for their kindness when my spirits were low.

Thanks to Shane, for providing much of the material, continually interrupting the process, etc. as he is aware.

I would like to again thank my husband, Robin Mookerjee, for his insightful suggestions about this book – and all the other good things.